A Field of Tulips and Bones

Haunting Tales and Withered Old Flowers

Cassandra Doon

Mimi Baptist

The Devil Whispered In My Ear, "You're Not Strong Enough To Withstand The Storm."

Today I Whispered In The Devil's Ear, "I Am The Storm."

ONE
ROMAN WATERHOUSE

5 Years Old

"Oi, Roman, mate," Grandpa's voice is all wobbly like the jelly we have for afternoon tea. "We gotta yarn about something real tough."

I'm sitting cross-legged on the floor, pushing my toy cars around, making them crash and zoom off the rug onto the shiny wood. That's when I noticed Grandma's eyes were leaking. She doesn't talk, just bites her lip hard, and there's this heavy thing in the air you can almost grab.

"Your mum and dad," Grandpa starts, and then he stops, his big hands shaking like leaves in a windstorm. He takes a deep breath, looking at Grandma. "They've been in a nasty prang, little fella."

"Prang?" I echo, thinking of my toy cars. "Did Dad's car get bonked? He'll fix it. He fixes everything."

"Ah, love, it's... it's more than a bonk," Grandma finally

pipes up, her voice all quivery. "Your mum and dad, they're not coming back home. Not ever."

"Whaddaya mean?" I scrunch up my face, trying to suss out what she's saying. "Not ever is a really long time. Did they get lost? Dad's got that GPS thing."

"Roman," Grandpa says, kneeling down next to me, his old knees cracking like the bark of a gum tree. "It was a bad car smash. They're gone, mate. Up to the stars."

"Stars?" I whisper because I know about stars. Dad used to say Mum sparkled like one. I glance through the window where the sun's just coming up from behind the hills, leaving streaks of orange and purple. But no stars yet. It doesn't make sense.

"Can we go get them?" My voice shakes as I look from Grandma to Grandpa and back again. "From the stars?"

"Ah, kiddo, if only we could," Grandpa's eyes are shiny too now. "But it's like they're on a trip they can't come back from."

"An adventure?" My fingers clutch the car tighter. Dad liked adventures.

"Yeah, an adventure," he agrees, though his smile looks like it hurts his face. "The biggest one there is."

"But who's gonna read me stories? And tuck me in?" The questions spill out like marbles, bouncing every which way.

"We've gotcha, Roman," Grandma says, pulling me into her soft, squishy hug. "We'll be here for every bedtime story and tuck-in."

"Promise?" I ask, the word feeling heavy and strange.

"Strewth, promise," Grandpa says, and somehow, even

though nothing makes sense and my chest feels all tight and funny, I reckon they might be telling the truth.

Grandma smooths down my hair, the way Mum used to. "You're such a brave boy."

"Am not," I mumble, but they don't argue, just give me these sad smiles that make my insides twist all funny.

)O(

One sunny morning, we go for a drive in their clunky car that coughs and wheezes more than Old Man Jenkins from next door. The city buildings grow taller as we get closer like giant kids playing who can touch the sky first. We stop at one so big its top gets lost in the clouds. I clutch Grandma's hand as we walk into this shiny place with floors so clean you could eat your breakfast off them.

"Right-o, Roman, we're here to see Mr. Kellerman," Grandpa explains. He's wearing his best jacket, the one he saves for church and funerals.

"Who's that?" I ask, tripping over a rug that's probably worth more than our telly.

"A very important fella who helps people with money stuff," Grandma says, squeezing my hand.

We ride an elevator that feels like it's shooting us straight into outer space. 'Ding!' The doors open and there's this man waiting, all dressed up in a suit so shiny it could blind you. He's got a smile, but it isn't reaching his eyes.

"Welcome, welcome!" His voice booms around the room like thunder. "Young Master Roman, I have some news for you."

"News?" I scrunch up my face. "Is it good or bad?"

"Good, very good," Mr. Kellerman says, bending down so he's eye-level with me. "Your father was a very smart man, Roman. He made sure you'd never have to worry about money."

"Money for what?" I'm still holding onto Grandma's hand as if it's the last chocolate biscuit in the jar.

"Anything you need, mate," he says, ruffling my hair which makes me flinch. "Toys, books, education—whatever you fancy."

"Can it buy back Mum and Dad?" I blurt out the question before I can stop it.

"Ah, mate, I wish it could." There's a twist to Mr. Kellerman's mouth like he's eaten something sour. "But it can make sure you're taken care of, and that's what your folks would've wanted."

"Right, then," Grandpa says, standing up straighter. "Let's get this sorted so we can head off."

"Indeed." Mr. Kellerman stands and shakes Grandpa's hand. "The paperwork is all ready."

I don't really understand all the talk about wills and trusts and heaps of cash. But I reckon it must be important 'cause adults always get all stiff and serious when they're talking about money.

"Oi, Roman, you gotta listen to this bit, it's about your old man," Mr Kellerman says, jabbing a finger at some papers that look like they've swallowed a dictionary. His eyes are sharp behind those shiny specs, and I reckon he's trying to drill the importance right into my skull.

"Everything," he continues, words marching out quick and no-nonsense, "your dad owned, every bloody cent, is yours now." He hammers the point home with a thump of his hand on the desk that makes me jump.

"Mine?" The word feels weird in my mouth, too big and strange. I mean, what's a kid supposed to do with 'everything'? It's not like I can stack it up and turn it into a race track for my toy cars.

"Every last bit, mate," Grandpa adds. He's trying to sound chipper, but his voice wobbles like a bike with busted wheels.

"And Mum?" I ask, squinting at them all. They shuffle and glance at each other like they're passing around a hot potato.

"Your mum," Mr Kellerman starts and then stops, clears his throat like it's full of gravel. "She set up something special —a trust. It's locked up until you hit twenty-one."

"Locked up?" My guts twist into knots. That doesn't sound good. Locked up means kept away, like when they put those kangaroos in the sanctuary and they couldn't hop free no more.

"Means you can't touch it yet," Grandma cuts in, smooth as butter melting on toast. "But it's there, waiting for ya. A nest egg, something your mum wanted to give you when you're grown."

"Like a surprise pressie?" I venture, trying to wrap my head around it. Mum always loved sneaking sweets into my lunchbox when I wasn't looking.

"Exactly like that, love," she nods, her smile crinkling the corners of her eyes.

"Ok," I mutter under my breath. All this talk about money and trusts and dead parents—it's like a game where everyone knows the rules except for me.

"Let's get goin', Roman," Grandpa says, standing up. "We can figure this out later, yeah?"

"Righto," I agree.

We scuttle outta that stuffy office, the carpet swallowing the clack of our shoes.

"Grub's up soon," Grandma says, trying to sound chirpy. "You hungry, darling?"

"Starving," I lie. My guts are in knots, but I ain't about to be a sook in front of her.

We pile into Grandpa's car, and I squint out the window, watching the world zip by like one of them fast-forward movies.

Two

Ackles Harris

8 Years Old

"Alright, my pretty charmer, are you ready for your bedtime story?" I hear Papa say as he enters my bedroom, making the door squeak and the floorboards creak.

It's just me and Papa, as Mama passed away 3 years ago. That's one of the tales my dear Papa never tells me. Maybe one day. He hasn't been the same since she left us to live amongst the stars. He's caring and loving to me but even I see the mask he wears, and I am only 8.

Papa is the head of police in our small town in Lancashire, England. When I grow up I want to follow in his footsteps and be just like him. Solve impossible puzzles with disjointed pieces, and set forth the gospel behind dark closed books. Paying the piper can bring you some sort of comfort, while not knowing can eat someone from the inside, he disclosed to me once upon a time. Since then I told myself I would rather bite the painful bullet than live in the shadows of oblivion.

According to the sign, as you enter our quaint little Newchurch town, there are only 248 of us, so everyone knows everyone and no secrets stay buried for long. Not that much ever happens here anyway.

"Papa, Miss Craft is not happy with you," I report to him from my cocoon of duvet and covers.

The house is freezing, since Papa refuses to turn the heater on for too long, saying that if we make the house nice and toasty, it's like sending an invitation for the Devil to come and live with us. Because you know, the abode of the dead is hot.

"What in the bloody hell is your head teacher not happy with now?" He asks me as he takes a seat at the end of the bed by my feet like he does every night for story time.

"She said you shouldn't be telling me scary stories. That they are not becoming of a young lady and something about maybe giving princesses tales a go instead."

"That old ha..." Papa clears his throat. As if I didn't know he was about to call my head teacher an old hag.

I giggle.

"Miss Craft would prefer I fill your head with fairytales and unrealistic expectations, it seems. Real life is filled with dark f... ducked up people."

"There are duck people? Now that sounds silly, Papa." I belly laugh, which makes Papa chuckle and give me one of his rare happy smiles.

"You do like hearing my chilling tales, my pretty charmer, don't you?"

"I do, Papa."

"Then screw Miss Craft, this is our thing," Papa says as he boops the tip of my nose. "How did this even come about?"

"Oh, I tried to warn the other kids at school about the Devil house, Papa. But Gigi George started crying halfway through and went to the head teacher to tell on me."

"Now there's a little girl that has a head jammed with cock and bull stories."

"Papa, you can't say co... o... ock." I stutter on the word.

"I can't say what a male rooster is called?"

"Maybe just call it that. A male rooster." I remark as I giggle again.

"That kind of ruins the saying, but alright." He shrugs. "What would you like to hear tonight, my pretty charmer?"

"Devil house down the road? Pretty please, Papa."

"Ok. Strap in for the dire and twisted ride, buttercup." He utters as he winks at me, placing his hand over my lower leg, moving it up and down, intuitively abating the words that are about to come out of his mouth. Papa should know I am not scared no more, as long as I have him by my side always, he will protect me from the duck people of the world.

This is my favourite; a sinister and troubling slander that sends shivers down my spine every time he tells it.

As claimed by many folks around town, Elizabeth Demdike, or as we call her the 'Demon Woman' - a crone already in her 80's, - allegedly met the Devil in a stone pit near Goldshaw Booth. He came to her as a boy, dirty and bruised, skin and bones, with messy dark brown hair, almost jet-black eyes, pale skin as if he barely had ever seen the sun, wearing just a brown and black coat, and calling himself Tibb. Demdike took him to her home, where one of her daughters Elizabeth fell in love with the boy, Demdike ended up adopting him and caring for him as her own.

Sadly it wasn't all sunshine and roses, as thorns began to take form and a few short years after, in 1612, 12 people around the Forest of Pendle were accused of maleficium, or to put it simply, witchcraft. Demdike, her daughters and illegitimate son Holgate, and Device's blood children Alizon, James and Janet, are some of the brought to trial and prosecuted.

Leaving as the sole survivor the lost boy Tibb. Who met the pretty Tulipa twins and fell in love with one.

In 1655, they built a house, the one we now call the Devil's house. A few extra homes were added to the property to house the growing family tree. But it's the main one that causes fright on every soul that comes across it.

The captivating stone-built exterior exudes an aura of the past, greying like Papa's hair, showing the signs of time. Its original Tudor elements are presently crumbling and being swallowed up by vines all over.

The landscape around is as dead and decaying as the people who summoned the home to existence.

"The Devices were a cult worshipping their father, and tainting the walls of that place with blood and gore. I am certain the foundation of that place is made out of bones and ashes. If only I could dig deeper and find out the truth it obscures."

Papa took a slight deviation there. Normally this is the moment he would forewarn me about the witches, and how if they see a child wandering around the grounds of their master's home, they would compel you to come in, condemning you to never leave that hellish place, and damning your soul to eternal suffering.

My 8-year-old brain is starting to think he spewed out that little white lie to keep me away from the Devil's house. But why?

"How come you can't, Papa?" I ask him instead.

"Because it's too dangerous, a sweet innocent girl like you should never roam those cobwebbed-covered walls."

"I didn't ask why I couldn't. I know the rules, Papa. But you're a grown-up, the witches have no power over you."

"Perhaps, but sometimes adults with frail states of mind can get lost in their spells too."

"You are not weak, Papa," I observe as I unravel myself from the cocoon I was in, jumping on my father's lap and throwing my arms around his neck, giving him a tight bear hug.

He embraces me back, as I cache my face on the alcove between his neck and shoulder, breathing in his scent of bourbon, vanilla and white oak.

"If someone can kick some witch's ass it's you." I voice, which makes Papa laugh.

"You should be sleeping, young lady."

I pull my head back to stare into a pair of eyes that look nothing like mine. I am told that I look just like Mama, and haven't taken much of Papa's genes. I have curly, rowdy red hair, and forest-green eyes and my face is painted with freckles all over my nose and cheeks. Meanwhile, Papa has golden walnut brown hair and hazel eyes, with no freckles in sight.

"You are the one that changed up the course of the story, old man."

"Watch it, my pretty charmer." He comments as he begins to tickle me.

"No, Papa. No." I breathlessly say between hoots of laughter. "I cede. I cede." I declare over and over again until he stops.

Papa lifts himself up with me in his arms, clasped to him like a spider monkey. He lies me back down on the bed, swiftly pulling all the bed covers on top of me and tucking me in nice and cozy.

"In due time, maybe. Nothing has happened in there for years that would give me a reason to break in and start poking around to uncover stuff that may not even be. The estate is still under the same family, I just don't know where the last living relative is or how to get in contact with them. Just like Tibb years ago, this person has vanished into thin air. We just gonna have to wait patiently for someone from the same bloodline to finally come around and..."

"Let us in on the family secret," I concluded Papa's sentence.

"Goodnight moon," Papa says as he kisses my temple.

"Night Papa."

Some secrets should stay enclosed in the rotten wooden box, under the dirt and smut they were buried for all perpetuity. But curiosity is a killer.

THREE

ROMAN WATERHOUSE

21 Years Old

The morning sun hadn't even bothered to slap some sense into the sky yet, but I was already up and at it. Today, I hit 21. Big bloody whoop. Not like I'd be smashing tinnies at the pub, though — had to leg it to work instead. The tool belt was snug around my waist, a familiar weight that screamed responsibility louder than any boozy chorus of "Happy Birthday" ever could.

"Roman, you old dog! Twenty-one, eh?" Grandpa's voice crackled through the phone.

"Cheers, Gramps," I grunted, scratching at the stubble that thought it could make a man out of me overnight. "Feel the same as yesterday, just with more people reminding me I'm supposed to be an adult or some shit."

"Ha! You'll always be that snot-nosed brat to us, won't ya, love?" Gran chimed in, her laughter wrapping around me like a warm hug. I couldn't help but smile, even if it was just a twitch of the lips.

"Guess so, Gran. But this snot-nosed brat's got houses to build today. New gig in Campbelltown, remember?"

"Of course we do, Roman. We're proud as punch, love. Your mum and dad would've been over the moon," she said, her voice doing that wobbly dance it did whenever she mentioned them.

"Righto, gotta shoot through. Love you both," I said, ending the call before the feels got too heavy. No time for that. There were frames to erect and concrete to pour. Fresh off my apprenticeship and straight into the deep end with a company that actually gave a rat's about quality work. That's what I needed.

Campbelltown wasn't exactly the arse end of the world, but it was getting there. Still, fresh turf meant fresh starts, and I was all about building something from nothing. Could almost smell the sawdust and sweat just thinking about it. Nothing gets the blood pumping like the promise of a day spent shaping the future, one beam at a time.

"Twenty-one," I grunted, yanking the front door open. There was already a sheen on my brow, just a hint of the day's heat to come. My hand had barely left the doorknob when the tyres crunched against the gravel of my driveway, and I squinted against the light to see some flash car rolling up.

"Strewth, what now?" I mumbled under my breath, impatient. Flies were already starting their morning dance around me, buzzing like they knew today was supposed to be mine.

The car stopped with a purr that screamed money and out stepped a bloke in a suit that probably cost more than my monthly rent. Out here, in Ingleburn? Had to be lost, or a bloody idiot. But he zeroed in on me, his face all business, and I knew this wasn't some random door-knock spiel.

"Roman Waterhouse?" He didn't wait for my nod, just barrelled on. "I'm Jameson Holt, solicitor. You are rather difficult to pin down."

"Builders tend to move around, mate," I shot back, not liking the interruption or the pompous tone. "What's it to you?"

"Your mother," he said, and damn if that didn't stop me dead. Not much could, but the 'M' word was a full-stop on any day.

"Go on," I growled, arms crossing over my chest as a shield.

"Her will," Holt continued, holding out a thick envelope sealed tighter than Fort Knox. "You've reached the age where it can finally be disclosed. Shall we?"

"Inside," I said, jerking my head towards the house. Couldn't stand there gawping in the drive like a galah while the world spun on.

"Of course," he murmured.

"Watch the step," I warned as we entered the dim rental.

"Thank you," he said, but I wasn't really listening. My mind was racing, wondering what ghosts were about to spill out of that envelope. What part of her was coming back to haunt me on my twenty-first birthday?

"Sit down, get it over with," I said, voice rough as

concrete. Steeling myself, I waited for the past to come knocking.

I slammed myself down in the threadbare armchair, the kind that squeaks betrayal with every shift of weight. The solicitor, Holt, perched on the edge of the sofa like a bloody crow – all dark suit and shiny shoes. He slit open the envelope with a flick of his wrist, precise, no messing about.

"Your mother's will," Holt said, voice low as he handed over the sheets of paper. They felt heavy like they were soaked in her absence.

"Cheers," I said, not feeling thankful at all. I scanned the pages quickly at first, then slower, each word etching itself into my brain. My eyes snagged on a sentence, and I read it again, and then a third time. "Bloody hell..."

"Something the matter?" Holt asked, trying to peer over, but I angled away from him, protective.

"Didn't know..." I started, then shook my head. My grandparents, bless them, had done their best after Mum and Dad died. Raised me with more love than I knew what to do with. But this? This was news to me.

"Her folks were Poms?" I blurted out, my voice rough as sandpaper.

"English, yes," Holt confirmed, nodularity to his tone that got right up my nose.

"Never said a word about it," I mumbled, half to myself. Grew up thinking we were as Aussie as they come. Meat pies, footy on the weekends, sunburnt Christmas days. And now, out of nowhere, I'm part Pom?

"Often, families have complexities that—" Holt began, but I wasn't in the mood for a lecture.

"Save it," I snapped, cutting him off. Finger jabbing at the text, I demanded, "What's all this mean, then? What am I supposed to do with a bunch of English... history?"

"Perhaps you should continue reading," Holt suggested, irritatingly calm.

"Right," I said, clenching my jaw. Because that's what you do, isn't it? You keep going even when life throws you a curveball straight to the face. Just another secret unravelling, another piece of the puzzle that was my mother.

I flicked through the sheets, each one a slap to the face of what I thought I knew. "Bloody hell," My voice hitched as I muttered those words under my breath, rough like I'd swallowed a chunk of drywall. I ran a hand through my hair, trying to piece together this jigsaw of family history I'd never heard my grandparents utter. The paper felt too crisp, too real against my calloused fingers—builders' hands that had never touched anything so life-altering.

"The gist of it, your mother was Australian born, but the roots, Mr. Waterhouse, as you can see, run deep through English soil." Holt's words were like a drill, boring into me with precision.

"Deep through English soil," I repeated, scoffing. "Sounds like the tagline for some posh gardening show."

"Quite." Holt didn't crack a smile. Probably didn't know how.

"Three properties, eh?" I squinted at the list, feeling the weight of the revelation. All in the same town—someplace I couldn't pronounce, let alone imagine visiting.

"Correct. A considerable inheritance," he added, as if I couldn't count.

"Never even been on a bloody plane before," I spat out, thinking of the furthest I'd ever been—some rundown beach shack up the coast, not a sprawling estate in merry old England.

"Perhaps now's the time to consider travel," Holt remarked, but I just shook my head.

"Travel..." I snorted. "Righto, mate. Let me just drop everything and bugger off to the Queen's land. Got bricks to lay, don't I?"

"Of course, Mr. Waterhouse, but these assets—they're not something to be taken lightly."

"Didn't plan on jugglin' 'em, did I?" The sarcasm dripped from my tongue, a defence mechanism when I felt cornered by the absurdity of life.

"Understandably, this is a lot to absorb—"

"Absorb..." I cut him off again, a bitter laugh bursting free. "Feels more like drowning, mate."

"Take your time," Holt said, standing up, ready to leave me with my newfound lineage sprawled in front of my eyes.

"Time," I echoed, watching him head for the door. "Yeah, reckon I'll need a fair bit of that."

As the door clicked shut, I sat back, alone with the ghosts of a family I'd never met and the dusty reality of properties left untouched. My birthright—or some twisted joke from the past. "Cheers, Mum," I whispered to the silence, a toast to the woman who'd left me more questions than answers. And now, apparently, a legacy hidden in the cobbled streets of a foreign land.

I flicked the thick cream envelope, disbelief etching lines in my brow. Three bloody houses. Here I was, sweating it out laying bricks, and there sat a trio of English ghosts on paper, just gathering dust. My fingers traced the faded ink on the will, the looping handwriting like a map to a hidden treasure I never knew I was hunting.

"Three bloody generations," I muttered, the words tasting like iron on my tongue. "Unlived in." The idea was mental, houses standing silent, watching the world change while they stayed locked in time, like bloody mausoleums.

"Trust fund's been coughing up for taxes all this while, eh?" I scoffed, thumbing through the legal jargon that made less sense than a roo hopping down George Street. Who the hell sets aside a pile of money for land tax on places nobody's sleeping in?

The air felt heavy in the room, thick with the scent of old paper and the lingering tang of my morning coffee. Shadows clung to the corners as if echoing the abandonment of those English properties. It was a lot—too much—and it gnawed at my gut like a starved dingo.

"Bugger me," I said aloud, though no one was around to hear. My voice bounced off the walls, a stark reminder of the solitude that matched those empty houses. Heritage or headache? That was the question.

"Should be chuffed, right? Strike it rich without lifting a finger..." My laugh was a harsh bark, the sound rough in my ears. But it's all a bit sus, innit?

My mind raced, thoughts jumbled like a mob of sheep in a pen, all baaing for attention. Power, hierarchy, the whole shebang—the weight of it pressed down on me, a heavy crown I never asked to wear. Roman, the accidental heir, with a lineage lost to time and an ocean away.

"Right then. What the bloody hell do I do with you?" I asked the silent room, addressing the legacy left by strangers who shared my blood. The question hung in the air, unanswered, as I reached for my phone.

"Need advice from the olds," I decided, thumb hovering over Grandpa's number.

With a deep breath, I dialled, bracing for the torrent of questions and exclamations. This birthday was turning out to be a real corker—one for the books, with a plot twist I never saw coming.

FOUR

ACKLES HARRIS

23 Years Old

It's an oddly clear dawn, with not a single cloud painting the sky grey, here in usually rainy England. I am on my routine morning run through the Newchurch Moors, a rich tapestry of floodplain meadows of grazed pasture and woodland flowers like wood anemone, primrose, bluebell and wood aven, giving my surroundings a prairie feel, with patches of marshland and denser woodland.

My long curly ginger hair oscillates from side to side thanks to my high ponytail, and even though the break of day normally means bitterly cold air, I am only wearing black biker shorts with a black cropped peekaboo long-sleeve hoodie on top of a black plunge sports bra. I like black.

As I get swallowed up in the midst of trees and shadows, the melody of songbirds echoes in the air, with the peculiar drum from woodpeckers here and there. Most of the time I am lucky and get a glimpse of a red squirrel leaping from branch to branch, or a bat fleeing the fading darkness as the sunlight starts to break through the cracks amongst the trees, or even a fox crossing my path on its hunt for dormice or human rubbish.

All of that beauty, yet, the only thing that makes me stop in my tracks is a towering slaved away rusty old iron gate. Every day, I place my hand on the neglected chain keeping the secrets beyond it locked away. Maybe, I think to myself always, I can climb over the gate or anywhere in the surrounding property fence, even though the top of the metal bars ends on a pointy spear that most definitely could do some harm by slashing some of my flesh off. But at least I would be walking amid the ghosts it hides.

What is it about this Devil house that screams to me in a soul-gripping and spellbinding siren song?

I drag my feet through the dirt below them, taking as many steps back as I need before I can break the enchantment and go on my merry way.

After getting home, taking a scalding shower and having a proper English breakfast of bacon, sausages, scrambled eggs, fried tomatoes and mushrooms, black pudding, baked beans and toast. I head to the police station where I work.

Today is the day. In the wake of years of going through the Police Constable Entry Programme, training and working under my Papa's wing, and 3 years of taking online classes on Criminology, I am finally getting promoted to Detective. Dear Papa, I hope you are proud.

Last year, he finally succumbed to his abuse of the Devil's drink. Following Mama's passing, Papa got driven to the bottle pretty much every day as a way to battle his demons.

You would think if anything he was feeding them. His liver decided to give up on him, the way he decided to give up on a clear of any hellish fog mind.

When you are a kid, you can't possibly see the signs for what they are. To me, it was just Papa drinking a funny-tasting and usually awful-smelling drink, a lot of it, which made him strangely numb but jovial. Ignorance is bliss, and as long as Papa kept telling me his scary bedtime stories nothing was amiss.

When you are a teenager, you don't want to see the signs and think paying no heed to it is the best way forward. Also, you have your own drama to deal with, like does Poe Phillips fancy you – news flash he didn't, he just wanted to pop my cherry. Parents should know better, after all, they should have it all figured out.

By the start of your young adult life, you finally see the errors of your ways and try to intervene, but by then it's too late, the damage is done, the plague has set in and it's consuming its host from the inside out.

Don't get me wrong, I loved my Papa, and if anything the illusion of happiness on his part did give me a blithe upbringing, but watching him waste away in a hospital bed at the end because I couldn't mend his broken heart, fractures mine in the process. Those were dark days, more blackened than when Mama died, at least she went so suddenly she didn't get to suffer – at least that's what Papa told me, - while you could feel the agony and pain sweep through my Papa's hazel eyes as the disease ate him alive.

"Morning, Hopps." Orwell, a fellow cop, says the moment I walk into the police station. I hate how the boys I work with keep calling me variations of Judy Hopps, a character from the Disney movie Zootopia, just because I am a girl cop. In a way, it's better than what the other kids named me growing up. Witch. Right now the worst one is...

"Bunny, there you are. Bargrave is waiting on you in his office." Doyle utters.

Byron Bargrave was my Papa's best friend and took over as chief of police once things took a nasty turn.

"Right, thanks."

I softly knock on the closed office door.

"Come in." I hear Chief Bargrave, command from the other side.

Once I do so, he informs me to take a seat as he gestures to the uncomfortable four-legged oak wooden chairs in front of his desk. Reluctantly I settle my ass on one of the very worn-out upholstered seat and backrest cushions.

"Chief." I call for his attention.

"Harris." He says as he looks at me with his dark brown eyes from the top of his reading glasses that are almost at the tip of his nose. He's a nice-looking man, in his mid-forties, his dark brown hair has started greying at the roots, and some lines of time are beginning to take shape around his face, but that actually makes him look more alluring. Not that I would hit that, he's like an unrelated Uncle, and his wife, Bridget, is like a Mama to me. They both have been my safe haven since Papa took ill.

My parents had me quite young; Mama was just shy of 18, and Papa was in his twenties, 22 I believe he was. And here I am at 23, never having left the quaint town I was born in, living in my parents' home – just with no parents, - single, no kids, and this, what's about to happen, is what I have yearned for since Papa first told me the tale of the Devil house up the road. What comes next, off the back of achieving your only dream? Where do I go from here?

"I drafted up a contract, once signed you will be Newchurch's newly appointed Detective." Chief Bargrave tells me.

"You wrote it up?" I playfully ask him.

"Well, Miss Bronte did, but I told her what to put in it."

I hum in agreement with his statement.

"That explains why it is not handwritten then."

"Don't you give me attitude, young lady." He voices in a disapproving tone.

"I didn't say anything... that wasn't verifiable. Everyone knows you and technology don't get along, Chief." I remark.

Chief Bargrave leans on his seat, crossing his arms over his chest. "You take that from your Dad."

"What? My charm?" I ask, batting my eyelashes. "Or my somewhat bawdy and raw way of dealing with the world?"

"That. Your heedless way of being and sassy mouth is sure to spill trouble your way sooner or later." He observes.

"You love me really."

"Not the point, Ackles."

"Just give me the paper, before you change your mind," I say as I overreach for the contract on the desk. When in my hands I start to read through it.

"I don't want you to be disappointed, Harris." The Chief speaks under his breath.

"What do you mean?" I question just as I am scribbling

my signature where the Barbie pink small sticky tabs indicate me to do so.

"Not much happens here. You know that."

He's not wrong. This backcountry little town doesn't see much of anything, lawbreaking wrongdoers or delinquents are scarce in this neck of the woods, which is not a bad problem to have. But that means that murder or any crime that needs a thought investigation is going to be hard to come by here. I think the last time this, as the Americans would call it, Hicksville had something happen was back in the 1600s when the witch trial occurred.

Perhaps, I am setting myself up for a letdown. Who knows, maybe down the line I might ask for a transfer to a bigger town, where there's more action, more drama, maybe even London where I could follow some tragic gory real murders. Wow, I am a terrible person for wishing someone to die horribly just so I can scratch an invisible itch.

"There are some cold cases that you can dig your claws in. Your dad was going through them before..." Chief Bargrave clears his throat, like something he's not supposed to tell almost slipped out of his mouth but he stopped himself just in time "... that bloody Devil house became his obsession. I am certain you could find the files for them scattered around your dad's messy office at home. But if you are not ready to go in there yet, you can just ask Miss Bronte, she will show you where the originals are in the archives, here in the police station."

"Or print them out for me?"

"Right. That. You're dismissed, Harris." Byron says as he

shoos me away. "On your way, you can give her your contract so she can do whatever she does with stuff like that."

I nod my head acknowledging his words, get up from my seat and head towards the door.

"Ackles." The Chief calls out.

"Yes, Chief."

"Just promise me you won't fall down the same rabbit hole your dad did."

FIVE

ROMAN WATERHOUSE

Present Day

The screeching of the saw cut through the morning air. I wiped the sweat from my brow, flicking it onto the sawdust-strewn floor. A few years back, Mum's will had hit me like a gut punch, all formal with its legalese and promises. Now here I was, 28 and still knee-deep in timber and nails, but the itch to bolt was getting too fierce to ignore.

"Oi, Roman! Shift yer arse, mate!" Jezza hollered from across the site, his voice gruff as sandpaper. I flipped him the bird without looking up, but a smirk twitched at the corner of my mouth.

"Steady on, you old bastard," I shot back, hefting another plank onto the workbench. Seven years with the company, seven years of breaking my back for someone else's dream. The blokes were decent enough, but the drone of hammers and the stink of labour had soured. It was time to carve out something that was mine.

Mum's will hadn't just left me some cash; there were properties halfway across the world, old English stone and mortar that could be my ticket to something grand.

I revved up the saw again, the whine drowning out the chatter. As the blade bit into the wood, I felt a piece of the chain that held me to this place break away. My own company. My name etched into the city bones'. That was the dream, and I'd be damned if I didn't chase it down.

As the sun dipped low, casting long shadows across the concrete, the idea niggled at me again. England. Mum's old lands. Could be a right ripper of an opportunity. Fix them up, flog them off, and build a portfolio that'd make any bloke jealous.

"Strewth, who am I kidding?" I scoffed, imagining the rolling green and stone walls of the motherland. It was gutsy, but didn't every mongrel with a bit of bite, dream of their own empire?

"Better than bustin' me hump here till kingdom come," I decided, slamming my hard hat onto the bench. I needed to get out and chase down the chance for something epic. Something mine.

"Oi, Roman! Knock off time!" yelled one of the lads.

"About bloody time," I shot back, grinning despite myself. Tonight, I'd sit down, crack open a cold one, and plan. Tomorrow, I'd start paving the road to my own bloody castle. And not just any pile of rocks – no, this would be a fortress built on my terms.

England. The thought sent a jolt of adrenaline through my veins. I could almost hear the chink of coins, the rustle of notes. A fresh start. A new legacy.

"Look out, you Pommie bastards," I whispered to the setting sun. "Roman's coming, and he's bringing the storm."

)O(

THE ROAR of the plane's engines was nothing compared to the racket in my head as I touched down at Heathrow. Jet-lagged but buzzing, I stumbled through customs, feeling like a scrappy dog that'd chewed through its leash. London was a beast of a city, but it wasn't my kennel.

"Ta," I said, slapping a few quid into the cabbie's hand. The black cab had seen better days, much like the bloke driving it, but it got me out there, away from the hustle and straight to the heart of Lancashire.

As we rolled into the small town, the sign loomed like a joke: 'Population 404'. Someone had slapped a fresh '404' on it, shining like a new penny against the rusted backdrop of the old digits. "Bit of a facelift on a corpse, that," I muttered, craning my neck to see past the peeling paint.

"Welcome to nowhere, mate," the cabbie grunted, his eyes meeting mine in the rearview mirror.

"Cheers for the lift," I said, hauling myself out with a duffle bag that carried more dreams than clothes. The cab took off, leaving me in a cloud of fumes and the tangible stillness of a town too tired to care.

The solicitor was waiting, a proper English gent with a shiny car and an umbrella, even though the clouds were holding their piss for now. His grip was firm, his smile tight.

"Mr. Waterhouse, I presume? Nigel Brompton," he introduced himself, giving me a once-over that didn't miss the steel caps on my boots or the tattoos peeking from under my sleeves.

"Call me Roman, mate," I said, cutting through the pleasantries. "Let's take a squizz at what Mum left behind, eh?"

"Very well," he replied, unlocking the car.

We drove in silence, the miles ticking away as I took in the green rolling hills, a crisp difference from the sun-scorched earth back home.

"Quite the inheritance," Nigel commented as if reading my thoughts.

"Quite" I retorted, my gaze fixed on the horizon.

Nigel didn't say another word, just offered a noncommittal hum. I didn't need his chit-chat; I needed to see those places with my own eyes and size up the bones of them.

"Here we are," Nigel announced as he pulled over.

The car crunched to a halt, gravel spitting beneath the tyres like it had a personal vendetta against them. My eyes scaled the large stone wall stretching before us, old as hell and twice as stubborn, winding through the countryside like some kind of ancient serpent. The rain had started pissing down again, blurring the edges of the stones into a grey smear.

"Jesus, look at that," I muttered under my breath, pressing my face closer to the window, fogging up the glass.

Nigel's voice cut through the drumming of water on the

roof. "Impressive, isn't it?" There was a note of something in his voice, something that was close to horror.

"Looks like something straight outta a bloody movie," I said, more to myself than him. It wasn't just impressive; it was intimidating like it held secrets and stories thicker than the moss clinging to its sides.

We had stopped in front of a gate—a towering wrought iron beast that looked like it could've given a medieval army a run for its money. A fat chain bound it shut, rusted but strong.

Nigel shuffled out into the rain, his jacket pulled up over his head as if that flimsy bit of fabric would do bugger all against this deluge.

I watched as he fumbled with the keys, cursing the heavens or the lock, I couldn't tell which. With a grunt of triumph, he unlatched the padlock, and the chain slithered to the ground with a clatter.

"Here." Nigel thrust the keys into my hand as he jumped back into the car, the metal cold and slick against my skin. "I guess these are yours now."

"Guess so," I replied, the keys suddenly feeling heavy like they were about to drag me down into the mud. This was it —no turning back now.

"Let's see what Mum's left me to play with, eh?" I said, more to brace myself than anything else, driving onto the property that was mine, for better or worse.

"Indeed," Nigel murmured, barely audible over the rain on the roof of the car.

He revved the engine and we rolled onto the estate, tyres crunching on the gravel path that seemed to have seen better days. To the right stood a small cottage, its windows like bleary eyes squinting against the daylight.

"Strewth looks like it's hangin' by a bloody thread," I muttered, eyeing the sagging roofline. But as we got closer, I noticed the stonework, solid and unyielding, like the backbone of some ancient beast. "Foundations are ace though," I added, more to myself than Nigel.

"Indeed, Mr. Waterhouse. Structurally sound, according to the last survey," he offered, his tone clinical, but I could tell he was trying to sell me on the idea.

"Needs a fair whack of elbow grease, doesn't it?" I observed the prospect of tearing into the work sparking something fierce in my gut.

"Quite." Nigel's agreement was curt, his eyes already shifting to what lay ahead.

He cranked the wheel left, and there it was—the second building, a stone doppelgänger of the first but two stories high, with a bit more meat on its bones. The windows were intact, at least, giving the impression it wasn't completely knackered.

"Looks like she might've been a beaut once upon a time," I said, a smirk playing across my lips. This one had potential, not just for a quick spruce-up but maybe a proper home. "A bit more room to stretch your legs in this one."

"Potentially quite comfortable after renovations," Nigel chimed in, though comfort seemed like a foreign word to him.

"Reckon so," I replied, taking in the mossy stones and the wild garden trying to swallow the place whole. "Bit of hard yakka and she'll be right as rain."

We continued to roll up the gravel path. I leaned forward, hands gripping the dash as the main house loomed into view —massive, an old beast squatting on the land. Stone and timber jutting out like the ribs of a long-dead leviathan. My heart hammered against my ribcage; this was it, the big score.

"Jesus, would ya look at that?" The words tumbled from my lips, breath hitched with the raw potential before me.

"Indeed," Nigel murmured, but his voice was a distant buzz against the drumming in my ears.

Three stories, maybe more if you count the attic space peering out like watchful eyes. I could see dollar signs in every crumbling brick, each splinter of wood. She was rough as guts, sure, but nothing a bit of elbow grease couldn't fix. And the money, bloody hell, the money. This wasn't just a fixer-upper; it was my golden ticket, my way out of the rat race.

"Reckon we could fence off the smaller plots, sell 'em separate." My mind raced ahead, plotting, and planning. "This one's the real prize, though."

"Quite," Nigel agreed, pulling out a hefty ring of keys and leafing through them. "It's been years since anyone took proper care of it. A significant undertaking."

"Understatement of the year, mate." I climbed out of the car, boots sinking into the soft earth as I craned my neck to take in the full height of the place. The air smelled of dampness and decay, but beneath it all was the scent of opportunity, rich and intoxicating.

"Can you get me everything you've got on these properties?" I said, already halfway to the front door, eager to inspect every inch.

"Of course, Mr. Waterhouse," Nigel called after me over the rain.

"Cheers." I didn't look back, too caught up in visions of what could be. The door groaned open under my hand, revealing shadows and dust motes dancing in the slanting light.

"Better find a local pub then, I need a place to crash and sort through this mess," I spoke mostly to myself, thumbing the peeling paint on the doorframe. It was going to be a mammoth job, no two ways about it, but I was ready for the challenge.

Six

Ackles Harris

Present Day

This is it, no going back now. As I sit here, on a stool by the counter, at one of our local pubs in Newchurch, drinking my usual virgin mojito and eating their homemade Lancashire butter pie, a flaky pastry filled with delicious potatoes, onions and lashes of butter. A sense of serenity takes over my body and soul. I don't touch the Devil's drink, in any way, not after what happened with Papa. So I made Austen, the bartender and owner of Yo Olde Boot & Shoe, learn how to do a medley of mock-tails. When we landed on the virgin mojito, which is a simple mix of lime juice, simple syrup, mint leaves, limes, club soda and ice, I was done for.

"What's new, buttercup?" Austen asks me now that there is a calm moment in the bar.

I love Austen, she is a badass bitch that takes no shit from anyone. She's the total opposite of me, tall – everyone is a fucking giant when compared to my pint-sized 5'1 – tattoos that cover up most of her pale skin, she has beautiful straight raven hair that just slips past her shoulders and alluring hazel eyes. She's only a few years older than me, at 32, whilst I just reached 26.

"I finally did it," I tell her with delight oozing out with every word.

"Hmmm, sorry to break it to you my teeny friend, but didn't you lose your V-card ages ago? With what's his face?" She clips her fingers as she tries to remember the guy's name "Poe Phillips." Austen says gun fingers pointing at me.

"That's not what I meant."

"Oh my God, you finally did anal," Austen shouts.

I shush her. Fuck, there is no way the whole bar didn't hear that.

"No." I howl back, making sure all prying ears hear that too. Rumours spread like wildfire in this little town of ours. That's how I found out about Doyle cheating on me. The asshat.

To be completely candid, there aren't a lot of options in this sea, most of the fish you can catch around this town are gross, to say the least. Mama used to say "If you can't say something nice, don't say anything at all", so I am going to leave it at that. Pretty sure she stole that from a Disney movie, Bambi maybe.

Either way, Doyle was the only decent man I could find. At a full 6 foot, well-built physique from going to the gym every day, caramel blonde hair, like Papa used to have, and dark brown eyes. The fucker was hot, ok. Don't give me shit for being a horny bitch looking for a pretty boy.

The thing with boys like that is there is always a joker in

the pack. Doyle is just that, he's a serial cheater. For 11 months we dated, and if the gossip around town is to be believed, he rolled around in the sheets with at least 7 different women in that time. The nerve of that guy. And there I was, bending to all of his kinky sexual needs like a fucking sex doll, and I still wasn't enough. Should've picked up that something was wrong when he wouldn't tell me that he loved me back. Because that's the truth, I fell, as water falls from the February sky – and any other month in this country.

"I handed in my transfer to the Edinburgh police force." I finally informed Austen.

It took a while to convince myself I needed a change. When I finally set my mind and heart on Scots for Old Smoky, Chief Bargrave was more than happy I asked for it and said he would do everything in his power to make sure I got it.

What was it he said to me? "A beautiful caterpillar-like you shouldn't be cocooned in a dump like this. It should spread its majestic butterfly wings out there in the big bad world." That's exactly what a woman wants to be called a larva. Not.

3 years of working as a detective in a town where the only disturbances are kids playing pranks on Father Demis by grafting weird runes and satanic symbols on the walls of St. Mary's Church. Or dear old Mrs. Payne hitting Mr. Payne with the rolling pin again, over a dispute about, well, last week it was over how he told her that the moon landing in '69 never happened and the footage we see is actually a Hollywood production, and she absolutely lost it. *"How dare*

you taint my credence in stuff with your silly conspiracy theories?" You know, I think Mr. Payne does it just so he can get her attention. He probably sits down at their 90's desktop computer, googles a tall tale deception, somehow, and just rolls with it to annoy his wife.

Is it weird that I want something like that? Maybe not the antagonising bit or the beating someone with a kitchen utensil, just to be with a person for that long where they know everything about them and them about you, because you are one another's other half.

Can't find that here. Not if he – whoever he is - doesn't come to me. Maybe out there I will have the chance to meet that someone.

"You can't leave, Ackles. Who am I going to tell my sexcapades to?"

"Everyone? I am pretty sure I hear about you dogging it in the Newchurch's Moors with that girl from the next town over, Agatha was it, from Christie." I remark.

"Right. But you are the only one that gets the juicy details."

"If only there were these things we could use to communicate with each other from a distance."

"HA, very funny, buttercup."

"Pigeon's. That's it." I utter all of a sudden. "I will get us one so we can send messages over to one another."

"Get out of my bar," Austen says amusingly as she points to the door.

"Nah, I don't think I will. I haven't finished my pie yet." I state as I stab said pie with my fork, gathering a big chuck, and shoving it into my mouth. "Honestly girl, I think Father Demis is just about ready to exorcize you."

"He would have to catch me first. And seeing that I'll never set foot in church again, that ain't going to happen."

"Priests aren't confined to holy ground. They can walk amongst us sinners too." I chuckle.

"Damn, now you tell me."

We both start laughing, as a group of previously ordained gross men walk in the bar.

"Hey Austen, can we get a round over here?" One of them orders, as they all take seats on the other end of the counter.

"Coming right up, boys." Austen yells back at them, as to me, in a murmur she remarks "Because saying please is too old fashion." I giggle.

"While you are at it, can you get me another drink?"

Austen crosses her tattooed arms under her chest, pumping those DDs up, and arching an eyebrow at me.

"Please?" I eventually offered up.

"Good girl." She tells me as she turns away to prepare the drinks.

"I'm telling you there was someone walking around the Devil's house with Nigel Brompton this morning." I overheard Eliot, one of the guys, say.

"The solicitor?" Another asks.

"Yeah."

The Devil's house? Like a fucking moth to a flame, my ears just perk up at those words. That place is my quiet obsession, not even Austen knows about it, and I consider the girl my best friend.

"That land is private property, still owned by the Device

family," I announce it to the group of guys. "Nigel should know better than to take random fellows in a merry-go-round of that falling-to-bits place."

"That's the thing, Ackles, apparently this guy owns it," Eliot informs me.

"Guy? What guy?" I question him.

"Aussie, and very much so. His momma left him the crumbling buildings of the Device estate in her will or something." One of the other boys tells me.

"He's a Device?"

"Waterhouse his last name is. Rowan? Or Roman, perhaps." Eliot says.

Are you fucking shitting me? Are you telling me the same morning I decide to take my life into my own hands and take a risk on something beyond this place, you send me a guy? And not only a guy, someone that owns the fucking Devil's house? Fuck, right, off.

"Apparently, he plans to fix the place up." Eliot continues on. "Split the three houses into different properties and sell them that way."

"He's fixing them? And selling them? Doesn't he not know the history of that place?" I cross-question poor Eliot.

"Like Nigel would ever spill the beans." He observes.

"The guy is in for a nasty surprise."

"Who in their sane mind is going to help him repair that land?"

"Who is going to buy them from him? Definitely not anyone from around Newchurch, that's for sure."

A few other guys comment. I mean, they are not wrong. This Australian guy has no idea what just landed on his lap here. The Devil's house, the Device estate, it's a haunting mare's nest, embedded with skeletons in every closet. I wonder if I can get him to let me snoop around, you know before I leave. Finally, scratch this itch I have.

Roman Waterhouse, ready or not, I am about to rock your world. Or just bedevil the hell out of you.

SEVEN
Roman Waterhouse

The solicitor's car growled away, leaving me in a puff of exhaust and small-town dust. I stood there, the local bed and breakfast looming before me like one of those quaint joints you'd see on a bloody postcard. Charming, with a weathered sign swinging above the double door entryway that creaked an invitation or a warning—I wasn't quite sure which.

"Righto," I muttered under my breath, hitching my bag higher on my shoulder as I trudged up the steps. The doors were ajar like the old girl was gaping her mouth at me, ready to spill secrets of past visitors if only walls could bloody talk.

I stepped inside, the scent of beeswax and something sweet hitting me hard. My eyes took a second to adjust to the dim interior, all decked out in lace and wood, like stepping into someone's overdone memory of their grandma's house.

"Can I help you, love?" The voice cut through the quiet, friendly as a slap on the back. She was an old sheila, parked behind the front desk, greying hair twisted up in a bun so tight it could've been winding her chipper smile tighter. "You look like you've come a long way."

"Sorta," I replied, giving her a once-over. Her eyes had seen things, I reckoned the kind that made them too bright, too eager to please. It set me on edge, but I kept my own grin fixed in place. "Just need a place to crash."

"Of course, darling." She beamed, keys jangling in her hand like some sort of bloody welcome tune. "We'll sort you right out."

"Reckon I might be stickin' 'round a bit," I muttered, scratching at the stubble on my chin. "How's the policy for a kip here? Might need a couple of nights."

"Two-night minimum, sweetheart," she chirped, tapping something ancient into her computer that hummed like an old fridge. "Keeps the riff-raff out, you see?"

"Fair dinkum," I said, curling the corner of my lip. "Let's make it three then, just to keep the bloody peace."

"Three it is," she echoed, her smile never faltering as she handed over a registration card. "And what brings you to our little slice of heaven, if you don't mind me asking?"

"Got some real estate tossed my way," I replied. "Plan to spruce 'em up, flip 'em quick smart. In and out, no mucking about."

"Ah, the renovator's dream," she cooed, her head bobbing like one of those dashboard dogs. "You'll find plenty of character in the bones of this town. Lots to work with."

"Character, eh?" I snorted. "We'll see if that pays off when the hammer starts swinging."

"Which bits of dirt did you get your mitts on then?" she asks, leaning forward like the gossip's just too good to pass.

"Device estate and the land around it," I say, dropping my gaze to the card I've just filled out. "Whole lot."

Her face goes as white as a cocky's feathers in a split tick. "Oh, that's nice, dear," she stammers, pushing a brass key across the counter with her now trembling digits. "Room eight, up the stairs, second on your left."

"Righto." I pocket the key, but can't help squinting at her sudden change in colour. "Everything copacetic?"

"Of course, love," she says, but there's a quiver in her voice. She ushers me off with a shaky hand. "Enjoy your stay."

As I head for the stairs, I can feel her eyes drilling into my back, sending prickles up my spine. Just what the bloody hell is up with this place?

)○(

SUN CRACKED the horizon and I was bolting down to the breakfast room like a joey with a dingo on its tail. My stomach was rumbling something fierce, but I wasn't just chasing the chow. No, mate, I needed answers. Last night's queer look from the old girl had been playing on my mind, making sleep skittish as a possum in a spotlight.

The dining hall was all dolled up like a sheila on Saturday night. Lace curtains, china plates—proper fancy. But there, shoved in the far corner like an afterthought, was a table sporting a slip of paper with 'Waterhouse' scrawled across it. Didn't take Einstein to twig I was being put out of earshot.

"Morning," I grunted, slumping into the chair that seemed to be carving out a quiet little slice of solitude just for me.

"Good morning, dear!" It was her, the grey-haired Sheila who'd checked me in, all chipper as if yesterday's spook hadn't happened. "What can I get you?"

"Whatever you reckon's the pick of the paddock," I said, leaning back and eyeing her carefully. Was there a twitch in her smile? A flinch in her eye?

"Right, love," she chirped, pivoting on her heel quicker than a wallaby on the run.

"Hey, wait up—" I started, but she was already halfway to the kitchen, not looking back. Something was crook in this town, and I had a hunch it was more tangled than a bush ballad. Whatever the hell was going on, it was clear as mud these folks weren't keen on chinwagging about the Device estate.

"Best be worth the bloody trouble," I muttered under my breath, drumming my fingers on the table. The plot was thickening, and it sure as hell wasn't just the gravy for breakfast.

The clatter of crockery yanked me back to the now as a platter heaped with grub landed in front of me. A proper English breakfast, enough to make a grown man weep with joy—or maybe that was just hunger talking. Either way, my stomach growled its thanks, and I dove in like a dingo at a butcher's shop.

"Ta," I mumbled, mouth full of egg and bacon, barely

glancing up as the old bird nodded and flitted away. Couldn't help but scarf it down; there was a riddle waiting to be solved, and I wasn't about to solve it on an empty gut.

Bangers and beans, toast so thick you could use it for a doorstop, eggs done just right—this meal was a ripper. My fork was making quick work of it, like a miner through pay dirt, when the thought struck: time's ticking, Roman. With a final swig of coffee strong enough to kick-start a dead kangaroo, I wiped my mouth and stood, ready to face the day.

"Cheers for the tucker," I called out, not waiting for a response. The streets were calling, and I needed answers.

Three streets—that's all it took to cross this blink-and-you'll-miss-it town. Felt like stepping back in time, each cobblestone whispering secrets if you listened hard enough. But they weren't spilling the beans on the Device estate, that's for bloody sure.

I pushed open the solicitor's door, the bell above giving a half-hearted jingle like it couldn't be arsed.

The solicitor's office had the stale air of a place that'd seen more deals gone sour than a milkman in a heatwave. The bloke himself, Mr. Brompton, was perched behind his desk like a vulture eyeing a carcass, envelopes in hand, a look of relief plastered across his weasel face.

"Roman, mate," he said as I walked in, thrusting those yellow packets at me like they were a hot spud. "Can't tell you how chuffed I am to be shot of this lot. That estate's been a right thorn in my side."

I frowned, taking the envelopes. "That bad, huh?" It didn't sit right, his eager-beaver act. A shiver ran down my spine, and not from the draft in this musty excuse for an office.

"Reckon it's cursed, do you?" My voice was light, but my gut was coiling tight. Something about all this was as off as a bucket of prawn heads in the sun.

"Ah, don't get yourself in a tie," he chuckled, but the laugh didn't reach his eyes. "It's just been... complicated."

"Complicated," I echoed, thumbing through the papers. They crackled with age and secrets. "Righto, let's hope the local library's got a bit more dirt on this caper."

He gave a noncommittal grunt, already shuffling papers, dismissing me. I left, feeling the weight of his gaze on my back.

Outside, the world seemed too bright, too normal. I shoved the envelopes into my jacket and made a beeline for the library. Time to see what the ghosts of yesteryear had to say about the Device mess I'd inherited.

The library was a quiet little joint, the kind where you could hear your own heartbeat echoing off the walls. I strode in, boots clomping on the polished wood floor, the sound out of place in the silence.

I marched up to the counter, my boots still singing the song of city grit against small-town polish. The librarian, a bird-like woman with spectacles slipping down her nose, peered at me like I was the main character in a plot twist she didn't see coming.

"Lookin' for anything on the Device estate," I said, dropping the name like a hot rock.

"Got any old newspapers, records, that sorta thing?"

Her eyes widened, and she sucked in a breath, quick and

sharp as if I'd just asked her to recite her own obituary. "Sorry, I have nothing in here on them," she stammered out, and with a swiftness belying her frail frame, she turned her tail and scarpered off into the labyrinth of shelves.

"Jesus, H. Christ," I muttered under my breath, eyebrows knitting together. "What's the bloody story with this place?" The stench of secrecy was rank. My gut churned, something about this whole song and dance felt off-kilter.

"Bugger it," I grumbled, whipping out my phone. A quick jab at the keys and the council's address pinged up. Conveniently located next door to the library. With a huff of frustration, hot on the heels of unanswered questions, I shouldered through the exit, my mind a riotous mess.

"Let's see if the council's got more than just bloody paperwork and red tape," I growled to no one in particular. The door to the council building loomed ahead, as inviting as a dentist's chair. But answers weren't going to find themselves, were they?

I barrelled into the council chamber, a whiff of old wood and musty paper. The place was as dead as a doornail, save for another bird-like woman perched behind the front desk, pecking away at a keyboard.

"Oi, I need to snag some paperwork you've got on file," I barked, no time for niceties anymore.

She looked up, eyes round as saucers. "A meeting will be necessary. May I have your name?" Her voice was a rehearsed chirp.

"Name's Roman. And I don't need a bloody meet and greet; just the docs. Someone's gotta be around to chinwag about it now, right?"

"Let me just call through..." she said, reaching for the phone with a sigh that told me she'd rather be anywhere but here.

"Make it snappy," I pressed, drumming my fingers impatiently.

With a click and a murmured conversation, she pointed me through a door to where a bloke sat hunched over a desk the size of Uluru. His cheeks were red enough to stop traffic, and he was built like a meat pie, all round edges and puffed-up pastry. But his mug was friendly enough, even if it was slicked with sweat.

"Roman, is it?" He didn't wait for me to nod, already shuffling papers like a croupier at a casino.

There was an earnestness to him that made me think he wasn't part of whatever cloak-and-dagger act this town was putting on, but I was about as trusting as a cat at a dog show. Something reeked, and it sure as hell wasn't just the damp council archives.

The council bloke had a handshake like a wet fish, but at least he was looking me in the eye. "I'm Barry—Barry O'Connor. How can I help you today?"

"Right, Barry," I started, leaning forward, elbows on his desk that looked older than time itself. "It's about the Device properties. I've inherited the bloody things and I'm looking to give 'em a spruce up, maybe flog 'em for a decent price."

His mug, which had been all politeness and pleasantries, went white as a ghost. He sputtered into his coffee, the dark liquid sloshing over the rim of his mug and onto the stack of papers he'd been thumbing through.

"Oh, um... okay," he coughed out, swiping at the mess

with a sleeve already stained with god-knows-what. "I'll just, uh, grab what we have. One sec, mate." And just like that, he bolted from the room.

"Christ," I muttered under my breath, raking a hand through my hair. What the hell was so cursed about these properties that had everyone in this town acting like they'd seen a bloody ghost?

EIGHT

ACKLES HARRIS

The rusty old chain lock is gone. Nothing is holding these gates to hell closed anymore. Why is it that these devilish playing grounds were eerily quiet just a few days ago, now seem to scream like a fucking banshee? I have this weird ringing in my ear, like static waves whooshing past it.

I could easily push on these cold heavy metal bars, sneak in and have a peek.

"You should never enter the Device's estate, the Devil lives there. His devoted witch servants will take your soul and drag it, kicking and screaming, to the deepest part of hell."

I can see now why Miss Craft wasn't too fond of Papa's stories; he wouldn't beat around the bush. He was always the type to say it as it is. God, I miss him. Now the question that plagues me, was his version of the tale webs he spun red-herrings just to keep a curious mind like mine away or is there some gospel to it? I mean why else would the whole town look at this place like there are bodies buried every-where amongst these grounds?

Witches aren't real. Most of these people tried and executed as so back in the day, were accused purely as scape-goats to church politics, property feuds or children's outbursts of stupidity. It was all a sick demonstration of the mentality of that time, where someone says I don't like you bitch, or I don't know you, or you have something I want, therefore I am going to say you are a witch so I don't have to look at your ugly face no more. It was child's play, the act of pointing a finger at someone, throwing whatever you could come up with at them and seeing if it would stick.

Books like 'Malleus Maleficarum', which translates to the 'Hammer of Witches', by Heinrich Kramer, and 'Demonolo-gy', written by a fucking king of Scotland (and later England), were like bibles used to diagnose someone as a witch, how to get them to confess they slept with the Devil and what to do with such a servant of Satan as a punishment afterwards.

Courts were simply a joke back then. Written laws that allowed such things as visions, dreams, and even the testi-mony of spirits permissible as evidence are almost laughable if they weren't so horrifyingly unjust.

Diseases that couldn't be explained other than the Devil caused it, wouldn't help the accused causes, and most of the places you read about where witch trials happened, outbreaks of unexplainable illnesses, needless to say, did occur. Failing crops and dire harvests didn't lend a helping hand either.

So many lives ended, thanks to mass hysteria over

anything and everything really. Either burned to a cinder at the stake, a noose around their neck or losing their heads as they were cut clean off. Debatable on the clean, I don't think the end of the sharp blades used ever saw any soap and water, and it took three blows to sever Mary, Queen of Scots head, that must've looked pretty jagged at the end.

When it comes to the story behind the trial of Pendle witches of 1612 that happened just around these parts, the outbreak of 'witchcraft' and the many allegations correlated to that resulted from accusations that members of the Device and Chattox families made against each other, perhaps because they were in competition, both trying to make a living from healing, beseeching, and badgering. Both of these families earned money as traditional healers, using a mixture of herbal medicine, talismans or charms; which may have left them wide open to charges of fiddling in the black arts and flirting with Satan.

In the end, all of these inquisitions and executions are an awfully sad tale that taints our history, and we have to grasp the errors of our ways and learn from them, or we are damned to repeat them.

One step. Two steps. Three steps back. And the noose around my neck ruptures and I can finally breathe again.

"Damn you, Devil's house, why do you entice me so?" I whisper in the wind.

I'm disappointed, I was kind of hoping I would cross paths with this Roman guy. It seems fate was against us on this one. And the previous few times I ran by the Device's estate in the past days. I am not stalking per say, I have been running this way for years so that's not new in my routine. I guess one would hope the opportunity to meet would arise.

Hmmm, actually, now that I think more carefully about it and as I peer down at myself, maybe coming face to face with him for the first time in my well-loved and well-worn black leggings and, also, black peekaboo sports bra, while all sweaty and my rats nest hair in a high messy bun is no meet-cute material or the first impression I want to leave on him. Thanks, fate, good call there.

As I head home I come across sweet old Sheila who waves me over. This better be because she baked a batch of her delicious Eccles cakes and wants to give me some.

"He's nothing but trouble, dear." She tells me the moment I am right next to her.

"Hello to you too, Shy-Shy. And aren't all men so? But who is this 'he' that has your knickers in a twist?" I ask.

Her wrinkles become more pronounced as she furrows at me.

"You're a gremlin too, missy."

I laugh at her remark.

"This entire town had a hand in raising me, so if I am trouble, then you are all to blame for it."

"The boy from down under," Sheila states all of a sudden.

"What about him?"

"Trouble."

"Ok," I chuckle.

"You should stay away from him. He's a Device." She continues on.

That's exactly why I won't stay away from him, but I

won't tell Sheila that. He has the key to the Devil's house. Literally.

"Isn't he staying under your roof? And Eliot told me his last name was Waterhouse."

"Does not matter what he goes by these days, the Devil's blood still runs deep in his veins." She tells me in a matter-of-fact manner like that's the holy gospel or something.

"You shouldn't judge a book by its cover, Shy-Shy," I inform her.

"I am not, dear. I am judging it by its contents."

"Right. Stay away from the Aussie. Got it." I say those words with as much conviction as I can master, but we both know they are lies.

"I mean it, Ackles. That whole family is a cul..."

"I have to go." I interrupt. "Work."

"You don't start for another 3 hours," Sheila remarks but I am already long gone.

Once home, freshly showered, I sit by my dining table. Breakfast has been discarded and left to go cold as I go through what little notes I have on the Devil house.

The old bad habit of biting my nails is back, just like this damn obsession. Having someone in town kindred to this haunting closed book that is the Device family and estate, has made me more invested in finding out further information on them.

My eyes move from the papers dispersed all over the table before me – mostly stuff that Barry O'Connor had in the council archives, some cold cases files that I find fishy and scribbles of my own of Papa's stories - to the door that holds, maybe not all but some, answers to my vastness of questions.

Papa's office. I am not allowed in there. At least that's what I have been saying for the past 4 years. He's gone. This is my house now, I am entitled to enter and exit every room in my own home. Except, maybe, the attic and the basement, one is full of spiders while the other is full of dampness and mould, so I won't go in any of those for my own health and safety.

Ok, Ackles Danneel Harris, this is it, get your sweet ass in that room this instance.

I get up so abruptly that the chair I was sitting on tumbles to the floor. The loud thud as it hits the black and white squared tiles echoes all over the house.

"Shit," I utter.

I make my way ever so slowly and silently to the door, which makes no sense considering that I already made a racket with the chair, and most importantly there's no one in this damn house apart from me. So who the hell is going to catch me with my pants down?

I stand before it, my back stiff and my palms sweaty, for a small number of seconds before placing one of my hands on the handle and turning.

"I'm sorry, Papa. A man made me do it."

This hiss of cold and stale air brushes past me just when the door squeaks and creaks as it opens. Fucking creepy. Dust particles dance in front of me, solely being brightened by a strip of dim light coming from the kitchen behind me, cutting through the darkness of the room. The room smells musty from being closed for so long but, there, well hidden in the midst of it all, a hint of Papa, the scent of bourbon, vanilla and white oak lingers still.

One step. Two steps. And just as I am about to take my

third step, I almost get knocked out of balance and fall on my ass. Amongst the full-shelved walls filled with dusty books, right next to a beautiful Victorian presidential mahogany desk, there's this crime board with the Devil house right in the centre of it and red string connecting it to an array of other clippings.

Oh my, "Papa, couldn't stay away either I see. You Holy Willie, telling me not to do something yet you go and do it yourself."

NINE
ROMAN WATERHOUSE

The stack Barry O'Connor gave me was hefty enough to double as a weapon. I dropped onto the bed, papers scattering like seagulls when you chuck a chip at the beach.

"Alright, let's see what the hell this is all about," I muttered to myself, rifling through the pages with fingers that twitched with impatience. The scent of dust and ancient ink rose from the documents, and somewhere in the back of my mind, I wondered if Tibb Device himself had touched them. That bloke and his missus, Lilith, started this whole mess back in 1655.

The oldest joint, crafted by their own hands, no doubt, was a testament to whatever madness drove people back then. 'Built to last', they'd probably said. Well, it did, and now it was mine to deal with. The scratching of my pen against a notepad echoed in the silence as I jotted down notes. "Tibb and Lilith Device, huh?" I read aloud, my voice bouncing off the walls. "What were you two up to?"

A shiver crawled up my spine, uninvited and unwelcome,

as I leaned back against the headboard. The air felt thick with history, each layer a story untold, secrets kept, lives lived and lost. I shook my head, trying to dispel the creeping sensation. "Get a grip, Roman," I snapped at myself. "It's just an old house. A really bloody ancient house."

I could almost hear the echoes of the past whispering around me, the rustle of parchment-like leaves in the wind. My focus sharpened as I tried to piece together the puzzle that was my inheritance, the legacy of the Devices. Something about being connected to these historical figures, these pioneers of their time, stirred a sense of dread in my gut. Or maybe it was just indigestion.

"Damn," I said under my breath. "1655, Tibb and Lilith. What a pair." I couldn't help but wonder what kind of people they were, living in a world so starkly different from my own. Did they walk around in those fancy, stiff collars and talk all posh? Or were they the rough-and-tumble types?

I tossed the papers aside for a moment, rubbing my eyes. The weight of centuries bore down on me, and I hadn't even scratched the surface. But one thing was clear – whatever happened here, it started with them. And now it was my problem to solve. "Crikey," I whispered. "You better be worth it, Tibb and Lilith." With a deep breath, I plunged back into the sea of paper, determined to unravel the mystery of the Devices and their damned, enduring house.

I stumbled on a family tree that looked old as hell. "Bloody Nora," I muttered, tracing my finger down the line of ancestors. Tibb and Lilith had popped out three sprogs before she carked it.

"Christ, Tibb, you didn't have much luck, did ya?" I

scoffed, half-expecting the ink to whisper back some cheeky retort. The silence that followed was unsettling though—like the room suddenly knew more than it should.

My gaze drifted to the next bit, the creepiest part: the family crypt. Lilith's name is etched in stone, her rest eternal under on the bloody estate. But Tibb? Nothing. No date, no stone, no nothing. "Vanished into thin air, did ya, mate?" I whispered, a shiver tiptoeing up my spine despite the balmy night.

"Spooky shit, this." I rubbed at the goosebumps on my arms, cursing the morbid curiosity nibbling at the edges of my brain. It was like Tibb Device was playing a sick game of hide-and-seek with death. And now, here I was, caught in the bloody middle of it.

"Where'd you go, you old coot?" I mused aloud, leaning back. The urge to bolt was there, to leave this eerie legacy behind, but nah I was invested now.

"Missing dead blokes and ancient secrets," I chuckled darkly, shaking my head. "Welcome to the family, Roman. Hope you survive the initiation."

"1705, huh?" I muttered to myself, tracing the date with a grubby finger. "Second place built for Mr. and Mrs. Device while the kiddies played house." Where the bloody hell did they stash all that coin? No mention of what kept the coffers full. Bootlegging? Smuggling? Witchcraft? The paper was tight-lipped, keeping its secrets locked up tighter than a nun's cunt.

"Typical," I grumbled, tossing the page aside, frustration nipping at my heels. Bloody cryptic ancestors. The Device clan were as elusive as a drop bear on a moonless night.

"1730 now, we've got a veggie patch masquerading as a farm." I laughed, short and sharp. A whole damn section dedicated to cabbages and spuds, yet not a single bloody clue about the green they were really raking in. This lot knew how to keep their cards close to their chest, alright.

"Strewth, you're all a bunch of cagey bastards, aren't ya?" I spoke to the ghosts of my lineage as if they'd pop out of the woodwork for a chinwag. The silence that answered back was thick enough to cut with a knife.

"Farm, my ass," I scoffed, pushing up off the bed. Veggie farm listed in the records, but no dirt-stained fingernails or sun-kissed necks among this mob.

"Fine, keep your bloody mysteries," I spat, standing up with renewed vigour. My head buzzed with questions, every unknown detail another jab in the side, prodding me along. I'd get to the bottom of it, crack the code of the Devices. It was personal now, a challenge etched into my very DNA.

"Let's see what else you're hiding, you sneaky pricks," I said, determination fuelling my next steps. With a final glance at the cryptic papers, I steeled myself. This was more than just an inheritance; it was a legacy laced with shadows, and I was diving headfirst into the fray.

I yanked open the drawer where I'd shoved the solicitor's paperwork, a bastard of a task that had me swearing under my breath. Another family tree sprawled across several sheets, looking more like the blueprint to a bloody maze than any sort of lineage. My eyes darted over the names, tracing the inked lines that connected one Device to another, a roadmap of stubborn blood and secretive lives.

"Three kids, all hitched, but two not a single sprog to

show for it," I muttered, my finger paused on the stark emptiness beside two of the siblings' names. "What the hell were you lot playing at?"

But there, in the corner—the youngest. A glimmer of hope? Nah, just another twist in the tale. She popped out three, the little rebel. "Good on ya, love," I conceded with a wry smile, despite the chill that crept up my spine. Maybe she was the anomaly, the break in the pattern. Or maybe she was the beginning of something else—something deeper.

The paper crackled as I turned it, every fold and crease echoing through the room like whispers from the past. And there it was—the continuation. Two of her offspring followed the path of barren matrimony, but the youngest, again, forked off another set of three. "You're kidding me," I breathed out, the repetition gnawing at my gut. It wasn't random; it couldn't be. This was calculated, a riddle etched into the very essence of the Devices.

"Carrying on the bloody legacy, weren't ya?" I said, half-expecting the walls to respond. No such luck.

The trail led me down to my great-grandparents, and wouldn't you know it? Three rugrats for them too—Three more sheilas. But here's where it gets really rich: the eldest pair, dry as a dead dingo's donger, with no offspring. "What did you do to piss off the fertility gods, eh?" I chuckled darkly, shaking my head.

Then there was my grandmother, the wild card of the bunch. Packed her bags and pissed off to Australia at the ripe age of eighteen. Never looked back. The thought of her, so young and gutsy, charging into the unknown with nothing but her wits and... what? What drove her? Fear? Ambition? Desperation?

"Bet you've got stories that'd curl my toes," I whispered, feeling an odd kinship with the woman who birthed my mum and left this twisted heritage behind.

She had one child, my mother. Just one. Broke the pattern, or maybe started a new one—who's to say? I let out a long breath, rubbing the tension from my jaw. The silence of the room pressed in around me, heavy with the weight of generations, their secrets bound up in these papers.

"Devices," I said with a shake of the head, "you're a tough nut to crack. But I'm onto ya." With a newfound resolve simmering beneath my skin, I folded up the family tree, tucking it into my back pocket. Might as well carry the ghosts with me—they seemed keen on haunting my steps anyway.

TEN
ACKLES HARRIS

I haven't slept. Actually, I haven't done much since walking into Papa's office other than go through everything that Cave of Wonders holds. But that board, that fucking board, that's the Genie's magic lamp amongst all the scattered mess.

Now, either those are the findings of a genius or the ramblings of a madman, I can't know for sure until I get my foot in that door, literally. I need to get in the Devil's house. I will suck the Aussie's cock if that will guarantee me entrance, and depending on how hot he is, I might even let him fuck me.

And then there is this stupid antique rusty cast iron floor safe, with no crevice only a wheel combination lock and a lever. That thing is like the large ruby being held by a monkey idol that consumes Abu's full attention, makes him ignore all of Aladdin's warnings and does something foolish that almost makes them perish in the desert sand of Agrabah. I am Abu in this scenario.

I tried every number of marriages I could think of that Papa would use. Nothing. I tried googling it and watched YouTube videos on how to open one of these things. Nothing. I even tried a crowbar to the impenetrable metal coffer, and all I managed was a pretty nasty cut on my palm. Ugh! What could Papa possibly be hiding in there?

I am overcome with temptation and I feel like I am burying myself alive by this Device obsession. The safe may not even hold anything related to that, but I opened this can of worms, accidentally spilled them all over the place and I can't seem to find or catch all the wiggly creeps and put them back in the fucking can. I blame Roman. Why, oh why, did he have to come to town and stir this dormant pot? I hate him.

"Wow buttercup, that's it, I am cutting off the caffeine here. Your leg hasn't stopped bouncing since you've taken a seat at my bar." Austen comments.

I am a bit jittery; I think I am on my sixth cup of coffee today, which doesn't help. I make an effort to stop my leg from bobbing up and down after her words.

"And I thought you had kicked that vulgar habit of yours to the curb a while back." She continues on as I lower my hand away from my mouth. My nails are mostly chewed through to the distal edge either way, not much left to bite there.

Austen looks me up and down, puckers her brows and places her hands on her hips like a very disappointed mother.

"You don't look so peachy. The last time you had bags under your eyes like this was when you were stalking Doyle for weeks to catch him with his trousers down."

"I did end up with pretty great pictures though," I remark.

Austen chuckles. "Right. But you already knew he was cheating so why put yourself through all of that."

"Why? Indisputable proof. That I could throw in his face."

"Literally." She rapidly adds to what I just said.

I give Austen a cheeky grin. "Yup."

It still gives me rousing goosebumps remembering how I tossed the vanilla envelope containing quite a few sexually explicit high-definition photos of Doyle and his... other girls. His face when I did it while shouting "We are done," made all the sleepless nights sitting in my car, alongside my Nikon D70 digital camera with a wide angle lens, worth it.

"What has gotten you foaming at the mouth this time?" She asks.

"You are making it sound like I have rabies or something."

"Some bunnies are wild." I gasp at her comment. The audacity of this bitch, she knows I hate the Judy Hopps analogy.

"Don't you start too, I am not a bunny," I utter in a grim voice.

Austen puckers her lips and says "But you are so cute and tiny," which makes her sound like she's talking to a baby. She then boops the tip of my nose with one of her middle fingers.

"Some bunnies can be savage too. If you are not careful I might bite."

"Don't threaten me with a good time my friend; I might take you up on it." There's a hushed moment right after

Austen speaks those words, where we just stare at each other's eyes, waiting to see who will break first, and then we both start laughing uncontrollably. God, this girl is a pain in my ass, but I love her. She will, no doubt, be the one I will miss the most when I leave for Edinburgh.

Once I gather my composure, I ask her, "Aren't you dating... what was the flavour of this week again?"

"Cheryl. Yeah. But you know I would leave anyone for you, baby. We are each other's kinda crazy. And those perky little boobs on you, lick-able."

"Grow a dick, and I might think about it."

"If you two ever wind up together then the end must be near. That certainly has to be a sign of the apocalypse." Orwell notes from his seat at the bar.

"Shut up, Orwell." Both me and Austen say in chorus.

That's when he walks into the bar. This gorgeous specimen of a man, muscular, at least a good foot taller than me, sun-kissed skin with some tattoos poking out of the collar of his Henley navy blue top and his rolled-up sleeves, messy dark brown hair and alluring jade green eyes. Who's that hunk?

"Oh no," Austen utters with alarm in her voice.

"What?" My attention snaps to her.

"I know that look."

"What look?"

"That." She says, waving one of her hands right in front of my face. "You are pulling your 'I want to fuck that guy' face right now."

"What?" I bark a bit too loudly. "No, I am not." I protest.

My eyes go back to the very attractive man, who is taking a seat at the front of the bar as well, right next to Orwell.

"That's him by the way?"

"Who?" I ask her without taking my eyes away from the beauty that is scrolling through his phone as he waits to be served.

"The Australian guy that owns the Devil house."

Turning to face Austen, I howl, "Fuck me dead." I cringe at my raucous words. Damn, Ackles, use your inner voice.

A very manly chuckle penetrates my ears, coming from where that guy is sitting. Fuck.

"You're the Kiwi guy, right?" Orwell asks Roman, who's about to reply when I interrupt.

"That's New Zealand, you dipshit."

"Isn't that in Australia?" Orwell asks.

"Oh my God, dude, shut up," Austen tells him. "What can I get you, hot stuff?" She directs that question at Roman.

"What's good?" Oh, settle down my sweet pussy. I think I just about came with solely the roughness of his voice. I shift in my seat to find some relief between my legs. Damn, I need to get some quick, if this is all it takes to get my motor up and running.

"Butter pie." Everyone in the bar, apart from me, answers him.

"That, I suppose. And a pint of whatever is on the tap."

Austen just stands there, arms crossed under her chest, staring him down. I know exactly what she's waiting for, which makes me giggle.

"You forgot something, Mister," I inform him. He peers at me, and for a fraction of a second, our eyes meet. I swear in all that is holy, a spark of something I never felt before just shoots through my spine, making me spasm.

"I guess they never taught you manners in the colonies."

I gasp and follow that with, "Austen, I don't think you can say that anymore."

"It's all good. And my gran most definitely did. I'm sorry. Could I have what I asked for, please?" Roman says.

"Coming right up, hot stuff," Austen announces as she disappears around the back.

"You're the bloke that owns the Devil house, ain't you?" One of the patrons sitting at a table close to the bar asks Roman.

"The Devil house?"

"The Device estate." I clarify to him.

"Why do you town folks call it that?" Roman puts the questions to the room.

"The Devil himself lives there." Someone replies. "Tibb is his name."

"Tibb Device is the Devil?"

Skipping right through what Roman just asked, someone says, "There's a portal to hell in the basement of the original house."

"That place is haunted," Orwell interjects. "Right, Hopps?"

All eyes in the room fall on me. "My Papa used to say witch servants to Satan would lure you in and drag your soul to hell."

"Damn, right." Someone else utters.

"You better knock that whole place down, son." Another patron adds.

"No, you idiot. He should just leave it alone."

"Run before they get you, boy."

"I think there was a cult there." The whole room falls silent to my statement. Austen had just come out of the kitchen with a steamy Lancashire butter pie for Roman and even she halted in her tracks. "What? Y'all have been saying it for years. The Devices were a cult. It makes sense, the family numbers don't add up, the history of some of the buildings in the estate is iffy, to say the least, and then there's a bunch of cold cases that I think…"

"Buttercup," Austen says in a forbidding voice which makes me come to an abrupt standstill in my words. She shakes her head at me.

"Let me get this straight. Tibb is the Devil, the Devices were a cult and the houses are haunted?" Everyone in the bar looks at Roman as he's done speaking but stays silent.

Until Orwell breaks the stillness by pronouncing, "Pretty much."

Roman laughs which throws us all for a loop.

"You are all crazy. They are just bloody houses." He says.

"Right," Austen utters. "Here." She places the plate of food in front of Roman and starts pouring his drink. "Just houses. Maybe once they are done up they won't look too spooky and the creepy stories will die down."

"That's the plan." Roman asserts as he takes the drink from Austen. "Thank you."

"You," Austen says as she points at me, "a word." And then she heads to the kitchen.

"Oh someone is in trouble."

I get up from my seat to follow my best friend, lifting my

middle fingers to Orwell's words, and then I am gone from the room too.

Once in the kitchen, she tells me in a stern voice, "What in the heavens, Ackles?"

"What?"

"Someone would think you would have learned from your father's wrongs. You saw what that devilish place did to him."

"That place? No. I saw what losing my Mama and the Devil's drink did to him though."

"He was obsessed." She remarks. Yeah, well, like father, like daughter I suppose.

"Oh, I know. I went into his office." I tell her.

"You did? That explains it then."

"Explains what?" I am getting a bit frustrated here.

"The unhinged buzz you seem to be in. The lack of obvious sleep. When was the last time you ate something? That, needless to say, wasn't your nails."

"I am fine, mother."

Austen gives me this pitiful once over and says, "I wasn't much in favour of you leaving me, but maybe getting away from here will do you good."

"It's just a bloody house," I repeat Roman's words back at her.

"You haven't even gone in and it seems it has haled your soul already."

If my soul is already damned then I see no hitch in going in.

And after seeing that pretty boy out there, I would not only suck this Roman guy off, I would drink up everything he gives, let him fuck me six ways to Sunday in every position there is, and God, if he's an ass guy and wants to stick it in there, he can have that too. He can have it all. Not that one thing needs to be the condition of the other. I do want in the house. I do want to get under Roman. If I get them both, then even better.

Eleven
Roman Waterhouse

"Fuck it," I muttered under my breath, a plan suddenly snapping into focus in my mind like the sharp crack of a whip. I was going to do it; no more bloody dilly-dallying. I'd pack up my life in Oz, shove everything that mattered into storage, and move here. The UK had some charm to it after all.

The cottage was first on the list—probably the most buggered piece of architecture I'd ever laid eyes on, but it stood solid in its own neglected way. It would be mine to transform, to breathe life back into. I could already see it: the worn stones resurrected, the twisted timbers straightened out. Yeah, I'd shack up in one of those grand old buildings, make it liveable, make it more than just a relic—it'd be a home, my base for whatever came next.

"An amazing start to my portfolio," I mused aloud, excitement bubbling up inside me like a good brew on a Friday arvo. This wasn't just about fixing up a derelict spot; it was about proving something. To myself, maybe. To any wanker who thought I couldn't hack it in this game. It was tangible, something you could run your hands over, stand back and say, "Yeah, I did that."

"Renovator, designer, bloody miracle worker," I chuckled, the sound echoing off the empty walls. My hands itched for the feel of tools, for the satisfaction of peeling back layers of neglect to reveal the bones of something great. It was a challenge, sure, but I've never been one to shy away from a blue. Plus, the stories those old walls could tell—if they weren't so tight-lipped.

STARING at the old leather suitcase, I couldn't help but think how bloody lucky I was. Not every bloke is handed a goldmine at twenty-one. Three decrepit beauties waiting for me to roll up my sleeves and claim the rights to their rebirth.

"Righto," I muttered, snapping the case shut with a satisfying click. "Time to pack it in."

The house felt smaller as I moved through it, each room stripped of memories, bare and echoey. Never had much, but what was there got boxed and labelled for storage. My fingers worked on autopilot, wrapping, tucking, sealing—every piece a silent nod to the past.

"Off to make your mark, eh?" Grandpa's voice startled me out of my reverie as I stacked the last box.

"Something like that." I grinned, hoisting the box onto my shoulder.

Grandma came out from the kitchen, wiping her hands on her apron with that look she gets—you know, the one that's all pride and worry mashed together. "Just promise you'll come back to us, love."

"Wouldn't dream of letting you down," I said, giving her a peck on the cheek.

"Bring some of that English rain back with you," Grandpa quipped, the corners of his eyes crinkling.

"Rather bring the pub," I shot back, and we shared a laugh that filled the small space, warm and homely.

"Fly over when I'm done with the place, yeah?" The offer hung between us, an unspoken pact.

"Wouldn't miss it for the world," Grandma said, pulling me into a hug that smelt like fresh scones and home.

"Go on then, show 'em what you're made of," Grandpa said, his grip firm on my shoulder.

"Will do." I squared my shoulders, lugging my life to the car.

"Be proud, Roman!" Grandma called out as I slid into the driver's seat.

"Always am, Gran!" I yelled back, firing up the engine. A final wave and I was off, chasing the horizon and the future waiting across the sea.

The plane ride back to the UK was a blur of anticipation and crappy airline food. Landed with a thud, the wheels screeching like a cockatoo at dawn. Dual passport, living rights—a fair dinkum Brit now, too. But the Aussie in me snorted, not about to let a piece of paper tell me who I am.

"Let's get this show on the road." I shouldered my bag, feeling the weight of it, the right kind of heavy. The kind that meant business.

"Renovator, designer, bloody miracle worker," I echoed my earlier thoughts, stepping into the crisp evening air. Smirked at the sky, a dare in my eyes.

"Bring it on."

THE MIDDLE PROPERTY was a bloody mess, but it stood there, sturdy as a kangaroo in a boxing match. I dumped my gear in the corner of what might've been a living room once upon a time and pulled out my phone. The list of local builders wasn't exactly inspiring, each name was followed by a question mark—might as well have been a bloody blacklist.

"Right, let's crack into it then," I muttered, thumbing the first number.

"Hiya mate, name's Roman. Got a job for ya, a big one. Fixin' up an old place. You in?"

"Whereabouts?" The voice on the other end had that cautious tone like he'd found a redback on his toilet seat.

"Device property."

"Ah, nah mate, not a chance." Click. Deadline. Stone the Crows, they weren't kidding about the local fear factor.

"Bugger this," I said to no one in particular, "I'll give it another shot."

Second call, same story. Third, ditto. The legends about this place must be thicker than Vegemite on toast. Tempted as I was to stroll down to the pub, the last time I did, the glares were sharper than a sheila's stiletto. Reckoned I'd need more than a slab to get them onside.

But then there was her. The fiery redhead who'd looked at me like I was a lamington at a school fete—plenty hungry. She didn't seem the type to shy away from a ghost tale or two. More the kind to laugh in the face of a bunyip if it dared cross her path.

"Feisty little she-devil," I chuckled, reminiscing about the way her eyes had challenged me, all spark and spitfire. If anyone in this town had the guts to take on a project steeped in spook, it'd be her.

"Could use a bit of that fire," I admitted, scratching the stubble on my chin. With a shake of the head, I shoved my phone back into my pocket. Builders be damned; maybe it was time to roll the dice at the pub again.

"Or maybe," I pondered aloud, "It's about time this town met a bloke who doesn't scare easily. Devil worshippers or not, this place is getting a facelift."

And with that, I grabbed my jacket, prepping myself for round two with the locals. It wasn't just about fixing up a building—it was about proving a point. About showing 'em that Roman wasn't some soft cock to be scared off by shadows and tall tales. No, this was gonna be my portfolio starter, and hell or high water, it was gonna be a ripper.

The evening chill nipped at my cheeks as I strode through town, hands shoved deep in my pockets. The warmth and buzz of the pub welcomed me like an embrace from an old mate. I sidled up to the bar, nodding to the regulars who eyed me with a mix of curiosity and something akin to suspicion.

"Evening, Austen, wasn't it?" I greeted the bar lady, her name rolling off my tongue like a familiar tune. She was pouring a pint, her movements efficient and sure, not even glancing my way.

"Roman," she acknowledged, sliding the frothy glass to some punter before fixing her gaze on me. "Back again? What will it be?"

"Pint, whatever is on tap," I smirked, sliding onto a stool. "Got a question for ya, too."

She raised an eyebrow, wiping her hands on her apron. "Shoot."

"Seems I can't get a single bloke in town to help out with the property," I said.

"Ha!" Austen snorted, crossing her arms. "Here's the thing, hot stuff, you won't find anyone in this town fool enough to go near your haunted little fixer-upper. You're better off calling someone from outta town. Less super-stitious."

I couldn't help but let out a laugh, shaking my head at the absurdity. "Fair dinkum, we're talking about bricks and mortar, not the bloody Boogeyman."

"Tell them that," she said with a shrug, a hint of mirth dancing in her eyes. "Old stories die hard around here. People have long memories and short courage."

"Strewth," I sighed, leaning back and taking in the hushed conversations that circled the room like willy-willies. It seemed I had more than just renovations to contend with. But like hell, I'd let a few ghost yarns scare me off.

Fingers drumming an impatient rhythm on the scratched wood of the bar. "But why's everyone here so dead-set against the place? There's gotta be more to it than just being a bit run-down and creepy."

Austen polished a glass, her movements steady, but the furrow in her brow spoke volumes. "Look, Roman, we all grew up steering clear of that property. The stories about it are as old as the hills—ghosts, hauntings, you name it. No one in their right mind from this town will set foot there." She glanced around, lowering her voice like she was sharing top-secret intel. "They say bad things happened there. Things that make your skin crawl."

"Fuck me dead, ghosts?" I scoffed, incredulous. But inside, a niggling curiosity twisted my guts. Why were these tough country blokes shitting themselves over a few cobwebs and creaky floorboards?

"Sure, the place might've been a magnet for some twisted cult donkeys back in the day," I mused aloud, ignoring the chill that tickled the nape of my neck when I thought about the desolate halls and shadow-lurking corners. "But that's all history now."

"Doesn't matter," Austen replied, her gaze sharp. "The past has claws here, Roman. And it doesn't let go easily."

"Christ," I muttered, pushing away from the bar. Whether it was the challenge in her words or the stubborn streak that ran through me like the Sydney Harbour Bridge, something lit a fire under my ass. I'd renovate that godforsaken spot if it was the last thing I did.

"Cheers for the heads-up," I grumbled, throwing a couple of notes onto the bar. "Looks like I'm on my own with this one. But I didn't come back to get spooked by a couple of ghostie tales."

"Good luck," Austen called out as I headed for the door, the pub's warmth giving way to the night's crisp bite.

"Ta, Austen," I mumbled, the word a rough scrape in my throat as I shoved through the pub's door and into the night. The cool air slapped me awake, sobering the edges of my beer-blurred resolve. With every step away from the warm buzz of the bar and into the moonless black, I felt the isolation of this rural English hellhole wrap tighter around me.

I trudged down the gravel driveway, boots crunching like brittle bones beneath my feet. It was quiet, too bloody quiet, and I couldn't help but snort at the ridiculousness of it all – grown adults scared shitless of some old bricks and mortar gone to seed. "Ghost stories," I scoffed to the dark, "what a load of cobblers."

But as the shadowy outline of the house loomed ahead, something about it felt off. Not just old or abandoned, but like it was waiting—brooding with a presence that wasn't quite right. I shook my head, trying to dislodge the unease creeping in. Maybe the stories were true?

Twelve
Ackles Harris

He's back it seems. Roman is back. For a second there I thought we town folks had scared him away with our talk of ghosts, witches, the Devil and cults. But it appears he's either too smart to listen to our crazy talk or too dumb and stubborn to hear the warning in our tales.

I ran past the Devil house this morning and there he was, in all his glory, walking around the grounds with a phone glued to his ear and a frown on his handsome face. I may have stood rooted in place with only an imposing rusty iron gate between us for a few heartbeats. And just like all the other times before, I had to snap myself out of the spell that place had on me and continue on my way. Only this time it wasn't the house that was the source of my bewitchment, but Roman.

What is happening to me? I don't get like this over boys. Ever. I mean men. That Aussie finger-licking good-looker is all man.

Poe Phillips falls short, a mere teenage crush shepherded

by the idea that he was as much into the blood-and-guts macabre horror-filled stories as me. Thanks, Papa for making me into a weirdo Goth girl that just loved her scary narratives.

Phillips had left a note in my locker that read, "There is no exquisite beauty without some strangeness in the proportion'. Fucking 'Ligeia' by Edgar Allan Poe, which was, and still is, my favourite poem by that man. A beautiful dark tale about an obsession over a lost love, and it coming back to life. Much better than Romeo and Juliet and them, spoiler alert, both dying in the end and that be it.

Who wouldn't want a love that drives you mad even before it begins, that haunts you while you are together and after it's gone, and that compels you to conjure it up and raise it from the dead?

"Ramblings of a madman high on opium." Phillips had said soon after he got exactly what he wanted from me. "And you are the fool for falling for it." The bastard had used my most-liked author and my best-loved narration to deflower me, the witch daughter of the drunken chief of police.

At least he got one thing right; the dark poet was probably being greatly affected by drugs when he wrote these words, doesn't make the poem any less alluring though. Maybe two things, actually. I was a fool, but not by falling for Edgar Allan Poe's stories, but by succumbing to Phillips's charms. What's worse? Hearing what you want to hear or hearing what's honest? Luckily the pretty boy that broke my heart, with raven black hair and the darkest eyes moved to London before the ink was even dry on the page.

Doyle pales in comparison too. Papa's disease had

finally moored him to a hospital bed and, because of that, the one-night stands with guys from surrounding towns were not doing it for me anymore. I needed something meaningful. I guess I just didn't want to go through it alone or end up all by myself once Papa was gone. Doyle is a player and a fucking cheater, but he was there for me, right by my side as it all went to shit, which is probably why I fell.

When Papa died, I latched on to Doyle like he was my salvation rope, but as it turns out he was my damnation noose. We were toxic together. What's worse? Being wanted and not loved, or loved but not wanted? It was a typical relationship where I would give and he would take, where he held more pieces of me than the desert has sand, yet what little I had of him, I could hold in one hand.

It's funny I don't even hate the guy, really. Because right after I found out he was cheating, the rope around my neck broke and I wasn't suffocating anymore. My little stacking excursion brought back my investigating and snooping bug back and that's when I requested to be promoted to detective.

I realised I rather be alone but be me, than bend to anyone else's wants.

Now for Roman, I would bend into any position he wants me. Which doesn't make sense, I was meant to have learned something from Doyle, and Poe before him, yet all of it seems to be going swiftly down the drain here. Maybe I have been in a dry spell for far too long. 3 years is a long ass time.

'There was now a partial glow upon the forehead and upon the cheek and throat; a perceptible warmth pervaded the whole frame; there was even a slight pulsation at the heart.' I whisper.

"What did you say, darling?" I hear Agnes Grey Bronte, our secretary, ask.

I reply from my desk, "Nothing. Just talking to myself." Or more like, describing what being in the presence of Roman Waterhouse does to me.

"Oh, no. That's the first sign of an unbalanced mind, Ackles. Be careful or you will end up in the mental hospital." Chief Bargrave's wife says as she walks in and comes to stand by the information desk.

"Hey, Bridget," I utter lovingly.

"Hello, my dear."

"I thought that place closed down years ago." Agnes Grey interjects. She's about Austen's age, I think. I remember going through Austen's yearbooks, and they were definitely in the same year at some point. But then I also recall my best friend saying something about failing a grade or two.

"There's an insane asylum in Newchurch?" I ask, my curiosity piqued.

"No, dear. I believe Miss Bronte is talking about Tear-smith Hospital in Hollin Hall."

"Hollin Hall? There's nothing there. It's just fields and glamping now." Both the ladies share a look that very much tells me I am wrong.

"So... he's back," Bridget announces, quickly dropping the loony bin subject.

"Who's back?" Agnes Grey asks.

"The Device boy."

"Waterhouse," I note. They gape at me with confused

expressions on their faces. "He doesn't go by Device, his last name is Waterhouse. Roman Waterhouse."

"Well, whatever his last name is, he must come from a Devil worshipper's ash, he is so good-looking." Agnes Grey declares as she fans herself with her hand. The spite I feel for our sweet secretary, in the wake of her spoken words, throws me for a loop. Why the hell am I jealous here? Roman ain't mine. "Ackles?"

"Hmmm?" Did she say anything else as I was trying to reel in my green-eyed monster?

"He's hot, right?"

"Right." I quickly respond to Agnes Grey. "I mean, I guess. It must be because he's not from around here, which makes him new meat, exotic, and almost like he is forbidden fruit."

"Is he meat or fruit?" Bridget teases me.

"What?"

"You were rambling there a bit, dear." She informs me.

"Oh, right."

"Aww, you like him." Agnes Grey observes, giving me the biggest most genuine innocent smile possible.

"What? No, I don't." I bite out.

"Who does Bunny like?" Of course, Doyle decides to make an appearance at that moment. He sits his ass down on my desk. Rude. I eat lunch on it sometimes.

"No one. Go away, Doyle." I snap at him.

"Since you are here Doyle, I am assuming my husband is free to see me in his office now." Bridget interrupts.

"Yup, he's all yours, Ma'am. Just no shenanigans, these walls are thin." You can hear Mrs. Bargrave laugh as she strides into the Chief's office.

I slap Doyle in the back of the head.

"Ouch." He utters.

"Have you got no shame? You can't say that to the Chief's wife, you moron." Agnes Grey giggles at my remark.

"Is it the kangaroo guy?" Doyle asks as he rubs the spot where I hit him. Oh my God, I can't have this conversation with an ex. I bury my face in my hands, which, it would seem, tells him all he needs to know. "It is." He asserts.

"I don't know the guy." I declare, lowering my hands to my desk. "And by the only interaction we had, he probably thinks I am an unhinged bitch with weird taste in stories."

"Bunny, you kinda are all of that." I punch him in the shoulder this time around.

"Ouch. Damn girl, where was this fire when we were dating?" He tells me just as he lifts himself up from my desk.

I scowl and point my finger at him. "Fuck you, Doyle." As I get up too, I direct that same finger towards the door. "Now get out of my face before I break something on that body of yours."

He lifts his hand in surrender. "You know, you two are possibly perfect for each other. You are as mad as one another. The idiot has been calling around for local builders to help him but to no avail. They have all turned him down, so far."

"And how do you know this?" I ask him, still pissed. My palms are now flat on the desk.

Doyle crosses his arms over his chest. "Lewis told me he got a call from him this morning. And that some of the other guys rang him as well to let him know this Roman guy was trying to get someone to flip the houses on the Device estate."

"Why the hell would they not take it?"

"You're joking, right?" Doyle chuckles.

"It isn't like they need the money around here." I taunt Doyle. "Oh wait. They do."

"It's the fucking Devil house. No one in their right state of mind is going to set foot in that God-forsaken place."

"It's just a bloody house." I use Roman's words once more. Honestly, it's becoming a bit of a chant that leaves my mouth any time anyone tries to tell me I shouldn't go in there.

"You of all people should know that it isn't." Doyle says bitterly.

"What is that supposed to mean?"

He shakes his head. "Nothing." And with that, he's out the door.

A low and gentle sight startles me from my reverie. "That went well." I shot Agnes Grey a solemn look. Fuck, I forgot she was still here.

THIRTEEN
ROMAN WATERHOUSE

I punched the numbers into the phone with a kind of savage glee, my thumb jabbing at the screen as if I were squashing bugs underfoot. The ringing on the other end was like some bloody taunting echo until a voice cut through, gruff and brusque.

"Whittaker Constructions, speak up."

"Roman here. Look, I got myself a bit of a fixer-upper a few towns over, in Newchurch. Heard you blokes are the ones to call if ya want somethin' done right." My words spilled out in a rush, each one tumbling over the last like they were sprinting for the finish line.

"Fixer-upper, eh? What's the damage?" There was a clatter of machinery in the background, the cacophony of industry that sang music to my ears.

"Two buildings for now - one's a cosy little cottage, the other's a beast of a place. Been left to rot and reckon they'll both need a fair dinkum going over," I said, leaning back against the weathered timber of the porch, the old wood creaking its own complaint beneath me.

"Sounds like you've bitten off a chunky piece. Send me the address, we can swing by next week, and take a squizz. Got a team that loves a challenge."

"Appreciate it. And don't worry about toughness; I'm after blokes who can handle a hammer and not piss their pants at the sight of a real day's work." The sun beat down on my neck, hot and relentless, as if it too was challenging me to get this job done.

"Ha! You're on, mate. We'll send our best. Two crews, yeah?"

"Dead right. One for the small fry and one for the big kahuna. The cottage is cute as a button but the other's gonna be a bitch to sort. It's got more issues than my ex, and she was a handful, let me tell ya."

"Gotcha. We'll come prepared. Ain't our first rodeo with tough nuts to crack."

"Good. 'Cause I wanna start yesterday. Time's burnin' and I'm not here to fuck spiders." I could already picture it – the transformation from dilapidated dumps to something that'd make the posh city folks' jaws drop. A revamp with balls, something solid as a rock.

"Next week, Roman. Lock it in."

"Cheers, mate." I hung up, the phone slipping slightly from my sweat-slick grip. The builders were sorted. Cobwebs would soon be dust, the rot turned to splendour. This was happening, and it was gonna be a helluva ride.

)○(

THE MOMENT the lads kicked into gear, it was like watching a platoon hit the trenches. Dust billowed, wood splintered, and every crash of the sledgehammer sang out like a battle cry.

"Look at this place," I muttered to myself, sidestepping a pile of plaster that looked like it might've been white once upon a blue moon. "More fucked up than a soup sandwich."

I'd hauled every stick of furniture out to the old barn, my muscles singing with the kind of ache you only get from honest toil. The air inside the barn was thick with the musk of aged wood and mothballs—a sharp contrast to the tang of fresh sawdust back in the cottage. My eyes roamed over the collection: chairs with spindle legs, tables carved with the kind of care you don't see anymore, wardrobes that could swallow a bloke whole.

"Christ, there's a fortune here," I said, running a hand over a dresser that had more curves than a coastal road. "These pieces have stories, reckon someone would fork out big bucks to keep 'em going."

The thought curled in my brain like smoke rising from a fire. "Gotta ring up an antique dealer," I decided, thumbing through my phone for a contact. "Some wanker in the city will go apeshit for this lot."

I tapped the screen, holding the phone between my shoulder and ear as I crouched down to inspect a rocking chair. No stamp, no maker's mark—just smooth, worn wood that whispered of nights by the hearth and hands that knew their craft.

"Hey, yeah, g'day," I greeted the voice on the line. "Name's Roman. Got a shitload of old furniture at the Device estate, some of it older than my Grandpa's jokes. Looks like the real deal. Reckon you'd wanna take a squiz?"

"Handmade, you say? No stamps?" The anticipation in the dealer's voice was palpable, even through the tinny speaker. "Certainly, Mr. Roman. Handcrafted pieces can fetch a pretty penny at auction."

"Good-o," I replied, a grin cracking across my face. "Bring your chequebook, mate."

Hanging up, I wiped my hands on my jeans, leaving streaks of dust and satisfaction in their wake. There was power in reclaiming what time tried to erode away, in breathing life back into something left for dead. And if I could make a dollar or two in the process, well, that was just sweet as.

My boots crunched over debris as I surveyed the cottage, now gutted bare, its innards laid out in the open like a battlefield surgeon had gone to town on it. Sweat dripped into my eyes, stinging 'em like a bastard, but there was a rhythm to the chaos, a dance of destruction that felt bloody right.

"Oi, careful with that beam, mate!" I barked at one of the

lads, who was teetering on a ladder like an elephant on a tightrope. "We need this place standing, not flattened!"

My voice cut through the din of hammers and chisels. The workers grunted in response, muscles bulging as they propped up the sagging skeleton of the old girl. Each thud of the mallet, each cloud of stone dust, was a step toward redemption for this forgotten relic.

"Roman, these stones are stuffed," called out the stone worker, a bloke with hands like sandpaper and eyes sharp as a hawk. "Gonna need some serious elbow grease to sort this mess."

"Then get stuck into it," I replied, clapping him on the back. "Make her sturdy again. She's been through the wringer, and deserves a bit of TLC."

I stepped outside, squinting against the harsh afternoon sun. A landscape designer, clipboard in hand, surveyed the wild tangle of greenery that had once been gardens. He was all business, jotting down notes faster than a punter ticking off a betting slip.

"Roman, this garden's more overgrown than a maiden's leg hair in winter," he said without looking up. "But we'll whip it into shape, give it some class."

"Good on ya," I shot back, cracking a wry smirk. "Just make sure it's got some spunk."

Striding back inside, I watched the beams go up, the crumbled stones get replaced. It was hard yakka, but worth every drop of sweat. This place was gonna have new life—my life—pulsed through its veins. Power surged through me; I was the master of my own bloody destiny, shaping it with calloused hands and sheer will.

"Let's get a wriggle on, boys!" I yelled over the racket. "Daylight's burning and this beaut won't fix herself!"

The sound of progress was a symphony to my ears, as raw and real as the earth beneath our boots.

FOURTEEN

ACKLES HARRIS

I am bent over the desk in my Papa's office; my upper body lay out flat on the mahogany cold wood. Papers and whatever else that was on top of the surface I am now on, is scattered all over the floor. My leggings and thong have been pulled down to my knees and my sports bra lifted all the way to my collarbone exposing my breasts.

Someone is ramming into me from behind, filling my pussy in a way it hasn't been before. We fit perfectly like we were made for each other. Hard and rough pounding in and out of me as big manly hands dig their nails into the flesh of my hips.

The sound of carnal pleasure is all that echoes in the small room. Flesh meeting flesh, moans and groans, my own nails scraping on the wood below me and marking the pristine and otherwise undamaged desk like a diary entry for this moment in time.

I turn my head slightly to peer at my partner in this crime. Between the veils of ginger curls, I manage to see his naked, very well sculptured, trunk with sun-kissed skin covered in beautiful intricate tattoos. Most are around his chest, collarbone and neck then cascade down into full tattoo sleeves, but just under his heart, this gorgeous handwritten message rests. As I look further up, I am met with the most intense jade-green stare. A little twitch of his lip, before it turns into a sinful smirk.

Roman Waterhouse. He's the one fucking me right now. Wait. How did we get here? Shit, I can't think straight with him thrusting into me like that. Every time he maxes out deep inside of me, my pubis bone hits the edge of the desk sending sweet vibrations to my clit. I am so wet down there that Roman slides in and out with great ease.

I try to call out his name, but no words form. All I manage is some cohesive jumble of sounds, mostly moans really.

"Ackles." I hear a faint voice call out my name. It wasn't Roman since his lips didn't move. "Ackles." It calls out again, this time louder, more distinctive. Mama?

I look in the direction of the sound, to the wide-open office door. What the fuck is going on? My Mama stands there, in a white lace high neck long sleeve full-length gown. Shit, didn't we bury her six feet under in that?

I reach behind me with one arm, as my other lay beside me, elbow and lower arm levelled with the top of the desk and my hand gripping the edge with vigour. Placing my palm on Roman's upper thigh I try to make him stop with the best damn pussy slamming I had ever received. But he doesn't, Roman just continues on. Oh my God, can he not see her? Can he not see the ghost of my dead Mama watching us fuck like wild bunnies in Papa's office?

"He's going to take your soul," Mama tells me. Roman has to have heard that right? That was loud and clear. Yet, there's no relenting on his part.

I can feel these little claws scratching up inside of my belly, furiously trying to break out.

"Roman." Finally, his name flees my lips, but it comes out more like a purr of pleasure than a warning. Fuck, I am so close to coming it's almost painful.

That's when shit gets weirder, as my Mama steps through the threshold into the room she turns into this distorted and disfigured black mass. Lights flicker making the shadow appear closer and closer with each blink. This isn't real. It can't be. Part of me wants it to be, you know, the one that is getting fucked right into the gates of heaven, or hell, like this is a nice wet dream. The other part, the one stuck in a ghostly horror movie, just wants to wake up from the nightmare.

The shadow morphs on the next darkened patch, just before it emerges right in front of me. Erect dead ahead of my face is the Devil. It has cloven hooves for feet, unusual hairy legs and a serpentine tail, yet its upper body is all man, apart from the curled goat horns protruding from the top of its head. Fully blackened, with a herculean physique, the beast is a disturbing merge between a goat, a serpent and a man. It's fully naked and its monstrous dick is standing to attention.

"Come for me, my pretty witch." It tells me in a forbidding and chilling voice, its snake tongue darting out as it speaks. The tail wraps itself around my neck, constricting it and cutting off my air supply. When I open my mouth seeking relief from the pressure the Devil is putting on my neck, gasping in desperation, it shoves its dick inside. At the same time, Roman growls like a man possessed, his dick settling in the pits of my pussy. Hot jets of cum fill me to the point of overflowing, gushing out and down my legs.

My orgasm rips through me, tears me almost in half it's that fucking intense. I feel myself squirt. My own juices now marry themselves with those of Roman, smearing my wobbly legs.

"Come for me." The Devil says again, getting its dick further down my throat. Wait, didn't I just cum? What does the beast mean by that?

The Devil then turns into a snake. Its head, I am assuming, is what's deepthroating me and the rest of its body is the choker I am wearing on my neck. The snake begins to move, slithering inside me completely. And that's when I woke up.

I jerk awake, full body spasm, lifting my head from my cross arms on the desk surface. I look around in confusion and panic, as I move one of my hands to my throat and the other to the edge of the desk. I almost strangle both with how much I clench my hands around them, making sure this is real. A scratchy whimper flees my lips. I'm in Papa's office, sitting at his desk with a sea of papers before me. I must've fallen asleep as I went through his stuff on the Devil house.

Closing my eyes, I take a few breaths in and out, trying to calm my fast-beating heart. That was heavy. It was such a vivid dream that even now that I am awake I can't really tell if the dream is really over or not.

"Fuck. I am losing my mind." I utter to no one.

Gazing around the room one more time, I gather the

courage to get up from my seat. My arms shot out to the wooden top of the desk to balance myself, as my legs felt like jelly. The worst is the throbbing in between my legs. What the fuck? You know, that soreness you get off the back of your pussy being properly and aptly stretched out by a more than agreeable cock. Yeah, that's what it fucking feels like.

Ok, let's think rationally here. I dozed off in quite an uncomfortable position so that explains the legs being dormant. As for the ache in my pussy, that was one hell of a sex dream. I can feel the residue of it, soaking through my panties and sleep satin shorts, dripping down my legs. This is the first time I've ever orgasm from a sleep fantasy like that. I wonder if Roman has anything to do with it. Roman Waterhouse. He's turning into a bigger obsession than the Devil house and that's scary.

After a cold shower to relax all of my strained muscles and a little session with my vibrator, since it seems that coming while in my sleep wasn't enough for my insatiable pussy, I go back into my Papa's office.

This is what I harvest from his probing into the Device family and estate. What a fucked up story? Not much makes sense. There are more holes in this tale than in Swiss cheese. It's almost like someone tried to write a bone-chilling chronicle over what is probably a very mundane actuality. From the old Demdike lady finding the boy Tibb, who by all accounts of the time was considered the Devil, to her daughter falling in love with him, and to the whole Device family being executed as witches apart from him, as if taking him in cursed the family or something. And it only gets messier after that.

Why wasn't Tibb ever put on trial for being a witch? Was it because he wasn't really of Device blood so the accusers never thought of pointing a finger at him?

Then there is Tibb's first wife, Lilith, and her twin sister Polly. Papa seemed to have a lot of interest in that particular and peculiar twin set, especially Polly, who from what I can flock together, doesn't really have anything to do with Tibb Device. She married someone else in the village and lived happily ever after until her death. So how does Polly fit into the Devil house's creepy tale? There's a note from Papa that says something along the lines of only girls like the Device family. How is that important?

My sixth sense tells me the answer to that last question is in that bloody cast iron safe that I can't seem to get open. I glare at the rusty thing, praying that the invisible daggers I am throwing at it will spectrally unlatch it for me. No such luck. Damnit.

Papa also alludes to the mystery of why, not counting Tibb in this, for all of these years, the town folks only saw the women in the Device family roaming around the estate grounds and our quaint little settlement. Where are all the other men?

Tibb's daughters – yes, because this family only seemed to be able to sire female offspring, until Roman that is - were married. There are documents all over my Papa's desk that prove it, but the male names in them don't match to anyone anywhere. How these papers even exist is strange on its own, since the couples tied the knot on the Device estate with a priest that no one ever heard about or ever really saw.

That's when I think Papa starts overreaching a bit and

the cult idea is brought to life. Papa believed these men were actually some of the missing people from the surrounding area, brainwashed or spellbound by the Device daughters. He keeps going from facts to fiction, from nutty as a fruitcake bunch of weirdos to witches. I have a headache from this entire ping-ponging. The cold cases do dovetail though. Not only do the dates correlate but there are testimonies that state these men were romantically involved with the women from that family at some stage in their past.

I know the Device estate has a cemetery, but by folklore, the only people buried there are the women, not even Tibb is under those grounds. Without bones, we can't bind any of this shit together.

The children are another tangled web. Tibb had three children with Lilith before she died, but only the third had children, three girls to be exact, and the cycle continues on until Roman's grandmother, who breaks the pattern and only has one. Roman is another wild card here. The first male heir to the Device bloodline.

Yet, there are stories, whispers in the cold haunting wind, of people walking past the Devil house and seeing some of the older daughters also being pregnant. No record of death, birth or miscarriage for any of these tall tales, just another question mark. I dread to know, if true, where those poor children ended up.

A single tear makes a break for it. I think that's enough on the Devil house and its many darkened secrets for now.

I rally some of the documents and newspaper clippings from the desk, making an effort to tidy the surface up a bit. That's when I saw it. Whatever was in my hands fell to the floor, flying and dispersing everywhere around me. I brush my fingertips, in a light as a feather touch, through the rugged five lines on the wooden surface. On the edge of the beautiful Victorian presidential mahogany desk, scratch marks. My scratch marks.

Fifteen
Roman Waterhouse

I'd been tearing through the overgrown brambles around the cottage for a good chunk of the morning, sweat beading down my brow like I was a bloody water feature. Grub's up, and the landscaper's waving me over with a look on his face that spelt trouble in big, capital bloody letters.

"Roman, you gotta see this," he hollers, voice cutting across the hum of nature gone wild.

"Strewth, what now?" I mutter under my breath as I stomp over. The ground's littered with debris, and I'm crunching on God knows what with every step.

"Look at this," he says, pointing down to the dirt where he's crouched, all wide-eyed and serious.

"Flamin' hell," I curse when I see it. There are bones, all arranged in lines straighter than a ruler and not half as innocent. Chicken bones, I first thought, but these have got more history in them than your nan's china cabinet.

"Reckon they're from some sorta animal?" The landscaper's brows are knitted together, fingers gingerly prodding the soil.

"Could be chook bones, or something weirder." I kneel beside him, the damp earth soaking into my jeans. They're set out like some kid's twisted idea of hopscotch, patterns that dance around in my head until I feel dizzy looking at 'em.

"Never seen anything like it," he admits, scratching at his stubbled chin. "It's like they're meant to be here... like someone put them here for a reason."

"Let's not get carried away," I say, trying to keep the unease from my voice. "Probably just some local kids having a go at being spooky."

"Kids with a collection of bones?" He stands up too quickly, knocking dirt back into the hole we've been eyeing off.

"Stranger things have happened," I reckon, but I can't help the shiver that races up my spine like a surfer catching the perfect wave. It's a grim find, but I'm not about to let it scare me off. Not when there's work to be done.

"Righto, let's keep digging then. Can't let a few old bones stop progress, let's see where they lead?"

"Sure thing, boss," he replies, but the tremor in his voice doesn't escape me.

We dig like madmen, flinging clumps of earth behind us as if the faster we move, the less the chill in our bones. The sun sinks lower, casting long shadows that seem to reach for the patterns laid out beneath our feet.

"Look at this," the landscaper pants, his voice strained with more than just exertion. "It's all... deliberate."

And bugger me, he's right. The bones curve and twist, leading us on a merry dance around the cottage. My palms are slick against the handle of my shovel; dirt stains my skin but it's the unease that's really clinging to me.

"Christ," I mutter, because there it is. The end of the trail —a bloody pentagram, clear as day and twice as sinister. You'd have to be blind not to see the intention in its lines.

"Roman, that's some dark shit." The landscaper drops his shovel, the clatter loud in the quiet that's fallen over us.

"Probably just some sick joke," I try, but the words feel like ash in my mouth.

"Joke?" He scoffs and backs away from the pentagram. "I signed up for a bit of landscaping, not... whatever the hell this is."

"Come on, don't chuck a wobbly now. We can sort this—"

"Sort it?" He's already shaking his head, backing away further. "Nah, not a chance. I'm done here. This is... It's—it's not right."

"Oi, you can't just bail—"

"Watch me." He doesn't even look back as he strides off, leaving me with the bones and the creeping dread.

"Fuck," I hiss into the growing darkness. Alone now, with the whispering bones and the secrets they keep. I was going to have to remove them myself, make sure no one else saw the bloody mess.

So there I was the next day, pushing the throttle on the bobcat like it owed me money. Dust and curses flew as I tore through the earth, unearthing those bones with a vengeance. Didn't matter if they were chicken bones or bloody dingo's breakfast; they were coming out. I kept my trap shut about it all and didn't even breathe a word to the blokes down at the pub. Just dug 'em up, ignoring the way that pentagram seemed burned into my retinas. Pretended the chill crawling up my spine was just the morning air.

"Strewth," I murmured, leaning back in the seat, trying not to acknowledge the pattern. I'd be damned if some old wives' tales were going to spook me. Roman Waterhouse doesn't scare easily. But, bugger me, the hairs on my neck were having a right rave-up as I worked.

Once the land was nothing but a churned mess of dirt and freedom from those eerie bone lines, I parked the bobcat and stood there for a second. The chill had settled into my bones now, making me feel like I'd swallowed a slab of ice.

"Get a grip, Roman," I told myself. "It's just a job."

Took a day, but I finally got the courage to ring up another landscaper. Met him outside the cottage, under the light sun that made every shadow sharp and every whispered superstition seem a bit foolish.

"Here's the vision, mate," I started, pointing at the sketches I had for the garden. "Nothing fancy, just good, honest greenery. A place to sit and sip a cold one when the day's done."

He scratched his stubble, eyes flitting over the land, over where the pentagram used to be, now just a memory under the raw earth.

"Can do," he said with a nod. I liked that—no mucking about, no sideways glances. He just took the job on, and before long, the garden was taking shape, looking like something out of a bloody home and garden mag rather than a scene from a bushranger's nightmare.

"Cheers, mate," I said once he wrapped up, clapping him on the back. He just nodded, packed up his gear, and left me to the silent company of my new, unhaunted garden.

The cottage, though... that was another story entirely. Bloody hell. Inside was like stepping into the belly of a beast that'd swallowed all sorts of random crap. I'm chipping away at the plaster, and out falls this bag, stitched up like a kid's lost lunch. I catch it before it hits the dirt floor—feathers, stones, and shit tumbling in my palm. And then, bloody oath, I see it—a finger, all dried up and gnarly like something out of a witch doctor's wet dream.

"Fuck," I mutter to myself, the word barely a whisper. I can't let the tradies see this; they'll bolt faster than a roo with a dingo on its tail. So I collect the bags, every single one, stashing them away like I'm hoarding secrets for the apocalypse.

When night fell. It was just me and the moon, and I'm back at it, painting over the symbols scrawled inside the walls. They're done in mud—or at least I tell myself it's mud. Could be something far worse, but I'm not keen to find out. My heart's thumping a hard rhythm against my ribcage, but I keep slapping paint over every mark like I'm smothering memories.

"Bugger this," I say under my breath, each stroke erasing more than just symbols—it's wiping clean a past that's better left buried. The air's thick with the smell of wet earth and the sharp tang of fresh paint, and somewhere in the dark, the cottage creaks like it's sharing a dirty joke only it gets.

"Keep it together, Roman," I growl to myself, ignoring the prickle running down my spine. "It's just a bloody building."

But even as I say it, I can't shake the feeling that the walls are watching, waiting, laughing at the bloke who thought he could paint away their secrets.

The cottage gives me the willies, I ain't gonna lie. There's a chill in the air that doesn't match the weather, and every shadow feels like it's got eyes. The bag with the finger—I should've taken it straight to the cops, but something knots up in my guts and tells me to keep shtum.

)O(

"BUGGER IT," I say the next day, stalking towards my ute I purchased when I came back, it was a simple black one, nothing fancy, something that wouldn't upset me if it got a ding or two. The police station's not far, and I figure it's time to spill the beans to someone who can handle this sorta caper. But the moment I step through the door, I'm hit by the stench of stale coffee and printer ink. A receptionist looks up, her eyes scanning me like I'm some kind of puzzle she's not sure she wants to solve.

"Can I help you?" she drawls all business.

"Uh, yeah, look, I need to speak to someone—important-like," I say, scratching the back of my head. "It's about a find on my property."

"The Device Property? I'll get Harris." She's on the blower before I can get another word in, and I'm left standing there feeling like a drongo.

"Detective Harris will be with you in a tick," she says, hanging up and giving me a nod that's all too dismissive for my liking.

As I wait, tapping my boot against the linoleum floor, the station door swings open and in walks a sheila I recognise from the local pub—a real sort. Lightly tanned skin, hair like that Disney character that I can't seem to remember, but it is all red and curly, and legs that don't quit. She catches my eye, and I can't help but think about the last time I saw her, at the pub with a smile that could light up the darkest barroom.

"Roman, mate, you're drooling," I chide myself silently, tearing my gaze away.

But damn, if she doesn't make me forget about the bloody bags and bones and all the eerie shit for just a second. And in that brief flicker of time, with her scent—a mix of wildflowers and something untamed—in the air, I can't help but wonder about the taste of her, about the secrets she might hide behind those come-hither eyes.

"Roman?" a voice snaps me out of my daze, and there stands Detective Harris, Copper Extraordinaire, looking at me like I've got two heads. "You gonna tell me what's going on, or are you just here to perv on the locals?"

"Right, yeah," I say, shaking my head to dislodge the filthy thoughts. "Got a bit of a situation out my way. Reckon you might wanna take a look."

Sixteen

Ackles Harris

"Roman?" Shit, his name just slips out of my lips like smooth butter. Did he ever properly introduce himself to me? I don't think so. But I am a bit taken aback by him being here, and I am still a bit shaken up from that crazy and dirty dream I had. Luckily he doesn't seem to pick on that little blunder, instead, he seems to be in a haze himself, just staring at me. "You gonna tell me what's going on, or are you just here to perv on the locals?"

"Right, yeah," Roman says whilst shaking his head. I wonder what plagued his mind then, probably not the filthy shit that does mine as I look him up and down. "Got a bit of a situation out my way. Reckon you might wanna take a look."

I nibble my lower lip, still assessing the goods. Damnit, behave, Ackles, you are at work.

"He's here about the Devil house, Ackles." Agnes Grey states all of a sudden, which makes me jump out of my skin. I keep forgetting she's around.

"Oh, right. Why don't you follow me into an interview

room?" This is a small police station, all of our personal desks are in the main room with the information desk, where Agnes Grey is sitting, gazing at us with a knowing smile on her face. "For privacy." I observe, throwing our secretary a grimace.

"Trying to get me alone already, Miss Harris." My eyes snap to Roman and the devilish smirk on his face takes my breath away and makes my legs weak.

I swallow dry, before replying. "Please call me Ackles. And what can I say? I want you all to myself, Mister Waterhouse." Facepalm! If it didn't make me look sillier I would've done the gesture on myself. What the fuck, Ackles Danneel Harris? Turning swiftly around I start leading him to the room, at least this way I can hide my flushing cheeks.

I hear him chuckle behind me as he follows. "Please call me Roman, pretty she-devil."

"What?" I stop abruptly in my stride, and as I am spinning to face him, this chunky piece of meat smashes right into me, pinning me to the door of the interview room.

"What?" Roman asks back, peering down at me. Fuck, he's tall. I need to tilt my head so far back, if we were to be a thing, I probably would have neck problems in the future. But then again so would he. One of Roman's hands is by my head, while the other is on my hip. I can feel his hand clench around my uniform, which makes me fist my own hands on his tee. They got trapped in the middle of me and him right on top of his six-pack abs. Seriously, I can feel every rig on his belly. I rub my upper thighs together, seeking some sort of relief for the itch between my legs. Fuck, I am wet. "Ackles?" He calls out my name in a low voice.

"We're here," I note, moving one of my hands behind me and twisting the doorknob, sending us flying into the room. If his arm hadn't sneaked around my waist, bear-hugging me fully against him, as with the other he held onto the door frame, we would have fallen to the ground. My arms have now crept around his waist too.

He chuckles again. "Wow, Sheila, you are a dangerous one."

"Who the fuck is Sheila?" I snarl at Roman. If I thought I was clinging to him quite vigorously before, then this is the kind of possessive latch-on that screams 'mine', so this Sheila girl can go fuck herself.

"Oh, easy there, firecracker. You are cutting off some important flow in my anatomy there." He sounds constricted when he says that, gulping for air in the end. "It's just an Aussie expression." His jade green eyes, which are staring at me with such passion, dilate for a split second.

I am just about to apologise, or not, I am not sure, when, "Bunny, what's going on here?" I hear Doyle's question.

Roman and I break apart but still stay in each other's personal space. I see Roman's hand drop down from the door frame as he begins to turn in Doyle's direction. I don't think I ever moved this fast in my life, grabbing the collar of his shirt with one hand and the door with the other. I drag Roman further into the room, as I take a few steps back saying, "None of your business, Doyle. Bye." Flinging the door which slams shut.

"Bunny?" Roman sounds mad when he repeats the nickname. Yeah, I don't like it either dude.

"The Devil house," I shout out of the blue, as I let go of his tee. "You are here to talk about your family estate." That part I say a bit more subdued.

"Are you reminding me or yourself?" He asks me as a smile pops up on his pretty face.

"Both of us, I guess," I utter, moving some wayward curls that decided to escape my high ponytail, behind my ear as I make my way to the table in the center of the room and take a seat. Peering back at Roman, he hasn't stirred from his spot so I indicate with one hand to the seat on the other side of the table, "Roman, why don't you take a seat." His eyes dance from the seat I pointed at to me a few times, presumably deciding what to do. He brushes his thumb over his lower lip, before shaking his head and then walks to the seat right next to mine. Moving the chair so it's facing me he flumps his nice-looking ass down on it. The pose he takes is all man, legs spread and arms crossed over his chest, making his arm muscles bulge. I think I am drooling from the forearm porn being displayed in front of my eyes.

"That douche, your boyfriend or something?"

I blow a raspberry. "Roman," I say his name with a mild hint of exasperation. "The Device estate."

"Is he?"

"No." I snap. "No, boyfriend."

"Good." Good? Wait. Is he glad I am single? Is he interested in me? "Are we addressing the pet name thing at all?" I roll my eyes at that. Roman is like a dog with a bone, he just doesn't want to let go.

"Not a pet name, more like an insult. Now can we please, just focus? I really want to know what about the Devil house brings you to my neck of the woods." My curiosity is killing me. Besides, if we keep up this line of conversation I quite possibly will just blur out that I am somewhat love-stricken with him, and we just kind of met so that's beyond weird. I don't want to scare him off.

"Well," he begins as he digs out something from his red plaid lumberjack jacket pocket, "I found this inside the walls of the cottage. Definitely not chicken bones."

"Chicken bones?" I question as he passes me this ragged bag. When I open it I see it contains a human finger, mostly bone, with some shrivelled dried-out tissue still attached in some parts. Unholy fuck.

"Unholy fuck, indeed." Damnit, did I say that out loud? "Look, Ackles, I don't believe in any of this juju Devil shit, but clearly someone did, if the pentagram made out of chicken bones I meticulously had to dig out around my property is anything to go by."

"You did what?" My chair scrapes on the polymer flooring, as I push on the edge of the table with my free hand, so I am fully facing Roman.

"Oh, I had to remove some bones that were buried in the dirt. It scared my landscaper shitless, and I couldn't hire another if they were just going to run with a tail between their legs after seeing it too."

"Roman, you can't just," I shut my eyes and pinch my nose before continuing on, "are you sure they weren't human bones?" I question fixing my gaze on Roman, who hums while massaging the nape of his neck.

"They looked too flimsy and small, so I assumed not."

"Right. I may need some of those bones to test. Especially

now that you found this." I lift the bag containing the finger to stress the point across.

"Got it, red locks." I furrow my brows at the nickname. I don't know how I feel about that one, but I can't deny that anything Roman calls me sounds almost pornographic to my ears. I liked she-devil better.

A pentagram, either made up of animal bones or human ones, what does that mean? It definitely solidifies the idea of a cult, right? Witches, a boy that everyone claims to be the Devil, all to say that if the Devices were a cult they weren't a Jesus-loving one. The five-pointed star represents good and it is used to protect against evil, unless, "Which way was the pentagram facing?"

"What do you mean?"

"The odd point, was if facing north or south?"

Roman takes a moment to think. "South, why?"

Shit. "That makes it an inverted pentagram, which makes it satanic. The symbol of evil. The sigil of Baphomet. Instead of repelling sinister forces it actually attracts them because it overturns the proper order of things and illustrates the triumph of matter over spirit." Roman is looking at me funny. "What?"

"Just," he chuckles, before proceeding with his words, "trying to figure out why you have that piece of information swimming around in that bewitching skull of yours."

"I should tell you right off the bat, I'm a Harris, I have a loose screw." I bluntly admit. At least that's what I overheard some of the old folks of Newchurch claim about my family. An obsessed father, and hmmm how does Mama fit into this statement? And why does something in the depths of my mind tell me she most certainly does, more so than Papa?

He leans his upper body forward, resting his elbows on his knees and intertwining his fingers as if praying. "Maybe I like crazy." Our eyes lock and the room seems to get hotter than hell, or perhaps is just my body catching fire with the intensity of his gaze.

I, at long last, gather the courage to note, "I want in." Roman lifts one eyebrow at my unforeseen revelation. "The houses, the grounds. I want to check out the Device estate. Someone needs to investigate whether or not other bones and secrets lurk in those walls. And let's face it, none of these scaredy cats are going to step foot in there. Especially when I tell them about the pentagram. These town folks would rather you shove this bag back in the wall and burn the whole thing to ash than find out the truth."

"I damn knew you were different." He tells me. A lopsided grin took shape on his face.

"Bad different?" I ask with apprehension over what he might say.

"Bloody damn good. You could be facing the Devil, but you are ready to jump right in bed with it for answers. I love it." The only person I want to get in bed with is you. Luckily those thoughts don't leave my lips. Roman words make me smile, finally, someone appreciates my polarity to the so-called normal around these parts.

"Does that mean I can come over?"

"Like you said, someone needs to look into the skeletons these houses hold. May as well be someone who actually seems to want to be there, amongst the fields of tulips and bones, and solve the mystery."

"Great. I will log this into the system and go to forensics to give them the bone. We won't get answers straight away but..."

"One condition though." Roman interrupts.

"Condition?" I ask, confused.

"You want in. I want a date."

SEVENTEEN
ROMAN WATERHOUSE

"I want a date."

The second the words left my lips, I didn't regret them. Ackles' eyes widened, and a deep blush spread across her pale freckled cheeks. Shifting uncomfortably in her seat, she stammered, "Um, I can't date people I'm on a case with..."

Her British accent sounded so bloody sexy when she was flustered. A cheeky grin broke out on my face as I leaned back in my chair. "No worries, love," I said, trying to keep my tone light. "How about we grab dinner sometime, as people who live in the same town as each other? I don't need a label of 'date' on it, but I'm getting one, name it what you want."

Ackles' blush deepened, but she seemed to relax a bit. Her eyes darted around the room before meeting mine again. The air between us crackled with anticipation, and I couldn't help but revel in the power play unfolding. This was our own little game, and I was more than ready to see how far it would go.

I watched as Ackles took a deep breath, and then she

smiled at me, tucking a stray strand of fiery red hair behind her ear. "Dinner sounds lovely," she said, her voice warm and inviting.

"Damn, straight it does," I thought to myself, barely able to contain the surge of desire that threatened to overwhelm me. Images of pinning her down on this very interview desk flooded my mind, but I knew that would be frowned upon. Still, I couldn't help but feel my dick growing in my pants at the thought.

"Let her see what she does to me," I decided, making no effort to hide my arousal. Ever since I laid eyes on her at the pub, I'd been craving some much-needed attention from this sexy redhead, and now it seemed like I might finally get my chance.

Ackles shifted her weight on the chair, seemingly unaffected by my growing arousal. Her voice was steady as she brought the conversation back to the case at hand.

"Right, I'll get these bones to forensics and let you know what they find," she said, her green eyes flicking down to the bag on the table. "As for dinner, I'm free tomorrow night."

I couldn't help but smirk. "Tomorrow? Why not tonight? Don't tell me you've got plans in this tiny town already, love."

Ackles raised an eyebrow at me, a teasing smile playing on her lips. "Needy much?"

"Oi, I'm just impatient is all," I countered, trying to maintain my cool demeanour despite the thoughts running through my head. Images of her body pressed against mine, the taste of her lips as I ate her out – it was enough to drive any man wild.

"Alright, I'll meet you at the pub at 7 then?" Ackles said,

her forest green eyes sparkling with mischief. "I'll grab a booth seat this time, and we can eat."

"Pub? Nah, love," I grinned, images of a more intimate setting forming in my mind. "What about that cute little Italian joint I saw on the outskirts of town? I'll make a reservation for 7, see you then." I stood up, leaning in close to her, her scent intoxicating me. "Underwear is always optional around me," I whispered, smirking as I saw her cheeks flush a deep shade of red.

"Roman!" she blurted out, flustered but still smiling. She was a tough one, but I could tell I'd gotten under her skin just a little.

"See you later," I said, turning to open the door and striding out with a huge smirk on my face.

As I made my way towards the exit, I noticed that Doyle fella hanging around, his eyes lingering on Ackles as she emerged from the interview room. The look he gave her made my blood boil – it reminded me of a predator eyeing its prey. What's the story between those two? Couldn't shake off the memory of him calling her 'Bunny.'

The sun was a bloody bastard, playing peek-a-boo with the clouds as I walked out of the police station. Shielding my eyes with my hand, as I walked towards my ute, left my dam sunnies at home. Right now, though, I had more pressing issues though - those damn chicken bones I'd hidden in the garden.

"Bugger it," I muttered under my breath, fumbling with my keys. The sooner I got those bones, the better. She had that fiery look in her eyes when we talked about it earlier, and I had to admit, it got me going.

"Right," I said to myself, starting the engine. "Get those bloody bones, bag 'em up, and then off to dinner." The thought crossed my mind to leave them at home, maybe as an excuse for Ackles to come back with me after dinner. My dick twitched in my pants at the idea, clearly thrilled at the prospect of some action that didn't involve my own hand for once.

"Steady on, mate," I whispered, chuckling to myself. "Let's not get ahead of ourselves."

As I drove towards my place, images of Ackles' long, curly ginger hair and those gorgeous forest green eyes filled my mind. She was a tough lass, no doubt about it, but I could sense her flirty nature just under the surface. Maybe she'd be up for a little fun after dinner if things went well.

"Blimey, Roman," I said to myself, shaking my head. "You've got it bad, don't ya?" But I couldn't deny it - there was something about Ackles Harris that had me wrapped around her finger, and I was keen to explore whatever connection we might have.

"Alright," I muttered as I pulled up to my house, determination setting in. "Let's find those bloody bones and see where the night takes us."

Eighteen

Ackles Harris

I watch Roman stroll out the police station doors. "Damn, that is a fine ass," I muttered mostly to myself while ogling his firm derrière. I wonder if he would let me take a bite, sink my teeth into the flesh and muscle of his delicious ass cheek.

"What did the Kiwi want?" I hear Doyle spit from his sitting position on the edge of his desk. And just like that my sweet daydreaming gets a sour taste.

"Roman is from Australia," I inform Doyle, lacking patience for this shit.

"Didgy then." Crossing my arms, I scowl at him in annoyance as I lift one of my brows in confusion. "You know, because of the didgeridoo thingy."

"If you have to explain it, that means it makes no sense and it's stupid."

"Just tell me what he wanted, Bunny." He says somewhat irefully, getting up and coming up to stand right in front of me.

"Don't call me fucking bunny, Doyle." My arms fall to my sides as I fist my hands. He's getting on my last nerves. "But if you must know, Roman found something in the Device property of interest and I am the detective on the case."

"Like hell you are." Doyle rasps at me.

"Fucking excuse me." Oh, help me God, this jerk is about to get sucker punched if he doesn't shut up.

"No one in their sane mind would set foot in there. It's a dangerous place. Especially for a girl like you. Chief would never allow it."

Oh, he's done it this time. "A girl like me?"

Doyle closes his eyes, taking a deep breath before uttering, "That came out wrong."

"You think?" His dark brown eyes meet my forest green ones. "I swear Doyle, if you try to get in my way, you will regret it. You and I both know I ain't right in the head, and by your words that makes the best person for the job. Y'all are just a bunch of chickens that are too scared of some decaying houses with a dark tale. I am going to get to the end of this story, just you watch me. Now get out of my way, I need to put Roman's findings through the system." I finish my rant and move past him to get to my desk, bumping his, well not shoulder, because tiny bitch here, arm, which makes Doyle stumble back a step.

After typing in all of the information Roman gave me into the system, I start getting ready to go to forensics to give them the bone he found, when I get stopped by Chief Bargrave. "Harris, a word in my office." He announces with a forbidding voice as he pokes his head through the gap in his slightly open office door and then disappears back inside. Fuck, I thought I was in the clear.

I enter his office, hot and ready to convey why I should be the lead in this case, "Chief."

"Close the door and take a seat." He interrupts me.

"No." I sharply utter.

"I'm sorry?" Bargrave asks from his seat behind the desk.

"This is my case. The only way you can take it away from me it's from my cold dead hands, Chief. I want it. I need it." I sound like an impudent child having a tantrum. But at least I didn't stomp my foot, that would've been a step too far.

"Are you done, Harris?" Chief asks as he leans back on his chair, crossing his arms over his chest and throwing me a strict look.

"Done? Hmmm, sure."

"Good. The case is yours, detective. There's no one better to solve whatever happened behind those closed doors than you, Ackles. I simply called you here to tell you to be careful and to remind you of what you promised me when I promoted you to detective."

"Not to fall down the same rabbit hole as Papa. I won't." I promise again.

"You better. Now go make your Papa proud. Dig all the dirt there is to exhume from the Devil house." Chief Bargrave wields at me like a father telling his kids that they believe in them. I won't let him down. I will make them both proud of me.

$$\smileymoon$$

. . .

THE MORGUE STINKS, but not in the way you think. Instead of death, it smells like chemicals from whatever they use to clean and preserve the bodies. I think I prefer the scent of decaying bodies to this. It's definitely triggering something within me, my hands are shaking and it's not from the cold temperatures of this space.

If you are wondering what I am doing in the morgue, well, that's where our forensic lab is. Small town remember? Our morgue guy is our forensic guy too. Speaking of, where's Doctor Huxley?

"Huxley?" I ask the seemingly empty of any living thing room.

"Ackles." A loud banging sound echoes in the dead silent room as Doctor Huxley pops up from below his desk to my right, rubbing the top of his head. "To what do I..." he tries to lean on the desk with an outstretched arm, placing his hand on a pile of papers that sadly for him slide away from underneath his palm and make him lose balance. He catches himself before falling to the ground, but now there's a mess of scattered papers everywhere on the floor. "... owe the pleasure?" He eventually finishes his sentence.

I like Huxley, he and I are the same age. He's cute with his messy, in desperate need of a haircut, dirty blonde hair, as ghostly pale as me with some freckles on his face too. Glasses, which cover his pale grey eyes, that he's now pushing higher up his nose with his middle finger.

He hasn't looked directly at me yet. According to Austen, he has had a crush on me since forever. It pains me that I don't feel the same way. He's the quintessential nice guy and obviously, that ain't my type, I am a sucker for having my heart broken it seems. Here's to hoping that perhaps Roman won't, even though he does give me bad-boy vibes. Ugh! It's just dinner, Ackles, don't get ahead of yourself there. But he did call it a date before I almost blew it.

"Guess what?" I say, crossing my arms under my chest and leaning with my shoulder on the door frame.

"What?" He at last looks at me.

I give Huxley a Cheshire cat grin. "Roman found a human finger in the walls of one of the houses in the Device estate," I tell him cheerfully.

"Roman?"

"The Australian guy." Huxley stares vacantly at me, giving me nothing. "The Device heir." Still nothing. "He's the guy everyone in town is talking about. They are calling him crazy for attempting to try and redo the Devil house and the others in the property." The doctor still has no Scooby clue what I am rambling on about. "Nothing? Oh my God, seriously dude? You have to get out more."

"Hmmm, a human finger you said." He's so awkward, it's adorable.

"Yeah. Here." I pass him the bag containing the remains.

"It might take a while for any results." He notes, slanting over his computer to type something.

"You have my number, just call the moment you have anything. I might have other stuff coming your way. I hope you are ready to see a lot of me." I see his Adam's apple bob up and down at my words.

"Right. I updated your report on the system saying I received it. I am going to place it in the fridge in the lab until I can get to it." Huxley states, moving around me to get to the room next door. Which is more like a janitor's closet, it's that tiny. But it has all the forensic equipment you'll need to solve a crime, so I guess size doesn't really matter in this case.

"Please tell me you don't keep your lunch in the same fridge?" I ask jokingly.

"Well, no. That's unsanitary. I have a cooler under my desk. I was looking for a drink when you came in." He replies and then he's just gone.

Finding myself truly alone in the morgue a shiver crawls up my spine, making me look around my surroundings. Something suddenly doesn't feel right. My eyes zero in on the embalming table. Was there a body in there before?

"Hey, Huxley?" I call out. "Huxley." No answer.

I don't know what compels me to walk until I am standing right in front of the table. Much like I don't know why I pull the mortuary sheet away from the body. I recoil back at the image before my very eyes. This grey flesh corpse, with opaque sunken-down eyes, stares back at me.

"Mama?" I say in a hushed tone.

"It's ok, my pretty charmer. I got you." I hear Papa's voice murmur as a shadow stops right next to me. I slowly peer at it, and there he is. Erect at my side as if he wasn't gone too, dead just like Mama. What is happening?

"Papa?"

"It's better this way. She's no longer trapped. Not inside her mind nor that place." Wait what? What does he mean by that? I want to ask but I don't seem to be able to, the words get stuck in my throat. Is this a memory? Or a bad dream? Before you can say knife, he reaches for my hand. "It's you and me, kiddo."

I am gazing down at our clasped hands. It feels so real, it's warm, and if I squeeze I can feel the muscles and bones beneath the surface. A passing breeze brushes some of my curls back and tempts me to look up at what's ahead of me. I am no longer in the morgue, in the presence of my dead Mama's body. Instead, before me stands an imposing red-bricked building, with vines climbing up the walls, and large Victorian windows everywhere. In big bulky letters 'Tearsmith Mental Hospital' is written above what I presume to be the main entrance to the building. I don't understand. I want to say, but once more words refuse to come out.

"It's you and me, kiddo," Papa utters again. "This is the only way that house won't get a hold of her. She can't hurt you no more." Wait, Mama is in there? And what does he mean by hurting me? Mama would never do such a thing. Right?

"No." Why do I sound like I am but a child? "No, Papa, please," I beg.

"Ackles?" Someone calls out my name.

"We can't leave her in there, please. She'll be good. Please." I am crying now.

"Ackles." Arms envelop me from behind and an ear-piercing scream flees my lips. "It's ok. Ackles, it's Huxley. It's ok."

I turn around in his arms. "Huxley?" Damn, I sound so broken. Revolving in his arms again, I look behind me. The building is gone. Papa is gone. And on the embalming table, my Mama ain't there. Actually, there's no corpse there, it's empty.

"Where did you go?" He asks me with alarm in his voice.

I don't know. That was pure bedlam.

Nineteen
Roman Waterhouse

As I sat in the Italian restaurant, nursing a cold beer and soaking in the cozy atmosphere, I couldn't help but feel a mix of anticipation and nerves. The window seat I'd chosen had a clear view of the carpark, perfect for spotting Ackles when she arrived.

"Come on, Sheila," I muttered to myself, tapping my fingers impatiently on the table.

Then, like a scene from an old film, a beat-up truck roared into the carpark, its engine sputtering and protesting as if it was on death's door. My heart leapt into my throat as the rusty door creaked open and out slid Ackles, looking like the embodiment of sin.

"Fuckin' hell," I breathed, feeling a shiver run down my spine. She was clad in a tight black pencil skirt and a crisp white blouse that hugged her curves in all the right places. She moved with grace and confidence, her fiery red curls bouncing with each step she took towards the restaurant.

"Keep it together, Roman," I told myself, taking a swig of

my beer for courage. As she approached, my heart thudded wildly in my chest, threatening to break free. I could feel the heat rising to my cheeks as our eyes met through the window, hers a piercing green that seemed to see straight through me.

"Here goes nothin'," I thought, bracing myself for the whirlwind that was about to enter my life – and boy, was I ready for it.

As I watched her through the window, her fiery red curls danced with every step she took, cascading down her back like a waterfall of embers. The moment she pushed open the restaurant door, I felt the air around me change – charged with an energy that could only be described as electric.

"Fuck me," I whispered under my breath, unable to tear my eyes away from her as she spoke to the host. He gestured towards me and her head turned in my direction. A smile spread across her face, illuminating it like a beacon of bloody temptation.

"Shit, Roman, you're really up shit creek with this one," I thought to myself. I'd never been into red-haired women before, but Ackles was something else entirely. She was perfection personified, and I suddenly found myself wanting to worship at her feet – and between her legs, if she'd let me.

"Keep a lid on it, mate. Don't scare her off."

"Roman," Ackles smiled, striding confidently towards me. Her green eyes sparkled with mischief, and I couldn't help but grin back at her.

"Evenin', Ackles." I stood up, attempting to play it cool despite my racing heart. "You look bloody fantastic, don't reckon I've seen anyone rock a skirt like that before."

"Flattery will get you everywhere, Roman," she teased, sliding into the seat across from me, her fiery curls cascading down her back like a waterfall of flames. She looked me up and down as if sizing me up, then asked, "How are you, Roman?"

"Same as when I last saw you," I replied with a grin, my eyes trailing over her body as she settled in. We'd been flirting since we first met, but I couldn't help myself – there was something about this woman that made me want to push the boundaries.

"By the way," she said, leaning in slightly, "I dropped your finger off at the morgue."

"Fuckin' hell," I blurted out, raising an eyebrow. "Morgue? I mean, sure it's dead, but shouldn't it have gone to forensics or somethin'?"

She laughed, her green eyes sparkling with mischief. "Small town, Roman. Our forensics guy, Huxley, is also the local mortician and morgue tech. One-stop shop for all your dead body needs, I suppose."

"Shit, that bloke must be bloody smart," I said, genuinely impressed.

"Borderline genius, actually" she chuckled. "But the daft prick can't tell his left shoe from his right. Saw him trip on his own feet more times than I can count."

I joined her laughter, trying to picture this brilliant mortician stumbling around like a clumsy kangaroo. But as the laughter died down, I felt the intensity of Ackles' gaze return. There was something driving her, something she needed from this estate of mine, and I couldn't help but be drawn into her world.

As Ackles scanned the menu, her forest green eyes seemed to dance with excitement. She glanced up at me, a question in her gaze.

"Know what you want to order?" she asked.

"Yep," I replied.

As if sensing our readiness, she raised her hand and, like magic, our waitress appeared at our table. Ackles smiled warmly at her, something familiar in their exchange.

"Hey, Grace," she chimed. "Can I get the mushroom gnocchi and a lemonade?"

Grace nodded before turning her attention to me. "And for you?"

"Chicken carbonara, thanks," I said, giving her a cheeky grin. "And the same beer." I said pointing to the one Grace had given me when I took my seat earlier.

With that, Grace whisked away the menus, leaving us alone once more. Ackles crossed her slender arms across her chest, her fiery curls framing her face as she leaned back in her seat.

"Right then, Roman," she said, her voice taking on an urgent tone. "Tell me all about this estate of yours."

Her directness caught me off guard, but it only fuelled my attraction to her. After a short laugh, I couldn't help but tease her a bit. "Why do you want inside so badly, love? It's just an old pile of bricks and secrets."

"Roman, you wouldn't understand," she insisted, her eyes burning with intensity. "It's like a siren call to me. I need to know its history, its stories, and the truth behind the legends."

I let out a low whistle, impressed by her determination.

"Alright, darlin', I'll bite. You're obviously passionate about this, and I'm curious to see where it'll lead."

As I watched Ackles' eyes narrow, I knew we were reaching the heart of her obsession. She uncrossed her arms, leaned forward, and stared straight into my soul with those piercing green eyes. "I need inside those walls, Roman. It's like a bloody compulsion. The stories, the legends... I've got to know it all." She hesitated for a moment, the vulnerability clear on her face. "It's hard to explain, but this estate has been haunting me for years now. My Papa was obsessed with it too. He left me all his notes, and now I need to get inside."

"Your dad?" I asked, curiosity piqued. "What's his story? Why was he so bloody fixated on this place?"

She shook her head, a wistful smile playing on her lips. "Dunno, really. He never told me much about it, just filled my childhood with heaps of scary stories. Now I need to sort out what's fact and what's fiction, you know?"

"Fair dinkum," I replied, taking a swig of my beer. A part of me wanted to protect her from whatever dark secrets lurked within the estate, but another part – maybe the more dominant one – couldn't resist the allure of joining her on this twisted adventure. We both had our reasons for wanting to explore the estate, but it was clear that for Ackles, this went far beyond simple curiosity.

I grinned at Ackles, my eyes crinkling with mischief. "Do you need some sort of written invitation? Or can I just say 'Open the door and let you in?" Her eyes widened, disbelief clear on her face.

"Really?" she asked tentatively as if she were afraid I'd suddenly change my mind.

"Sure, why not?" I laughed, feeling a surge of excitement.

"Actually," I continued, struck by a sudden idea. "Why don't you bring all the notes that you have over to mine? You can use the middle house I'm staying in as your home ground and just roam the property as you please. As long as you stay away from the builders and don't get in their way, it should be fine."

"Thank you, Roman," Ackles breathed, her relief palpable. But I wasn't done yet.

"And," I said, leaning in close and covering her hand with mine, feeling the warmth of her skin against mine. "Why don't you take me along for the ride with you? I've always had a thing for scary stories, ya know?"

Her green eyes sparkled, and I could sense the thrill rising within her as she squeezed my hand. "Deal," she replied, her voice filled with determination.

TWENTY

ACKLES HARRIS

I can't believe I almost bailed on Roman tonight, on this date, I mean dinner. But after what happened in the morgue it's as if something's been eating up at me, consuming me from within, from the depths of my subconscious. I should know something important, however, I don't, my mind has decided to block it out. Why? Those were definitely memories, right?

I was 5 when Mama died, and my recollection of stuff before that has always been blurry at best. Is it because I was young so things just didn't creep into my still flourishing brain and nestle themselves in there? Or because of darker, perhaps traumatising, shit?

"She can't hurt you no more." The Papa in my hallucination had said. Did Mama try to harm me? Why? And did he mean physically or did he mean it as in scar me mentally by acting strange and deranged? Is that why she ended up at the Asylum?

Papa kind of insinuated that the Devil house made her do

it. Sometimes adults with frail states of mind can get lost in the spell of that devilish place. Papa told me that too, a long time ago. Was he talking about Mama? Was that why he was obsessed with the Device estate because something or someone in there made Mama act crazy? So many questions, more so than answers. But now I have the opportunity to dig for some of the secrets buried there. And it looks like I will have a partner in crime, Roman Waterhouse.

My mind was troubled the whole drive to the restaurant, my thoughts loud and obnoxious, but the instant my eyes landed on the gorgeous Aussie guy it all went quiet. Roman's presence can calm me like nothing else can subdue my inner demons. When I am this close to him, everything else fades to hollowed insignificance, meaningless when weighed up against him. He can distract me in the best way, with his killer charm and flirty remarks. It's as though we've known each other forever, yet we just met. It's as if there's this intricate web binding us to one another beyond our comprehension. Like a moth to a flame, I am drawn to him, even if getting near him means death. I still rather risk it and maybe get the biscuit than live not exploring this.

Roman telling me he has a thing for scary stories, icing on the fucking cake. Can someone fall this hard and fast for someone else? Because I think I have.

"Are we having dessert after this?" I ask him, once we finish our main.

He was taking a sip of his beer, but it seemed the liquid decided to deviate and go down the wrong pipe, as Roman began to choke on his drink. Once he gets some control over his cough, he says, "Are we?"

"Well, they do a mean tiramisu here. We can share."

"Oh, that type of dessert. Right. Yeah."

"Roman Waterhouse, whatever did you think I meant?" I question teasingly. He looks away from me, staring out the window, as he does that thing where he rubs the back of his neck. "I should tell you I don't sleep with guys on the first date," I inform him. Only if they are intended to be a one-night stand, but I really don't want Roman to be that.

"I thought this wasn't a date, detective?" Roman observes, his green eyes meeting mine.

I lift an eyebrow and toss a crooked smile his way, before replying, "You ain't helping your case there, mister."

"So, just to be clear, you don't want to sleep with me?" He says, crossing his arms on top of the table and leaning slightly forward towards me. Wow, direct much. Damn.

I bite my lower lip, trying to hold in the words that ought to flee them. Oh, fuck this. "No. I mean, yes, I do. I want to jump you like a bitch in heat, but," I let out a long deep breath, "I am trying really hard to remain professional here, Roman."

"I don't see a badge, Ackles. What's more, I don't kiss and tell."

"Roman, let me introduce you to a small ass town and its outskirts. Everyone knows everyone else's bloody business. I am sure Grace already texted all of her friends to tell them that the hot Australian guy is wining and dining the crazy cop, by tomorrow we will be branded a couple."

"More reason to make it so, don't you think." Roman brazenly notes, giving me a cocky smile, and shooting his eyebrows to the sky and then back down in a 'come on' kind of way.

Grace picks that moment to enter the scene. "Dessert?" I peer at her, and subsequently at Roman.

"We'll have the tiramisu. To share, please?" He requests.

Grace looks at me with bulging eyes and asks very much aghast, "You are sharing your precious coffee-flavored dessert?"

"Grace," I don't have time to say what I intended to tell her, because she interrupts me.

"I knew it. I have to tell Millie." And she walks away from our table.

"What just happened?" Roman asks, a bit dumbstruck.

"My bad. I did say we could split it, but the last time someone tried to take a bite of my tiramisu I stabbed them with a fork. I think Doyle still has the scar on his hand." In my defence, the asshole said he didn't want any dessert and then attempted to steal mine. Yeah, I don't think so. Don't mess with an unhinged woman and their pud.

Roman groans, which wow, I just love that sound coming from him. "Can we not mention him?" Is that jealousy in his words?

"Doyle? Sure." I announce nonchalantly.

"Good. Even though hearing you disclose that you bore a sharp object into his flesh gives me a weird but nice tingle in my spine."

"Oh, yeah?"

"Yeah." You know how people say looks could kill? The one Roman Waterhouse is tossing in my direction is stripping me bare and fucking me raw.

We are making our way to our cars after going halves with the sweet course. I was a good girl, at no point did I seek to wound my good-looking date, I mean... oh, fuck it, I am just going to call it what it was, a fucking date. Roman even paid for the meal like a gentleman.

"So, you are coming over, right?" Roman asks as we get to my truck.

I spin around to face the pretty boy, "Roman, I am not having sex with you tonight. It's our first date."

He grins, getting really close to me. His eyes lower to my lips, coming back up to my jade colour eyes shortly after, as his hand lunges out to some of my badly behaved curly strands that keep falling over my eyes, to brush them behind my ear. "I heard you loud and clear, pretty she-devil. I meant with your daddy's stuff so we can go over it."

"Oh." His palm is now resting on my cheek, his thumb leaving sweet caresses on my freckled skin. "There's a lot of stuff. From police files on cold cases and missing people to official documents on most members of the Device family tree, like birth and death certificates, and wedding documents. There's also ripped pages of books on the Pendle witch trials, legends and lore from around this area, shit on cults."

"Keep teasing me with a good time, Sheila, and see what happens then."

"Some of these things are confidential, Roman. I could get in trouble if the Chief finds out I showed you the goods." When did my hands thrust up from being droopy by my sides, to come and grip Roman's shirt with such a strong fervour?

"Baby, my lips are a tomb. It's you and me, and that bloody house. Now stop dangling shit like forbidden fruit, making my curiosity gnaw at my insides and gimme what you got." Roman's other hand comes to my waist, clinging on to me as I am to him.

"Ok." I don't know what came over me at that moment, but I stand on my tippy toes, using his sturdy body for balance, as I reach for the nape of his neck with both my hands to pull his face down to mine. Shutting my eyes I kiss him.

We will definitely be the hot gossip of the town in the morning now.

We kiss softly at first, him caught by surprise, and me testing the waters before diving deeper. As I sense him freshly spilt-open like a fig, I dart my tongue inside and that's when the real fun begins. Roman releases this animalist grunt, a sound that emanates from the bowels of his throat, and he begins devouring me, establishing dominance and taking complete control of the kiss. Dear God, yes. I moan, but it gets eaten up by his mouth on mine.

The hand that was on my cheek gets tangled up in my mess of ginger curls, tugging and pulling on my strands, while his other, skims to my ass and seizes the flesh there with a wolfish rigour.

His tongue penetrates in and out of my mouth in a maniac dance. It strokes the tip of mine and we twirl them together, all so he can suck it and drag it into his own mouth. We do this rockabye a few times over, until Roman eventually takes mercy on my swollen lips and we go about meekly rubbing our lips together. As we give each other little pecks he ends this riveting freak show by sinking his teeth in my lower lip, enough so to draw blood.

"Fuck." I whimper. Once I open my eyes I see that Roman is already looking at me, his eyes fully dilated, licking his lips, certainly tasting the tanginess of my life essence on them. "Kiss me like that again and I might consider second base tonight."

"Pretty charmer, you fucking tease." He utters.

"What did you just call me?"

"Pretty charmer?" That was my Papa's nickname for me. Is this a joke? How did he know? What sick trickery is the universe playing on me right at this moment? "Would you prefer a beautiful enchantress? Stunning sorceress? Alluring siren? You have me under a fucking spell, Harris."

I swallow dry and step away from him. "You should follow me. I might need help boxing up the amount of papers I have." I announce, turning to open the driver-side door of my truck, and climbing, in a haste, into the seat. I am about to close the door when Roman gets himself in the gap, stopping me from doing so. He holds the door with one hand as the other rests on the roof of my car.

"Hold on. What just happened?" He asks. Is that panic in his voice?

"Nothing." Everything. "You didn't call me a witch." I think I love you.

"Should I have?"

I shake my head at his question. With a small smile on my lips, I stare straight into Roman's forest-green eyes and say, "Thank you. For seeing me, and not what everyone else does."

Nevertheless, what's a witch but the most capable character in a story? A witch sees the darkness of the world concealed at its core with curious eyes instead of fearful ones. A witch can turn humans into monsters and monsters to humans. A witch doesn't ask for what she wants, she just gets it. Maybe I have been looking at it all wrong. Maybe it's not so bad to be one.

Twenty-One
Roman Waterhouse

The taste of her lingered like a bloody tease that was driving me mad. I was hard as a rock, my jeans cutting into me with an urgency that was near painful. Blimey, did she have any idea what she was doing to me? That kiss, flaming hell, that kiss had me wondering if her pussy would be just as sweet, just as intoxicating. My mind went feral with the image of me diving between her thighs, getting lost in her, drinking from her like she was the last bloody drop of water in the Outback.

Stepping out into the cool night, the streetlights of this English town flickered like distant stars. I glanced back at her, her silhouette framed by the dim glow of her car's interior light. Fuck it. I wanted to bend her over the hood of her bleeding car and take her right here, right now. Show every bloke passing by that I laid claim to her.

"Easy there, mate," I muttered to myself, trying to shake off the raw desire that was clouding my head.

I climbed into my ute, the leather of the seat sticking to

my skin. I revved up the engine, feeling that familiar power surge through me. It was more than just the machine; it was the anticipation of what was to come. With a quick glance in the rearview, I saw her pulling away from the curb, and I followed suit, tailing her to her place.

The streets were quiet, almost too quiet, save for the purring of our engines breaking the silence. The drive felt like forever, each second stretched out, filled with visions of her body pressed against mine, her breath hitching with every move I'd make. My grip on the steering wheel tightened, knuckles turning white as I fought to keep control—not just of the ute, but of myself.

We finally pulled up outside her house, the quaint little building looking all respectable-like in the moonlight. Little did it know the filthy thoughts that were racing through my head. But there was a hunger in me that wasn't about to be sated by thoughts alone.

"Roman, you're playing with fire," I whispered to no one, parking up behind her car. Her taillights bathed the driveway in a red hue, like a stop signal that I had no intention of obeying. All I could think about was claiming her, marking her as mine. The animal in me wanted to roar, but I kept it caged...for now.

The door creaked open to Ackles' place, and the sight that unfolded before me was a bloody organised chaos. Papers were everywhere—on the floor, desk, spilling over from boxes like they were tryna escape. But there she was, in the thick of it all, her ginger curls wilder than the mess around her.

"Damn," I muttered under my breath, eyes following the

curve of her back as she bent over, shoving papers into boxes without so much as a glance my way. The thought of her, arse in the air, face pressed against the paperwork while I took her from behind sent a rush straight to my groin. I shifted, tryna adjust the strain in my jeans, picturing the desk cluttered beneath us, every thrust sending another sheet fluttering to the ground.

"Roman, can you help me with these?" Her voice, sharp and commanding, snapped me out of my dirty reverie. Fuck me dead, even her ordering me about did things to me I wasn't prepared for. Thoughts of her tying me up, taking control... I could almost feel the rope biting into my skin, her hand leaving marks that would tell anyone who looked just who I belonged to.

"Sure thing, love," I said, my voice a low growl, the bulge in my pants now impossible to hide. I caught her eyeing it, her cheeks flushing a shade that matched her hair. Was she thinking what I was thinking? Or was it just my cock leading the charge, making a right fool outta me?

I didn't bother to disguise it, let it stand proud as I started stacking boxes, our arms brushing every now and then, sending jolts of electricity up my spine. With each touch, I imagined her hands not on cardboard, but on me, claiming me, driving me mad with want.

The last of the boxes slammed shut with a thud, my hands working quickly as if they were tryna outpace the dirty thoughts racin' through my head. Ackles shot me this look, her green eyes sparkling with somethin' fierce, and I knew right then I had to get a grip or I'd be on her like a dingo on a baby.

"Let's get these buggers in the car, yeah?" I muttered, hoisting a box up under each arm, tryna focus on anything but the way she moved.

"Right behind ya, Roman," she called, her voice all flirty-like, but I'm pretty sure she had no bloody idea what kind of dark corners my mind was crawling through.

Boxes all strapped in her car, we drove back to mine, the ride nothing but torture. My jeans still tight as a nun's vow, I kept picturing the most messed-up shit just to keep from embarrassing myself further. Hairy nuns... Jesus, mate, what's wrong with ya? But it worked a treat, kept me from acting like some horned-up teen.

Pulling up at my place, I hopped out and started unloading Ackles's car. Ackles followed suit, her gaze drinking in every inch of the old house like it was the bloody Taj Mahal.

Watching her explore my space, touching things with delicate hands, made me want to show her more—of the house, of me, of everything. But for now, boxes. Just bloody boxes.

The tick of that bloody clock was the only thing I heard, over the rustle of papers and boxes. Her fingers danced across book spines and knick-knacks, every bit of her attention snagged by the relics of my life. And it stung, mate. Like a bloody jellyfish had wrapped itself around my chest. She was supposed to be looking at me, not my dusty collection of inherited trinkets.

"Oi, Ackles," I said, my voice rougher than I meant it to be. No response, just her lost in her own world. Righto, enough of this shit.

I closed the gap between us in two strides, planting myself right in her line of sight, blocking out the rest of the room. "You're missing the best part."

Her forest green eyes snapped up to mine, startled, like a roo caught in the headlights. That's it, darl, back here with me.

"Roman, what—"

Didn't give her the chance to finish. I leaned down, my lips claiming hers without waiting for permission. She tasted like wild honey – sweet, rich, bloody addictive. I pulled her close, my hands finding the curve of her waist, and she melded into me, soft and pliant.

Each kiss was a hit, a shot of the good stuff straight to the veins. With every press of our mouths, the world got a bit smaller, until it was just the heat of her body against mine, her breath mingling with my own.

She fit right there in my arms, like the last piece of a puzzle you've been working on for yonks. Her hands, those curious, flirty hands, they found their way to my hair, tangling in the messy brown locks and pulling me deeper into the kiss.

"Roman," she breathed out, her voice a mix of warning and want. But I wasn't listening. All I could think about, all I could feel, was the need for more of her—the taste of her lips, the sound of her heartbeat racing against mine.

"Fuck the boxes," I muttered into her mouth, part of me hoping she'd be on the same page, another part too far down the rabbit hole to give a damn if she wasn't. In that moment, all I craved was to get lost in the euphoria of her touch, to submerge myself in the ocean of her smooches, and sod everything else.

She pulled away from my lips reluctantly, my breath hitched and my heart pounding like a wild drum. "Alright then," I managed to say through a voice roughened by desire and a kiss that had nearly sucked the life out of me. "Where do you reckon we should stack these bloody boxes?"

"Over by the window would be good," Ackles replied, her voice steady but her hands telling a different story as they trembled slightly. She reached for a box, her slender fingers brushing against the cardboard as if she was trying to ground herself.

"Mi casa es tu casa," I said, chuckling at the cliché, watching her movements with an intensity that bordered on obsession. It was bloody obvious she wasn't just shaking because of the cold air nipping at us through the open door.

Twenty-Two

Ackles Harris

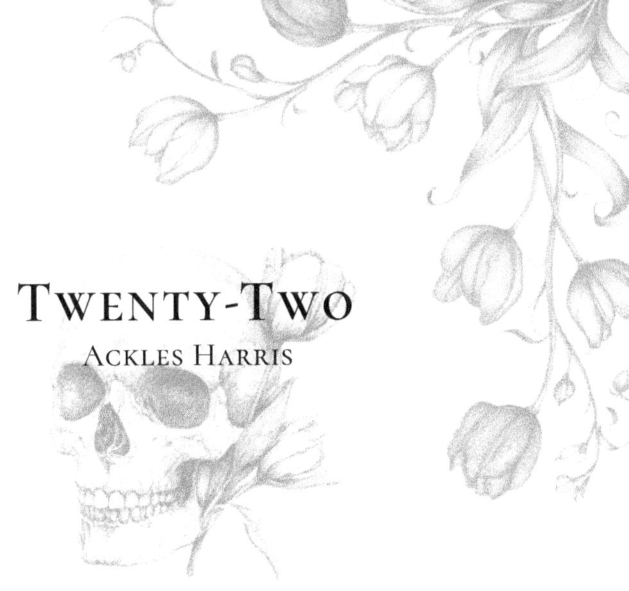

This is getting tempestuous. I can barely hold the box in my hands, I am shaking that hard. But not from cold, no, from this fucking abstinence I am imposing on myself, this stupid attempt at prudence and sobriety. Why? We clearly both want it, if the erection that Roman hasn't tried to keep in the dark is anything to go by.

When we got to his, as my growling truck crossed the rusty gates that set apart the outside world from this dark-ridden fairytale scene, I might've gotten a bit engrossed by the dilapidated bones that give rise to the Device houses.

"I have done it. I am finally in the belly of the beast." My hushed words filled the silence inside my car before I stepped out of it to an awaiting Roman.

I meandered around the house that the pretty Australian hunk has taken sanctuary in, like a kid in a candy store. My eyes skimming through my surroundings trying to get a glimpse of everything at once. My fingers brushed over things from the past hoping that the dust it has gathered would clue me in on the secrets of this place. I don't think Roman liked not being the centre of my full attention, because the kiss we shared amongst these old four walls was beyond needy and full of urgency. That didn't help with the flourish burn in the pit of my belly, this need to let him consume me, make me his.

I feel like I am losing my grip on reality by virtue of being this close to Roman.

I hear him chuckle before asking, "Are you going to let go of that box at some point, pretty she-devil?" Shit, how long have I been holding on to it? I drop it all of a sudden, which with the laws of physics, and it not being a freaking cat, it doesn't land on the floorboards straight. Nope, it just topples over and spills its contents everywhere.

"Oh, fuck." I mumble.

"That's one way of doing it." Roman remarks.

"Well, I am making myself at home. You saw my house. I like it messy. And this way I know," I slant forward to get a good look at the papers scattered on the floor, "where the stuff on dear madam Demdike is."

Roman laughs at my lame excuse, and I revolve around so I am staring at him head-on. "You are just too cute.' My face twists like I just tasted something sour at the word 'cute'. "But honestly Harris, I am all for you leaving your things all over my floor, especially if they are perhaps items of clothing that you might be wearing right now." Well, that turned my frown upside down in a second.

"Bad boy. Stop tempting me." I try to sound stern and

sober when I say that, yet, I am sure the smirk on my face and the lascivious hoarse tone of my voice tells another story.

"What would be the fun in that, baby?" This man is playing with fire; I think he might need a spanking. I nibble at my lower lip, ogling Roman up and down, as a succulent but diabolical plot comes to my dirty mind.

I dig my hand in the pocket of my black leather jacket, making sure I have what I require there. I don't tend to leave the house without them since you never know when you might need them. When I feel the cold metal of my hand-cuffs, I give myself a thumbs-up in my head.

"Oi, Roman, why don't you take a seat?" I gesture towards one of the chairs at the dining room table. "We should go through the box you have in your very manly hands. It's the one about your family. I think." I honestly don't know we didn't really label the boxes, just tossed stuff inside. Not that it matters what's inside, I just need him to sit his nice-looking ass down in the three ladder back wooden chair. Do you see where I am going with this, yet?

Roman sweet Roman looks at the chair with wariness, probably trying to assess where I am going with this. "You're a tough nut to break, aren't you Ackles?" He states, stealing a glance at me. Oh no, baby, you made the first dent the moment you stepped into this town, you then managed to turn that depression into a small fissure when you walked through the police station doors, and ultimately you cracked me wide open the instant we kissed. "Fine." He cedes, almost sounding like a beaten-up puppy, making his way to the table. Once there, he dumps the box with a thud on the surface and takes a seat, legs spread and arms crossed over his chest. I giggle. Roman is so adorable when he thinks he's not getting what he wants.

I walk to him with deliberate and unhurried steps, taking my sweet ass time, and let this tension simmer for a bit. As soon as I arrive at his side, I gently brush my fingertips up his right arm. Roman's eyes zero in on my hand and follow my movement like a hawk.

"Harris, what are you doing?" He asks me, his voice full of suspicion.

Once at his rear, I make my other hand mirror what the other is doing, now both descending from his shoulders to his wrists, compelling his arms to fall limply at his side. Leaning forward so my lips are by his ear I whisper in a suggestive manner, "Ever played cops and robbers?"

Roman chuckles. "Can't say that I have. What does it entail?"

"Mainly me handcuffing you to a chair and getting whatever I want from you?"

"What?" He asks, somewhat taken aback by what I said, and seeks to spin around, but sadly to late buddy. I had already handcuffed one of his wrists and forced the chain around one of the ladders on the back of the chair and I am now holding his other wrist captive by the other strand. He's stuck. "Ackles, what the fuck?"

I quickly tread around him and sit on his lap, my back to his front, my head resting on his shoulder, rubbing my ass on his not-so-little friend. "You don't want to play with me?" I whine and pout.

"Fuck me." He heaves, jerking slightly and tugging on his restraints.

"Oh, now you get it," I utter in a husky voice, angling my head so I can lick his earlobe, sucking it into my mouth and biting it, all while undulating my hips over his dick, he feels big. My left arm goes around the opposite shoulder my head's at, and bends so I can bury my fingers in the messy dark brown hair at the nape of his neck.

"Foxy, if you keep that up I am going to blow my load like a fucking virgin boy that has never seen a vagina. I would hate to embarrass myself like that, coming by you dry humping me." Roman observes, grinding his teeth.

I hum, yanking vigorously on his strands. "Maybe that's what I want, so I can suck it back to life later."

"Damn," flees his lips, "ok. Can we at least lose some clothing here? If I am going to make a fool of myself can I do it with your beautiful porcelain skin touching mine? Please, baby." He begs between huffs and puffs.

"Since you said please, I guess I can give you this one thing." I place a foot on the edge of the table, as the other stays rooted to the floor and pushes us back a little, making the chair scrape, what I am hoping is, the old parquet he's not keeping. That definitely left a mark. Ups.

I lift myself and kick off getting undressed before Roman, swaying my hips as if an erotic tune is echoing in the background. I lose my jacket first, and with a hand on either side of the waistband of my black pencil skirt, I start lowering it down as I slant my upper body forward, granting Roman a great view of my ass in a thong.

He grunts, "You got to be fucking kidding me."

With my skirt, presently a puddle at my feet that I step out of as I stand up straight, I peer over my shoulder and ask all innocent-like, batting my eyelashes, "Something wrong?"

His Adam's apple bobs up and down, prior to him saying, "Nice underwear."

"You don't have the full picture yet, baby. It's a set." I am wearing a matching white lace bra and panties. With a white button-down shirt, I had no choice about the colour of my undergarments. I could've gone with a nude hue, but this was prettier. I spin around so I am facing Roman, and one by one I undo the buttons of my shirt.

"Are you sure you're a cop?" Strange question, but I'll bite.

"What do you mean?" I query, getting rid of my top.

"Hmmm just that this feels a lot like a striptease. And before it felt just like a lap dance."

I chuckle at his remark. "Yeah, Austen really likes her strip clubs." I acknowledge, kneeling between his spread legs. "The girls at our usual joint are really nice and give me a lot of great recommendations on how to please a man without having him insert his dick in one of my holes." I unfasten his belt, pop the button off his jeans and lower the zipper. "Ass up." I request, and tug his pants down when he does so. "Roman? Why are you not wearing any underwear?" I ask a bit dumbstruck at what sprung free the moment there was no barrier there.

Fuck, he has a thick long trunk, and I'm a tiny skinny bitch. I don't think my inner walls can fan out that much. Not to say, it can probably reach my stomach when penetrating me fully.

"I'm a commando kind of guy." His words make my eyes jump from his monstrous dick to his forest green pools.

"Good to know I will have easy access whenever I am in the mood," I tell him, getting up and straddling him. His dick is nicely tucked in the middle of us both.

"We barely started this, you are already thinking of the next time. Someone is greedy."

"You have no idea." Draping my arms over his shoulder, with a hand on the back of his head tangled in his hair, while the other sinks into the collar of his shirt to touch the skin of his collarbone, I resume rocking my hips, so I am rubbing myself on his cock.

This position is better since I can caress my bundle of nerves on his tip and brush my wet pussy on his length. I bounce up and down against Roman's dick. Fuck, I might come just from this as I feel the flame he ignites within me become an uncontrollable inferno quite fast.

Burying my face in the alcove of his neck and shoulder, breathing in Roman's all-dark musky scent with hints of lavender, I begin to roll my hips in trance-inducing circles. He groans, which in turn makes him moan. I suck on his flesh, kiss it and lick it, as I increase the speed of my movements.

"Come for me." I hear a distant voice say, and I whimper. I am so close.

I lean back using a hand on Roman's knee for support as my other proceeds to stroke my clit, whilst bobbing close up to his cock. I bore my nails in the flesh of his knee as I begin to cum. I am struggling to stay upright thanks to my body convulsing like crazy.

"Roman." I moan his name.

I refuse to close my eyes as my orgasm hits me full force, in the fear of missing the moment he ejaculates. When he does cum, his penis jerks, shooting up jets and jets of pearly white fluid up in the air, landing all over his stomach.

"Fuck me dead, Ackles."

Twenty-Three
Roman Waterhouse

After a quick hose-down and shimmying into fresh clothes, I parked me arse on the chair Ackles had cuffed me to not long ago. I couldn't help but grin like a loon; this bloody chair was my new throne.

"Strewth," I muttered under my breath as Ackles settled opposite me, her ginger curls a fiery halo in the dim light. She was flicking through her stack of files, her fingers dancing across the papers like she was playing some secret tune only she knew. The sight of her, all business and focus, had me stiff as a board again. Bloody hell, she was casting some kind of witchy spell over me, no doubt about it. My mind raced, a mad dog chasing its tail, drunk on her. Pussy drunk and bloody needy.

"Oi, Ackles," I called out, half-cocky smirk, half-desperate plea. "You sure you don't need a hand with that?" But who was I kidding? I could barely keep my thoughts straight, let alone help with whatever mystery she was piecing together from those worn-out sheets.

"Keep your eyes up here, Roman," she teased, without even lifting hers from the parchment-like pages.

"Never," I shot back, my voice a mix of jest and raw yearning, I needed to break the spell — her spell — that had me by the balls. But for now, I'd settle for the rush of her gaze locking onto mine, green eyes clashing, igniting something feral within.

Ackles flicked through the pile of papers, her ginger curls bouncing with each movement. "Wanna hear a story?" she asked, not looking up.

"Sure, why not," I grunted, shifting in my chair to find a more comfortable position.

She leaned back, one leg crossing over the other, the green of her eyes darkening with something that looked like grief. "This land," she started, her voice dropping to a whisper, "it's soaked in blood, Roman. Older siblings from the family who owned it met with... accidents. Untimely ends."

"Accidents, huh?" My interest was piqued despite myself. "Tell me more."

"Tractor accidents, falls off ladders, heart attacks." She counted them off on her fingers, and I couldn't help but notice the slight tremble. "But, they weren't random. There's a pattern."

A chill settled in my gut as I listened, the air in the room feeling heavier, like the ghosts of those stories were seeping into the walls around us. "The husbands?"

"Dead, all of 'em," she said flatly. "Reported to police as misfortunes. All buried on this slice of heaven you have here. Or so we were told."

"More like hell." I muttered under my breath, as I

frowned, my mind racing. I was not a fan of crypts or cemeteries. "I need to check that place out," I muttered, already plotting an exploration. The thought sent a shiver down my spine, not all of it fear.

"None of them saw their fiftieth birthday," Ackles continued, her tone edged with a note of dread. "It's like death had them all earmarked."

"Self-reliant lot, were they?" I asked, trying to keep the unease from creeping into my voice.

"Never hired help. Kept to themselves." Her gaze locked onto mine, intense and searching. "Makes you wonder, doesn't it? What secrets are rotting out there with them?"

"Too right," I agreed, feeling the hairs on the back of my neck stand on end. This was no ordinary tale; this was a legacy of death, wrapped up in the very soil of this cursed land.

"Scared yet?" Ackles teased, though her smile didn't quite reach her eyes.

"Fuck no," I lied, my heart pounding a tattoo against my ribs. But deep down, I knew fear had sunk its claws into me, and it wasn't letting go anytime soon.

The air in the room had gone still as if even the ghosts of this accursed land were leaning in to hear Ackles's tale. Her words dripped with a history so dark it could blot out the sun.

"Did you know," she said, her voice low and steady, "the original owners of your sprawling estate were pegged as witches back in the 1700s? The locals were a superstitious bunch." She flicked her gaze up at me, those forest eyes holding me captive.

"Strewth, witches, eh?" I scoffed, trying to sound unfazed, but my pulse hammered like a warning drum. "Wouldn't be surprised if they cursed the bloody place."

"Seems the curse didn't leave with them," Ackles mused, flipping through another page. "It lingered, wormed its way into your family tree."

A shiver ran through me, despite the bravado I was putting on. This wasn't just a yarn; this was my heritage unravelling before my eyes, thread by bloody thread.

"Your gran, what happened after she left here?" Ackles's question cut through the tension that had thickened between us.

"Buggered if I know," I answered, a bit too quickly. "She just buggered off, didn't she? Like a bloody ghost. Not a peep about it, and Mum kept her trap shut too. All I know is that the old chook lived in Melbourne before she popped out Mum."

Ackles just nodded, scribbling something down in her notes, but I caught the look in her eye. It was sharp, probing like she knew there was more to it. And hell, maybe there was.

"Let's focus on the now," I deflected, eager to steer away from the gaping hole where my family history should be. "What else you got in that Pandora's box of files?"

"Plenty," she replied with a wry smile, "but nothing that'll put your mind at ease, Roman."

"Wasn't expecting it to, love," I shot back, the unease growing roots inside me. This house, these lands—they were tainted, and somehow, I was the next chapter in its bloody saga.

"You know," Ackles started, her voice trailing off as she thumbed through the ancient papers spread before us like the sinister petals of some long-dead flower. "There's nothing. Not a bloody thing on your great-great grandparents—no death certificates, no records. It's like they vanished into thin air." She glanced up at me, those forest-green eyes piercing through the veil of mystery that shrouded my lineage.

"Strewth, that's messed up," I muttered, scratching at the stubble on my chin, feeling the weight of unspoken stories pressing down on me. The void in the Waterhouse history was unnerving, a dark spot where the light of truth should have been shining. "Makes you wonder what sort of skeletons are lurking in the closet, hey?"

"Or under the floorboards," she added with a grim chuckle, though the humour didn't quite reach her eyes.

I felt the itch to keep digging, to unearth whatever cursed secrets were buried alongside the bones of my ancestors. But then Ackles started packing away her notes in piles on the table, the motion brusque and final, snapping me back to the present.

"I can't stay tonight, Roman," she said, her tone apologetic but firm. "I've got to feed my cat."

"Cat, huh?" I raised an eyebrow, knowing damn well it was a flimsy excuse at best. When I'd been over at her place, there wasn't a whisker or a paw print in sight. But who was I to argue? The lass needed space, and I wasn't about to crowd her.

"Fair dinkum," I replied, standing from my newfound

favourite chair and stretching my arms above my head. "Gotta look after the little critters."

She offered a small smile. We walked to the front door, the silence between us thick with unsaid words and lingering tension.

"See you around, Ackles," I said as she stepped out onto the porch, the cool night air sweeping around us.

"Goodnight, Roman." Her voice had softened, and for a moment, I caught a glimpse of vulnerability.

On impulse, I leaned down and pressed my lips to hers —a brief, electric kiss that held the promise of more secrets shared and nights spent between the sheets. She tasted like the mysteries we'd been poring over, sweet and intoxicating.

"Think about me, will ya?" I whispered against her lips, a cheeky grin spreading across my face.

"Ok," she murmured, a hint of a smile tugging at the corners of her mouth.

With that, she turned and walked down the path to her car, leaving me standing in the doorway watching the taillights fade into the distance. I shoved my hands into my pockets, wondering if the heat I felt was from the kiss or the burning questions that still smouldered between us.

"Feed her cat, my arse," I chuckled to myself, shaking my head. Maybe it was all part of the dance we were doing, two people circling each other, drawn together by desire and the haunting allure of the unknown.

I turned back inside, the house seeming emptier than before, filled with shadows that whispered of things long hidden. I knew one thing for sure—tonight, as she lay in her bed, I hoped she'd be thinking of me, just as much as I'd be lying awake, thoughts consumed by her.

THE SUN HADN'T EVEN CRACKED its first yawn when I found myself pounding on the solicitor's door, my mind ablaze with last night's goodbye and the gnawing need for answers. Ackles had already nicked off to work, leaving me to chase down these bloody ghosts alone.

"Mr. Waterhouse, this is quite early," the solicitor muttered as he peeked through a crack in the door, looking like he'd been wrestled from the arms of sleep, and dragged into work by my earlier call.

"Got any more of them files?" I asked, pushing past him into the stale-aired office that smelled like dust and decayed paper.

He shuffled behind me, a weary look stitched across his face. "Roman, I've given you what I had. There's nothing left."

"Come on, mate, there's gotta be something." I didn't bother hiding the frustration boiling in my gut.

"Here, take these," he sighed, thrusting a stack of yellowed documents into my hands—land rights, building plans, all smelling of secrets and mould. "I've only been at this gig for fifteen years. These things... they came with the office."

"Cheers," I said, flipping through the papers, feeling the weight of dead ends pressing against my chest.

Leaving the solicitor's office, the morning seemed darker, the air thicker. The bloody legacy of my family felt like a shroud wrapped tight around my shoulders. As I walked back to my car, the papers clutched in my hand, I couldn't shake the feeling that I was stepping further into a web, each strand a question without an answer, each corner shadowed with half-truths and lies.

Twenty-Four

Ackles Harris

"**F**uck, I think I might have to get a cat," I mumble to no one in particular.

"What did you say, darling?" Agnes Grey asks me from her seat by the information desk.

"Nothing. Just mentally doing a shopping list." Ugh. It's been a long day. Or mostly it has felt like one because all I can think about is when can I go and see Roman. Should I call him to ask if I can come over tonight? Should I just show up? Is it too soon to see him again after our date? Bitch, clingy much. What's the standard amount of time you should wait before texting or calling? Three days, is that what the Cosmopolitan magazine classifies as normal? No more than a week I am sure. I am driving myself crazy here.

Agnes Grey snaps me from my inner turmoil by saying, "So there's a rumour going around town." Oh, fuck. "That you and Roman went on a date last night. And kissed. Actually not really a hearsay, there are pictures."

"Pictures? Fucking Grace." Who does she think she is? A Paparazzo? Fuck.

"You almost gave sweet old Sheila a heart attack. She wants Father Demis to set up an intervention for you at church." I groan, reclining on the backrest of my desk chair and covering my face with my palms. "She's not happy with you." My hands drop at those words.

"Ackles Danneel Harris, forever the disappointment," I utter with vex in my voice. "Don't know why the folks in this town keep being surprised by it. You know, this is my life, if I want to make mistakes; I am going to make them." I announce standing up, slapping both of my hands on the desk and leaning my upper body forward. Not that Roman is a mistake. What is wrong with people? Meddling in shit that is not of their concern. "I love Shy-Shy, but sorry not sorry, she doesn't have any say in this."

"So you two are a thing?" Agnes Grey asks, her words wavering a bit.

"Sure." Fuck if I know. But I certainly want us to be.

As soon as I got home I took a very, very, long shower. Mostly to keep myself away from my phone. My fingers keep hovering over the call button under Roman's name.

"You are a grown-ass woman. Act like it." I tell my reflection after brushing my hand over the fogged-up mirror of my bathroom. "Damnit." Still wet and wrapped in a towel I go into my kitchen to grab my phone from the dining table. "You are not going to call him," I say over and over again. So I don't. I text him.

ACKLES:

Hey hot stuff, how are you doing?

Send. Oh my God, did I just Joey Tribbiani the shit out of Roman? You absolute loser.

HOT DEVIL: (Yes, that's the name Roman is under on my phone)

 Pretty she-devil, finally.

 I have only been patiently waiting by the phone all day.

He has? I was expecting a call, but I guess this will do.

ACKLES:

You know, YOU could've called me instead of dilly-dallying.

HOT DEVIL:

 Nah, I asked you on our first date.

 This time, it was your move.

 This is the 21st century, Harris, you ladies can ask us guys out too ;)

. . .

ACKLES:
I made you cum.

HOT DEVIL:
Indeed, you did.
Your point?

ACKLES:
Doesn't that count as a play on my part?
You know what, forget about it.
I am coming over.
Give me 5 to get dressed.

HOT DEVIL:
Hold one a second.
Are you telling me you are naked while texting me?

ACKLES:
No.
I am wearing a towel.
Just got out of the shower.

. . .

HOT DEVIL:
   No need for clothes.
   You are fine as you are.
   Get your ass here NOW.

I giggle. Roman's eagerness through those messages almost makes me want to do it. Wait. Should I? Would that be insane of me to do, arrive at his in only a towel? What if I get stopped by a cop? Oh, silly me, I am one. I can just lie through my teeth, and mention lady time, which should get all my colleagues who happen to be manly men and get squeamish at the idea of menstruation, of my scent. It's not like they don't know I am a little unbalanced, so I could definitely be the type of gal who goes to the shop in a towel to get some tampons. What if I get in an accident? Wow, dark though alert. I guess that would give the paramedics easy access to save my life. Hmmm, there's enough food for thought there, that's for sure.

)〇(

My headlights flood the porch of the house Roman is staying in with light. I have been parked here for over ten minutes overthinking my stupid decision. Is it too late to go back and change? Or get dressed?

My phone pings, from its holder on the dashboard of my truck, with a text notification.

HOT DEVIL:
   Are you staying out there all night?

LOOKING at the ground floor of the house I don't see any movement by the front door or any of the windows at that level, so I slant slightly over the steering wheel to peer up through my windshield. Roman is at a window on the first floor. What is he doing up there? And how long has he been staring at me from there? Also, why the fuck is he shirtless?

He types on his phone and a message pops up on my own.

HOT DEVIL:
   It's open, so just come on in.
   I have something to show you.

IS IT HIS DICK? Is that his bedroom? Calm your titties, Ackles.

Roman turns away from the window disappearing from my view, but not before bestowing me with that panty-melting smirk of his. I wonder if he knows I am not wearing any.

"Right. What's the worst that can happen? He won't fuck you senseless?" And with that pep talk, I am out of my car.

I make my way inside and up the stairs. Not that I know where I am going, but I can assume he is in the only room with a light shining off of the slightly open door. I push the door the rest of the way open and halt in my tracks. Roman is sitting cross-legged on top of an unmade king-size bed, with paperwork scattered everywhere around him. Can I just remark that this bed doesn't scream Roman, at all? Most of the furniture doesn't, to be honest. I guess the antiques came with the house. The bed though is this beautiful 1800s French-style mahogany bed, with a hand-carved headboard and footboard. Very 'boudoir elegance' shall I say.

"I went to the solicitor this morning," Roman informs me, whilst staring at a paper in his hand. "I think Mr. Holt is getting a bit tired of me, but what he tossed my way today has some pretty juicy stuff about…" He stops talking when he finally looks up at me. "Ackles."

"Roman."

You can hear him swallow dry in the otherwise silent house. "Why are you in a towel?"

"Why are you in your bedroom wearing a pair of wet dream-inducing grey joggers and nothing else?"

"I asked you first." He remarks.

"I thought that maybe we could continue what we started last night," I say all cool and collected, when inside there is a little moth on fire trying to break out so she can burn this whole place to ashes with steamy sex.

"Read more of your father's notes?"

I chuckle. "No, silly." I sashay my way to him, putting

emphasis on the sway of my hips with each step I take, only pausing at the end of the bed to undo the tremendously sturdy knot on my towel and let it fall to the ground. I am completely naked before Roman when I get on all fours on the bed and start crawling to him. "I did say I wanted to suck your dick back to life. Even though it seems your monster of a friend doesn't need the help of my mouth to flourish for me."

"Nobody warned me about how much of a fucking troublemaker you are, Harris." He declares, as I lift and wrap my arms around his neck, and straddle him.

"Funny, everyone keeps warning me about you." Roman hands land flat on my ass cheeks, massaging the flesh and muscle quite roughly.

"Yet, here you are."

"Yet, here I am." My green eyes dance from one of his to the other and back again. I do this a few times.

"Why?" He eventually asks.

"It seems we are both under a spell we can't split from. Not that I want to either."

"Neither do I."

"Well, then." My hands brush his sun-kissed skin from the back of his neck over the shoulders to his chest. "How about I take you for a nice ride? I do like a rowdy rodeo, what do you say?" I question, as I push him down so his back is on the mattress. His legs straighten at the same time.

"Condom or no condom?" Aww, that's actually sweet of him to ask.

"I am clean. And I really want to feel you stuff my pussy so full of your cum it spills out." I am not usually this dirty-mouthed, am I? I might need to wash my mouth with soap after this.

"Fuck, Ackles. I am clean too."

"Good. Since that's out of the way, how about we lose the joggers?" It was rather difficult to remove the joggers fully, seeing that I didn't want to budge from my position on him. We gave up with them midway down Roman's upper thighs. His dick is out, that is all that matters.

I spit on my hand, rise slightly on my knees and grip his cock. I pump it a few times, smearing my saliva all over his dick so it slides smoothly inside my narrow pussy. I mean, I am dripping, but with his size, it's undoubtedly going to sting when I impale myself on it, so every little thing helps to make it less painful. The tip meets my pussy, and I withdraw my hand, settling it opposite to the other on his chest. Inch by delicious inch I lower my body until he's all the way in.

I whimper.

"Damn, Harris, you are so tight." Roman grunts, his voice emanating with a deep throaty vibration.

"Well, you are not exactly small, Waterhouse." Beyond my walls having to spread to accommodate his length, I am positive my organs definitely had to rearrange themselves for him to fit. I honestly didn't know my pussy was that deep.

"You make it sound like it's a problem."

"No. No problem. Lucky for you I am all for being sore in the morning." Or for the rest of my life, because I don't think I am going to be able to let go of this Roman fucking Waterhouse obsession now that I felt him far in my core.

I begin to move, bouncing slowly up and down his dick.

Roman assists with the movements. His hands were still on my ass, his nails leaving half-moon indentations on the surface of my skin from how vigorously he was holding on, forcefully propelling me further on him. I am using my hands on his chest to stay steady as I haul myself up, his dick on the verge of entirely vacating me, only to shove back down, swallowing it whole once more with my pussy lips. My inner moth's ablaze wings are flapping like mad in the pit of my belly, making the fire scatter throughout my body.

I give my knees some rest from the hopping, relocating my hands to Roman's knees and leaning back on them, as I kick off simply undulating my hips. Holy fuck, this way his cock rubs against the sweet spot inside my pussy that, well, makes me lose it.

"Roman," I scream his name in euphoria as I cum undone, my body trembling ferociously.

I love this position, being on top, I feel like I have the reins over the wild beast below me. I am in control until I am not. In one swift move, Roman's hands ascend from my backside as his arms hug me around my lower back, pulling me down to him. Unforgiving and unbreakable is how I would describe his grasp. I am somehow pinned down to him, my arms prisoners between us. And then he just starts hammering into me in a fast and furious manner.

"Holy fuck." I gasp out.

I do not believe these beds were made for rough sex, because it sounds like it's about to break beneath us with the amount of squeaks and creaks and scraps that it howls.

I hum, because I am falling completely apart, the inferno

within me is raging yet again, and can't manage anything else. This time is with a violence I never felt before, ever.

"Fuck. Fuck. Fuck." Roman repeats as my body locks up, certainly milking his dick, and I begin to convulse. He thrust into me with some hassle, since my pussy walls just became narrower than a hangman noose. In the wake of the third push-in, he settles deep inside my pussy, his dick jerking as spurt after spurt I get flooded with his pearly juice. "You belong to me now, Ackles."

"My seed is inside you. You belong to me now, Ackles." A strange yet familiar voice echoes in my mind.

I slowly open my eyes but it takes a while for them to adjust and let the moonlight swamp the dark corner of the room enough for it to take shape. Where am I? I ask myself. There's a body against my back and this heavy arm rests over my waist. Peering down at it, I follow the line of beautiful intricate drawings on bronzed skin from this man's fingers to his shoulder until I reach his face.

I am staring at Roman's sleeping features when the same voice says, "Come for me, Ackles." I gaze towards the wide open door and see this shadow peek through from the corridor. What the hell? Is this another fucked up weird dream?

I rustle up from the bed, my bare feet touching the cold

floor. I think I hear Roman groan from amongst the sheets and papers. My eyes lower as this shiver consumes me. That chill felt very real to me. I notice that I am wearing a massive white tee that reaches my upper thigh, covering me up nicely. When did that happen? Oh, yeah, Roman kindly, but reluctantly, lended me one to sleep with after we had sex. Damn, that was the best fuck I had in my life.

"Come and find me." The voice speaks again.

I focus ahead and start treading to the doorway. Once there I peer down the corridor. Is that a fucking goat? Why is there a goat in the house? And why is it staring straight at me like it's getting ready to ram me with its curled horns?

"Ackles." Was that Roman mumbling my name? I am about to peer over my shoulder towards him but the goat decides to rush down the stairs then. Shit. I run after it. Why the fuck do I do that?

As I get downstairs and out the fully open front door, everything changes, like stepping into a portal into another world, another time, another life. Ok, I am without a doubt dreaming. The grey clouded night sky turns into a bright sunny day. The houses are erect before me now without a single crack or brick out of place, no longer decaying, in a terrible state of disrepair, wrecks. The odd thing about it is I can even hear crows sing, I can even smell the fields of tulips on the estate, and I can feel the breeze caress my skin and brush away my hair.

I have been dawdling in the direction of the main house, in a daze almost. But I stop dead in my tracks when from the Devil house this man walks through the front door. Roman?

Wait. It can't be. He's asleep in the other house, right? Much the same as a shimmer, the image in front of my eyes morphs in and out from someone who looks just like Roman to the goat man from my bad dreams.

"Lilith my darling, your home."

TWENTY-FIVE
ROMAN WATERHOUSE

I'm a light sleeper at best, so the sudden chill that snuck under the covers had me blinking awake in an instant. The bed beside me was empty, and I knew Ackles had left it. For a second, I thought she might've been on the hunt for the loo, but then I heard the telltale creak of the floorboards.

"Bugger," I muttered to myself.

Through the dark, my eyes tracked her shadow moving across the room, not towards the ensuite but to the blasted door. What was she up to? I shoved off the blankets, the night air prickling against my skin like icy needles.

"Ackles" No response. She was out the door faster than a roo on the hop.

"Shit."

I threw my legs over the side of the bed, muscles complaining from yesterday's slog in the yard. Didn't matter. I snatched up my sweats, dragging them on as I pushed through the confusion fogging my brain.

"Where the bloody hell are you goin'?" I called after her

again but got nothing back. Not even the echo of my own voice bouncing off the old walls seemed to reach her. She was all movement and haste, a flash of ginger curls disappearing down the staircase.

"Strewth..." My heart thumped a wild rhythm in my chest, part worry, part something else — something that felt a lot like dread.

Bare feet slapping against the cold floor, I made it to the landing.

"Dammit, girl," I hissed under my breath, taking the stairs two at a time.

"Wait up, will ya!" But she didn't. Couldn't? Who the hell knows? It was like she was bewitched, drawn by something unseen, unheard — by me, anyway.

"Christ on a bike, this isn't good." My gut twisted, a coiled snake ready to strike, tightening with every hurried step she took away from me. And in the dead of night, in this place, that could mean anything.

"Talk about a bloody cryptic midnight wander," I muttered, adrenaline fuelling my movements as I sprinted after her shadow. The old wooden floorboards creaked an urgent rhythm beneath my feet, each step a loud proclamation of my growing panic.

"Hey! Ackles!" The urgency clawed at my throat, raw and ragged. Still no response — just the echo of my own voice ricocheting off the walls, mocking me.

That's when I saw it — the front door wide open, swinging in the night breeze like a silent alarm bell. "Shit."

"ACKLES!" This time it was more than a call; it was a roar,

tearing from my lungs as I dashed outside, bare feet slapping against the dew-slick grass.

"Where are ya, darlin'?" My gaze darted left and right, searching the dark for her fiery curls, my mind racing with all sorts of grim possibilities. "Don't muck around!"

The cold bit at my skin, but the chill in my bones wasn't from the night air. It was fear, pure and simple. There she was, Ackles, just a stone's throw from the main house's entrance, her silhouette etched against the pale moonlight. She looked like she'd seen a ghost, all pale and shaky.

"Oi, Ackles! What in the blazes are you doin' out here?" My voice cut through the stillness, sharp as a knife. But she didn't so much as twitch, just stood there looking lost as a sheep in a paddock.

I closed the distance between us in a few strides, heart hammering like it wanted to break free. The closer I got, the more I saw how her eyes were wide, searching the darkness for something that wasn't there.

"Love, talk to me. You're scaring the daylights outta me." My hands reached out, hovering over her like I might spook her if I touched her.

Then I clocked the open door in front of her, swinging with a creak that set my teeth on edge. "Bloody hell," I muttered, taking it in. That door should've been locked up tighter than a drum. No way I'd have left it like that, not with all the critters about, looking for a cosy spot to kip.

The night air wrapped around me, cold as the grave, sleeping through my sweats like they were nothing. A shiver ran down my spine, not just from the chill. My gaze fixed on the open door, a dark maw that shouldn't be gaping wide at this ungodly hour. Something in the pit of my stomach stirred—this eerie feeling of belonging, like the house, was whispering, 'Welcome home, mate.'

"Christ," I muttered under my breath, the sensation sitting uneasy with me.

I shuffled closer, eyes still clung to the yawning doorway, when the sight of Ackles jolted me back. Her small frame trembled in the moonlight, her ginger curls wild and untamed against the stark white of her skin. Bloody hell, she looked more like a ghost than a woman.

"Ackles, baby, what are you doing out here?" I reached for her, hand snaking out fast. My fingers curled around her icy arm, dragging her body against mine. She was solid, real, but it did little to shake the sense of unease that crawled up my spine, settling heavily in my shoulders like a bad omen.

"Come on, let's get inside." My voice came out low, guttural, filled with a mix of worry and an odd protectiveness I couldn't quite place. The darkness beyond the door beckoned, whispering secrets I wasn't sure I wanted to hear. But right now, all that mattered was her, safe and sound, away from whatever madness had pulled her from my bed.

She swivelled her head to peer up at me, her forest-green eyes wide and distant. "Why did you call me Lilith?" Her voice was a whisper, floating through the cold like mist.

"Whatcha on about, Ackles?" I frowned, my gaze drilling into hers, searching for some sign of the fiery woman I knew. But there was something off, her eyes glazed like she was caught in a dream, but not quite dreaming.

"Never mind that," I grumbled, spinning her round, with

urgency nipping at my heels. We needed to get back inside before the house decided to spill more of its secrets.

Her feet shuffled against the gravel, compliant yet distant as I steered her through the open door. The warmth of the house wrapped around us—a contrast to the chill that had settled in my bones. I didn't know if she was awake or dancing with the Sandman. Either way, I got her back to bed, tucking her under the blanket's embrace.

She curled into me without protest, her body moulding to mine like two pieces of a puzzle long missing. A soft murmur escaped her lips, barely audible above the howling wind. "...why did you turn into a goat?"

"Goat?" I blinked, the word hanging heavy in the silence. Buggered if I knew what games her mind was playing. With a heavy sigh, I let the question dissipate into the darkness, deciding some riddles were best left unsolved till morning.

I watched over her as she drifted deeper into slumber, her breathing evening out, and I couldn't help wondering what demons chased her through her dreams, calling her by names of ancient myths. For now, though, she was safe, and that's all that mattered. I'd deal with whatever madness the daylight brought when it came.

The morning sun was just peeking over the horizon, spilling a soft glow through the kitchen windows when I caught sight of Ackles shuffling around in my old t-shirt. She looked like she'd been dragged backwards through a bush but still managed to be the prettiest thing I'd ever woken up to.

"Morning," I mumbled, scratching at my bedhead and pouring myself a cuppa that was strong enough to knock a bloke sideways.

"Hey," she chirped, though her voice was tinged with that just-woke-up huskiness. She glanced out the window, lost in thought, as she nibbled on some toast.

"Got somethin' to tell ya 'bout last night," I said, leaning against the counter, watching her reaction closely. "You went for a little midnight stroll—scared me half to death, you did."

Her eyes snapped to mine, and she blanched, nearly dropping her toast. "That happened? I thought I dreamt that."

I shook my head, taking a swig from my mug. "Nah, you were up and about, wanderin' like a ghost. Gave me a real fright."

She ran a hand through those wild curls of hers, looking a bit sheepish. "Used to sleepwalk heaps as a kid. Stopped after Mama got sick, though." Her green eyes clouded over, shadows of old memories flickering behind them.

"Rough go of it?" I asked, trying to keep my tone light but showing I cared.

She swallowed hard, looking down at her fingers wrapped around the mug. "Mama... she had a few screws loose. Ended up being put away in an asylum. That's where she passed." She shrugged, but the weight of her history was there, hanging heavy between us. "Was just a wee lass, so it's all a bit blurry—just flashes here and there."

"Shit, Ackles, I didn't mean to drag up old ghosts," I muttered, scratching the back of my neck awkwardly. She brushed it off with a wave of her hand, leaning over the kitchen table cluttered with paperwork.

"Roman, I'm not some delicate flower, am I?" Her eyes sparkled with that tough-as-nails glint I'd come to admire. "Besides, look at this mess here." She tapped a finger against a yellowed sheet among the pile. The solicitor's words printed on it looked like bloody hieroglyphs to me.

"Righto, what's catching your eye then?" I leaned in, catching the scent of her shampoo mixed with the mustiness of the documents—a strange combo that somehow worked.

"Your grandmother," she began, her digit poised delicately above a paragraph. "Departed when she was but a slip of a girl, around eighteen. Collected her belongings and relocated to Australia." She cast an upward glance at me, eyebrows gently knit together. "It appears she met her end at the tender age of thirty-five, by her own doing... And your grandfather wasn't long in following suit."

"Bugger me..." I exhaled, the words knockin' the wind right outta me sails. Didn't matter how rough 'n tumble you were; news like that could floor a bloke.

"And then there's this bit," Ackles continued, her voice soft but steady. "She'd only had your mum a few years before all that went down. She broke the three-daughter cycle."

"Okay, well it's definitely broken then," I grumbled, thumbing the ancient parchment that spilled a history as tangled as the roots of an old gum tree. "I'm the only bloke popped out in over three centuries if this paperwork is on the money."

Ackles was staring out the window, lost in her own world. Her lips moved silently, and I caught the word "goat" just hanging in the air between us. A shiver ran down my spine—something about that was off.

"Oi, Ackles, you alright?" I asked, my brows pulling together like crumpled paper. She turned to me, a smile lighting up her face that didn't quite reach those forest eyes of hers.

"Yeah, I'm fine," she chirped, though I wasn't fully buying it. "Just gotta dash or I'll be late for work."

She made to scoot past me, but I couldn't let her trot off half-cocked. "Hey, don't go flashin' your bits to the whole precinct," I called after her, lobbing my offer upstairs. "You can nick my sweats and shirt."

The sound of her laugh trickled down like rain on a tin roof, easy and free. Moments later, she bounded back into the kitchen, wearing my gear like it was made for her—loose and comfy, yet somehow making a statement that screamed all mine.

"Thanks, Waterhouse," she said, her voice a mix of mischief and something else—something deeper. She leaned in close, and our lips met in a kiss that could've set the room ablaze if we weren't careful. The taste of her, the heat from her skin... bloody hell, it was enough to make a man forget his own name.

"Later, hot stuff," she winked, throwing the words over her shoulder as she strutted out the door, leaving me with nothing but the memory of her touch and the echo of her footsteps.

I stood there, a daft grin plastered on my dial, watching

as she disappeared into the day. Ackles had this way about her, didn't she? Like she could walk through fire and come out smelling like roses.

"Roman Waterhouse, you've got it bad," I muttered to myself, still feeling the ghost of her lips against mine. But no time for daydreaming. There was work to do, even if the thought of her in my clothes was enough to derail any bloke's train of thought.

THE SUN HADN'T EVEN PROPERLY WOKEN up yet, but there I was, standing at the foot of the freshly minted cottage. The place looked like a bloody treat—walls as white as Bondi sand and floorboards that gleamed like they'd been kissed by the sun itself. Not gonna lie, pride swelled in my chest like a bloody big wave ready to break.

"Damn fine job, Roman," I muttered to myself, hands on hips as I gave the joint one last once-over. It wasn't a massive gig, nah, but it was mine, every nail and lick of paint. And now it was time to slap a price tag on her and send her into the world.

I needed to get this beauty listed for sale, pronto. My mind was still buzzing with thoughts of Ackles though—her fiery hair, the way she fit into my old sweats like they were made just for her, and that kiss... Christ, that kiss could've powered the whole of Sydney's New Year's fireworks.

"Focus, mate," I chided myself, shaking off the distraction as I grabbed my phone from my pocket. Gotta get this done, then who knows? Maybe celebrate with a cold one later.

I punched the numbers in, the phone cradled between my ear and shoulder as I flicked through the paperwork. "G'day, Sheila. Roman Waterhouse here. Got a cottage to list —" But the line went dead quicker than a kangaroo on the highway. Not the first to hang up on me today, either.

"Bugger this," I muttered, thumbing the end call button with more force than needed. Local real estate agents were all the same—spooked by some ancient ghost yarns about my property. The place was a bloody gem, but they couldn't see past the cobwebs of old tales.

"Fine then," I grumbled, scrolling down the list of real estate agents I found on Google. If these local yobbos wouldn't take the bait, I'd cast my line in deeper waters. Dialled the number, mind already picturing the convo—sell 'em on the history, the mystery.

"James Beaufort, how can I help you?" The bloke on the other end sounded chipper, not a hint of fear in his voice.

"Roman Waterhouse here. I've got a cottage that needs selling. Locals are too chicken because of some daft ghost story." My patience was wearing thin as an eel's wetsuit.

"Haunted, you say? Well, city folks eat that up!" He laughed—a hearty, belly-deep sound. "I reckon we can spin it. Haunted or not, there's no such thing as bad publicity."

I cracked a smile for the first time today. "That's the spirit. Reckon you can get a listing up pronto?"

"Swifter than a fox in a gale. Transmit the specifics, and

we'll have those urbanites forming an orderly queue posthaste."

"Cheers, mate." I hung up, feeling a bit more chipper myself. "Let's see how you like them apples," I said to the silent room, a smirk tugging at the corner of my mouth.

The city real estate was onto something—everyone loves a good scare, a brush with the unknown. And if it gets me property sold, well then, ghosts be damned. They can haunt the cheque all they like, as long as it clears.

)○(

THE MOMENT I set foot in the main house, the air buzzed with urgency, like a nest of hornets stirred up by an unwelcome boot. "Get a bloody move on, lads!" I shouted, my voice echoing off bare walls. The builders I'd wrangled for the cottage were back, tearing through the place with the efficiency of a cyclone.

Wood splintered, plaster crumbled, and dust danced in sunbeams like mischievous spirits. I couldn't help but smirk at the thought—mischievous spirits were about to become this old house's selling point.

"Roman, where would you like these placed?" One of the blokes gestured to a pile of bags, just sitting there. Ackles would be here soon to collect them.

"Over there, by the stairs," I said, pointing. "And watch your step, don't need any twisted ankles on my conscience."

As if on cue, Ackles sauntered in, her police uniform hugging her frame, authority radiating off her like heat from bitumen on a scorcher. She didn't even bother announcing herself anymore; her presence was a given, as sure as the sun rising and setting.

"Got another batch for me?" Her voice held that lilt that could make a man think of less... professional engagements.

"Right there," I nodded toward the bags, all too aware of the chair back in my house—my makeshift 'throne'. Some days I'd park myself in it, just to see if she'd take the bait and cuff me again. A dangerous game, but damn, it was worth it.

"Roman, you're spoiling me," she teased, bagging the bags with practised hands. Her gaze met mine, green eyes sparkling with something wild. It was enough to make a bloke forget his own name.

"Anythin' for my favourite copper," I shot back, leaning against a wall, arms folded, watching her work.

"Flatterer." Ackles winked and hefted the bags. "Forensics will have a field day."

"Find out anything juicy yet?"

"Well, the ones you unburied from the dirt outside were definitely chicken ones. You were lucky. These specimens though, are another story. Definitely human. Ancient as time itself, not a single new one among them," she expressed nonchalantly, seemingly unperturbed by the morbid nature of our conversation. "It's believed they were all severed after death, following mummification. Quite a chilling thought indeed."

"From the crypt, no doubt." The words slipped out before

I could stop 'em, and a shiver chased up my spine like a spider up a drainpipe.

"Ah, the infamous crypt." She looked at me, all cop now, curiosity sharp as a knife. "Have you checked it out yet?"

"Been... busy," I muttered, feeling the lie sit heavy on my tongue.

Ackles narrowed her eyes, sensing the dodge. "Roman Waterhouse, scared of a few old bones, are we?"

"Scared? Pfft. Just haven't got around to it," I bluffed, hoping she'd buy it. Truth was, cemeteries gave me the heebie-jeebies ever since Mum and Dad passed. But Ackles didn't need to know that.

"Sure, sure," she drawled, clearly not convinced. "I'll swing by tonight." With a final nod, she was out the door, leaving me to the silence and the dust and the ghosts of what once was.

"Bugger," I whispered to the empty room. "Gonna have to face that crypt sooner rather than later." But for now, there was work to do, a house to gut, and a cheeky copper who had me wrapped around her little finger—mummified or not.

Twenty-Six

Ackles Harris

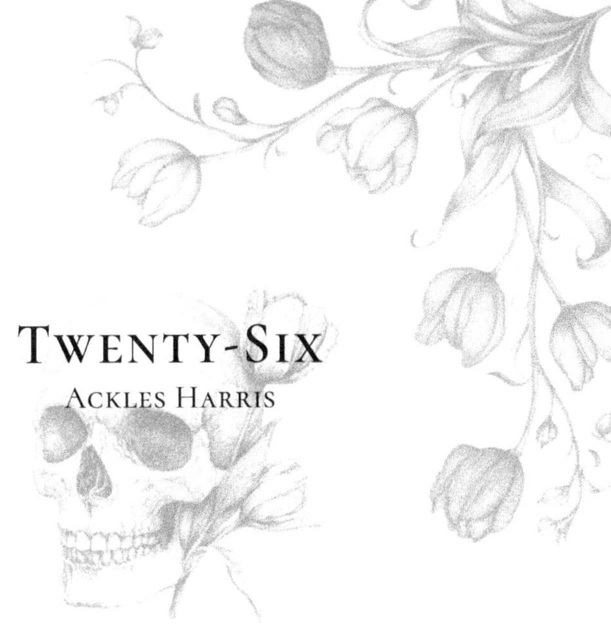

"I feel like I have seen more of you these past few days, than when we were back at school," Huxley remarks, bent over one of the embalming tables in the morgue, examining with a sharp eye the fingers Roman found buried in the walls of Device houses. Shrivelled mummified index fingers all of them, posthumously cut off from whoever they belong to.

"Tired of me already, Huxley?" I ask him teasingly as I come to stand right next to him, outstretching my arms to the table and placing my hands flat on it, leaning forward to see what he's doing.

"Never. I like having you around, you know that." Huxley says, peering at me but hastily looking away as a blush pops up on his cheeks. "You are a better company than these guys." He vaguely points at the cold lockers, without a doubt talking about whoever they have inside. "They are not very talkative."

"I would be concerned if they were," I observe.

"I just don't want your boyfriend to come and beat me up 'cause you are spending a lot of time with me."

"Roman? Nah, he's fine. You're fine. Just don't get too handsy with me like you seem to be with those fingers there, and he won't lay a finger on you. See what I did there?" I utter, elbowing him playfully.

"Funny." He utters, pushing his glasses up his nose with his middle finger. "So hmmm he is your boyfriend then."

Oh, shit, did I just imply that? I hum before replying to his not question but statement, "We haven't exactly labelled it anything per se." But I am over there pretty much every day, and spending at least every other night with him. We like each other, we like being in each other's company, we love each other's bodies, and the sex is just to die for. What more is there to it? Do we need to put a label on it? I am not insecure like that, so I don't see the point in having the boyfriend and girlfriend talk with Roman.

"Did you know that in olden times people used to stick around after an accused witch's execution in order to cut one of the fingers from the still-warm corpse? The index one was the most sought after." Huxley burst out all of a sudden.

"How come?" I ask.

"Folks believed it was the best charm to use in a protection spell."

"Protection against what?" This is why I like Huxley; he has an insatiable curiosity for everything, and an instinctive ability to appreciate the macabre and the unexplained. Also, the guy is like a walking Google; just ask him anything, and I am sure he will know the answer.

"Evil doings, perhaps." He notes as he straightens up and, believe it or not, looks me in the eyes.

"These are index fingers, right?" Huxley nods. "Of a time not long ago when witches roamed amongst us."

"They probably still do. We just don't go around accusing them for stupid reasons, making them go through senseless trials and killing them in the most inhumane ways."

"What I was trying to lead to, before you, my cute mortician, interrupted me, was that the Device family members were said to be hexers. What if they gave credence to what you just told me and the fingers were deliberately put in the walls like gris-gris to ward off or to guard something?"

"You think these belong to the Device kin?"

"Only one way to find out. If I get Roman's DNA can you test it against that?" Why, as I say that, am I grinning like a kid who just got exactly what they wanted for Christmas?

My phone pings as Huxley states, "For sure."

"Ha, speaking of the Devil."

HOT DEVIL:

Harris, I need you.

Get your peachy ass over here NOW.

ACKLES:

Baby, you seriously need to work on how to request a quickie.

This isn't the way.

. . .

HOT DEVIL:

Remember the basement the builders found in the main house?

ACKLES:

Vaguely.

I do promise I try to pay attention, but you are just so pretty I get distracted sometimes.

ACTUALLY MORE THAN as near as dammit, I remember every little occurrence in that plot of land. I am just trying to act casual about it.

HOT DEVIL:

Well, I told them to dig up the dirt for plumbing.

ACKLES:

Ok. Waterhouse, the suspense is killing me.

HOT DEVIL:

They unearthed body parts.

ACKLES:
More fingers?
I am starting to think your family had a fetish or
something.

HOT DEVIL:
No, more like full skeletons.
In pieces. Scattered. Everywhere.

"Fuck." I utter.

"What?" Huxley asks, his voice dripping with concern.

)〇(

It's a filthy goddamn horror show. What the hell happened here? There's an incomplete jigsaw puzzle of human remains all over this dirt-filled ground.

"You didn't tell me the morgue guy was a nice-looking dude?" Roman comments from right next to me. I got to Roman's in record time, with Huxley at my heels since he insisted on coming the moment I mentioned a basement, possibly, full of bones.

I lift my gaze from the mess at our feet to look up at the Aussie hunk, who just happens to be glaring at poor Huxley. "Seriously?" I ask, a bit perplexed by Roman's priorities. This basement just became an active crime scene and he's more concerned with the attractiveness of Newchurch's mortician?

"What? I might've been less inclined to let you spend that much time with him in a small space if I knew he looked like that." Oh my God, is Roman jealous?

"Oh, yeah. Because I am definitely going to do the deed with dead people around me." Roman spreads his arms in a "look around you" gesture. "Excuse me. It's not like I knew these were here." I announce crossing my arms under my chest.

"I'm sorry to interrupt," Huxley says as he approaches us, which makes Roman groan whilst giving him the evil eye. Wow, down boy down. "We might need some help here. I deal with meaty bodies, not bones."

"Ok. I will talk to Chief Bargrave. See if we can have a forensic anthropologist come here to give us a hand. Have you taken all the photos deemed necessary? If so can we kick off bagging these bad boys up?"

It took us hours to scoop up every single bone, days of filling out boring paperwork and reports, and a good few weeks before a specialist arrived. Kennedy Brennan a young bone expert from the big city. She walked into the morgue like an untameable wildfire. In her defence, Doctor Huxley was leaving the morgue to go grab something from the lab right next door and as he opened the door she just fell on him and with him. What I mean is, when I gaze from the array of body bony chunks I see Huxley Davies on the white terrazzo floor with a cute redhead on top of him. Whatever she had in her hands before she stumbled inside, flew everywhere at the contact, and was raining down on them at the minute.

"Now that's what I call a big entrance into the story?" They both seemed a bit lost in each other's eyes before those snapped at me at my remark.

"Oh," Kennedy utters, getting quickly up from her entanglement with Huxley, "I am really sorry. I was leaning against the door, trying to work out how to open it with my hands full, and then the door wasn't there to support my weight anymore."

"Because knocking is overrated?" Huxley observes from his sitting position on the floor, his legs lay out flat as he inclines on his hands behind him.

"Knocking, right," Kennedy says, a blush painting her cheeks.

She's pretty, kind of reminds me of me, but way taller, maybe 5' 7, slender, fair-skinned, with meadow green eyes and wavy natural ginger hair at the roots and bright orange and teal ombre highlight effect at the ends.

As Kennedy seeks to remove her double-breasted beige trench coat, her hand bumps with Huxley's mug on his desk, sending the object crashing to the floor. Dark brown brew lands on the mortician's lap, making him howl, "Fuck," whilst broken pieces of ceramic are dispersed all over the morgue, along with her papers from before. What a mess! I like her, she's a beautiful hurricane.

"Oh, you clumsy witch." She tells herself. "I'm so sorry, again." She says kneeling in front of Huxley and cleaning his crotch with her jacket. I guess that's one way of doing it.

I think Huxley might've spaced out for a second there, but when he comes to his senses he yelps, "I'm good," shooting to his feet so fast that Kennedy almost gets whiplash from the move. "I'll take care of it in the bathroom. I mean wash it. Excuse me, ladies." And with that, he's out the door and disappearing down the long corridor.

Well, that was a pretty massive bulge in his pants. Someone is packing a punch between their legs, and I think the anthropologist may have noticed that too, because she declares, "I probably shouldn't have rubbed it so hard."

I belly laugh at that, before joining her on the cold flooring, helping harvest everything scattered about. "Welcome to the madhouse, Kennedy. Something tells me you'll fit in just fine in this hellhole." I tell her.

The girl is amazing. In just a few days, Kennedy, not only pieced together every single skeleton in its entirety, but also concluded that the bones were all Caucasian males, around the age of 40 to 50, and that their possible cause of death was decapitation. All of them. That last bit she was able to gather from a small knife indentation on the cervical spine. She reckons someone slashed these guys' throats with such brutality and strength that led to an almost complete beheading in the moment of the killing. After that the bodies were cut into lumps and the rest is history.

In the back of my mind, something kept telling me that these might be the husbands. But they are buried alongside the Device daughters in the family crypt, right?

Wrong. Roman and I went to investigate the old burial chamber underneath the imposing muss-covered mausoleum, with stone that turned black in places due to the passage of time and the lovely damp British weather. Nestled amongst the fields of tulips that surround the property, the flowers mask not only the haunting structure but also the smell which is all-consuming once you step inside. Rot and decay. Clearly who constructed this didn't think of drains and air vents that get rid of the yuckiness of a decomposing corpse.

From the monstrous ornate blue cast iron doors, stairs shot straight down, and after that, a long corridor with either side wall made up of tomb after tomb. The writings on the walls claim that both husband and wife are inside the ossuary, but as soon as we break through the same dark raw marble, which hide the holes the coffins lay upon, we only find one body resting peacefully inside. Those lone corpses, they are all women.

Roman was the only living relative of the Device family and with the deed to the land the mausoleum stands proudly on, meaning that the papers we needed to exhume the remains were quite easy to obtain. I thought that maybe he would feel bad about disturbing his ancestors' sleep, but that wasn't the case. I mean he's the one that swung a sledge-hammer to the walls and later shoved a wrecking crowbar through the lid of the wooden coffins.

"Bloody hell, Harris, they are all missing an index finger." Roman had noted the instant every casket laid open before us. And indeed they were. I guess we won't be needing Roman's DNA to prove that the fingers we found on the walls belonged to the Device daughters. What we did require it for was to match the bones from the basement to his lineage. Hold and behold they did, which means they are the husbands.

Roman's whole family, and the estate itself, are all buried in secrets and lies, tulips and bones.

Twenty-Seven
Roman Waterhouse

As soon as the last of the bodies was yanked from that godforsaken crypt, I was on the blower to the local cemetery, sorting out a place for the poor bastards to rest. "Yeah, g'day," I said, my voice echoing a bit in the empty space. "Need to plant some bodies your way. No fuss, right?"

The cemetery was adamant about not accepting the bodies without the proper paperwork, so I told them firmly that Detective Ackles Harris would handle it. The bureaucrat on the line, all stiff and formal, agreed reluctantly. "No worries," I responded before ending the call, a bead of sweat rolling down my temple. The crypt – that bloody eyesore – had been lurking on my property since I got here, giving me the heebie-jeebies every time I thought about it. It wasn't just the sight of it; it was the air, thick with whispers of the past, enough to make your skin crawl.

But now? With Kennedy and Huxley playing matchmaker with finger bones and corpses down at the morgue, it was high time to get rid of the damn thing altogether. The thought of tearing it down sent a shiver of relief through my creaky frame.

I couldn't wait to see the back of it. To know that the land would be clear, free from the shadows that clung to it like cobwebs. And once those bodies were tucked away nice and neat on hallowed ground, maybe I'd sleep a bit easier.

"Let's get this done," I muttered, more to myself than anyone else. The sooner that crypt became history, the better.

The builders rocked up at dawn, their boots crunching the gravel as they filed through the gate to where the crypt sat like a bad memory. The morning mist curled around the neglected tomb, but I just hitched up my sleeves and nodded. "Let's rip into it."

"Righto, boss," one of the blokes called out, a stocky fella with a grin that said he didn't scare easily. They got to work, shovels biting the earth, pickaxes swinging. The sound of stone cracking was music to my ears.

I kept a keen eye on Ackles as she moved about, snapping photos with clinical precision. Her ginger curls were pulled back, and her green eyes flicked over every detail, her freckled face all business. She caught my gaze and flashed that flirty smile of hers. "Documenting history, Roman," she quipped in her British lilt, camera clicking away.

"History be buggered," I grunted, grabbing a sledgehammer from the pile. The walls of the crypt loomed, damp and dark, but not for much longer.

"Here goes nothing," I muttered and swung the hammer with all my might. The thud of metal against stone echoed, a satisfying crunch following. Again and again, I smashed into the walls, each hit a release of the dread that had filled me since setting eyes on this damned place.

"Careful there, mate!" one of the builders shouted as a chunk of wall nearly clipped his ear.

"Sorry, cobber," I called back, not slowing my assault. Dust billowed, the air thick with the smell of disturbed earth and old secrets.

It didn't take long for the crypt to crumble under our combined fury. Stone after stone, we dismantled the beast until it was nothing but a heap. A sweet, vicious victory.

"Good riddance," I breathed, looking over the ruin. We buried the remnants, erasing the monstrosity for good. The last of the rubble carted off, the land finally felt like it could breathe.

"Nice job," Ackles said, sidling up next to me, her voice softer now.

"Thanks to you too," I replied, tipping an imaginary hat. "For all the meticulous work."

"Ah, part of the service," she grinned, tucking her camera away. "I need to add to the paperwork we already have after all,"

"Of course you do," I replied, chuckling despite the ache in my arms. It was done. The crypt was gone.

"Rumour-mongering bastards," I muttered under my breath, marching towards the local cemetery with a determination that matched the storm brooding overhead. The grey clouds seemed to weigh on the spires of the church like an accusation, a fitting backdrop to the dispute I was about to have.

"Roman, keep your cool, yeah?" Ackles' voice cut through, her British lilt a stark contrast to my Aussie grumble. "We need them on our side."

"Righto," I conceded, but my jaw clenched tighter than a vice. The cemetery gates loomed, ironwork as twisted as the town's bloody gossip.

The cemetery's groundskeeper, a weasel-faced bloke with beady eyes, met us at the entrance. "Mr. Waterhouse," he sneered, "the Council may have given you permission, but these grounds are sacred. We can't have known demon lovers buried here."

"Known? You're all talk, no evidence, mate," I shot back, leaning in close enough to see the shiftiness in his gaze. "Council says yes, so you lot can shove your superstitions where the sun doesn't shine."

Ackles gave me a sidelong glance but said nothing. She knew as well as I did that this was more about old grudges than any real concern for sacrilege.

"Fine," the groundskeeper spat, clearly realising he was outmatched. "But they'll be buried in the back. Technically not on hallowed ground, but part of the cemetery all the same."

"Technically is good enough for me," I replied, smirking. "Just get it done."

"Follow me," he relented, leading us past rows of weathered headstones.

The land sloped downwards, away from the polished marble and chiselled angels, to a patch overgrown with brambles and thistles. It wasn't much, but it was disconnected from the main cluster – a limbo between the living and the dead.

"Here," he declared, stopping short and gesturing broadly at the neglected parcel. "This is where they can rest."

"Perfect," I said, though the word tasted sour. I didn't care for their peace; I just wanted those bodies off my property and out of my life.

No grand tombs this time. No bloody marble angels weeping over the dead. Just earth, shovels, and simple pine boxes - austerity in death as it should be. The men were laid to rest beneath their wives, an odd sort of chivalry for a family with a reputation dark as pitch.

"Got the last husband matched," I grunted, wiping sweat from my brow as I looked at the dirt-streaked faces of the workers and groundskeeper, reburying nearly twenty bodies, wasn't easy work. "Rest are unidentified individuals, but we have their DNA to compare with unsolved cases. Perhaps there's someone out there who will mourn their absence," Ackles states, noting that among the discoveries were ten additional bodies. These remains were being cross-referenced with missing person reports associated with the Device estate spanning years, yet justice had never been served.

"Seems like the town's full of their kin anyway," Ackles piped up, her curls plastered to her forehead, a smirk on her lips betraying the grim work. "For a bunch of folks scared shitless of the Device legacy, they sure didn't mind sharing their beds with the women."

"Blood's thicker than water, but lust's thicker than both, seems like," I replied, chuckling at the thought.

As the sun dipped low, casting long shadows across the freshly turned soil, Ackles sidled up next to me, her forest green eyes catching the last light. "You know," she said, flipping through the tattered paperwork, "papa used to spin yarns about the Device women."

"Is that right?" I asked as we watched the groundskeeper lower the caskets into the holes, around the now cleared patch of land, thanks to Ackles, myself, and the workers.

"Said they were like sirens, luring blokes with whispers and promises. Once any man crossed the threshold of the estate, he'd never leave. Like bloody will o' the wisps leading travellers off the path into the marshlands."

"Old tales to keep kids from nicking apples from the orchard, I reckon." I exhaled a breath.

"Maybe," she mused, her gaze distant, thoughtful. "Or maybe there's truth buried deeper than these graves."

"Either way, it's done now." I replied, "They're all six feet under where they can't bother anybody. Estate's clean, and I can move on."

"Move on to more secrets, you mean." Ackles' grin was back, sharp and promising trouble. "There's always something more with this place, Roman. Always."

"Let's hope not," I muttered, though deep down, I knew she was right. There was always something more, especially with a woman like Ackles by your side. She was a force unto herself, impossible to ignore, harder still to control.

"Come on," she said, tugging at my arm. "Let's grab a drink at the pub. I reckon we've earned it after playing gardener all day."

"Lead the way, siren," I replied, following her into the encroaching darkness, away from the graves.

Twenty-Eight

Ackles Harris

While Roman wanted to have the remains of his ancestors buried in the local cemetery mostly so they are no longer on his property, so their dead presence was no longer looming and lurking over the estate and him, out of sight out of mind. I wanted them there to show the old folks of Newchurch that the Device family are, in part, just like us, human, made of flesh and bones. They lived, they died, and yes they killed too and are undoubtedly worse monster's than the spooky stories about them led us to believe, but they are corpses enshrouded under six feet of dirt now.

It's an uncontaminated assumption that the Device ladies are the ones that slashed the husbands' throats, considering that no one else stepped foot in those grounds but them and whichever males they lured in. It is the only possibility that makes sense. They wouldn't make the other men kill one another; they would be giving away their ill-fated impending doom away. No. The woman did it, I am 100% sure.

Sadly what all of this means is that Kennedy Brennan is no longer needed. No bones. No Kennedy. Huxley, the poor guy, has been sulking since he came to that same realisation. I think someone likes the bubbly, yet clumsy, forensic anthropologist.

Honestly, the girl is a whirlwind even in the way she dresses. She combines pieces that normally don't go together, with a non-matching explosion of colour like a unicorn just puked a rainbow all over her. Kennedy thrives in breaking the conventional rules of fashion and celebrates her individuality with fearless experimentation of out there ensembles, with her very eclectic style. And everything she wears seems to have a story. "I got these earrings in Egypt doing a dig. And I got this top from someone I traded a burger with in Iraq while doing another dig. Then I got these pants handmade by a man in China while doing a dig." She does a lot of digs.

As it happens Kennedy is a talented artist too, and she does beautiful forensic facial reconstruction. So we got to keep her for an extra few weeks to have her help us do one for every single guy that dared enter the Devil house. Not that we need it, DNA has been enough to match it with most of the missing people cases from around these parts, but I thought it would be nice for these guys' families to see what they looked like before their tragic end.

When I arrive at the morgue, Kennedy is sitting cross legged on top of one of the embalming tables in the morgue, drawing up by hand what I presume is another husband's face. She has headphones on, but in the dead silence of the room you can hear the faint whisper of Courtney Love singing 'Doll Parts'.

Huxley's body neighbours my own at the door, and as I peer at him I can't stop the laughter that escapes my lips. "Oh my God, Huxley, what happened to you?"

"I think the universe is telling me I should give up coffee." His white doctor's coat and Nirvana tee underneath have this massive dark brown stain in his chest area.

"Did hurricane Kennedy cause this? Or is this just storm Huxley's doing?" I mean, these two are as bad as each other, little accidents and small mishaps are the standard when it comes to them.

"Hmmm a bit of both, I was leaving the lab when she was passing through heading to the morgue. She bumped into me, her drink slipping all over my front as she landed on her ass on the floor."

"Oh, so at least it wasn't your coffee this time." Huxley grimaces at my words.

If you are thinking that Huxley is the one that ends up with the mess on him every time, think again. When they were examining the Device daughters' corpses, Huxley cut something he shouldn't and Kennedy winded up with some foul smelling fluid on her pretty pink blouse. What she did next was the best thing ever. Kennedy just takes the top off, standing before Huxley, and me, in her gorgeous black lace bra. I swear if this was a cartoon, Doctor Davies eyes would've turned heart shaped and bulged out of the eye sockets.

"Hey, Huxley, you keep extra shirts around right?" I asked

our forensic technician. There was nothing for a moment, until I called out his name, "Huxley?" That's when his very much dilated eyes snapped to me.

"Yeah," He cleared his throat as his eyes dropped to the body on the embalming table, that usual blush of his appearing in his cheeks, "top drawer in my desk."

The way he looked at Kennedy in his Linkin Park tee, I've only seen one other guy have that sort of longing look. Roman when he glances at me. It looks like Newchurch's mortician has a type pale as a ghost redheads with green eyes.

"She's leaving tomorrow, right?" I ask Huxley out of the blue, turning my attention to the girl just sitting where dead bodies normally lay.

"Yeah, her train to London departs early in the morning." Huxley sounds so downhearted when he says that.

"You should ask her on a date," I tell him.

"What? No. Didn't you hear me, she leaves tomorrow."

"Which means you still have tonight." I gaze back at him. "Now, get your cute ass over there and ask her out," I order, pointing at Kennedy.

)○(

"Tell me again, how did we get reeled into this date?" Roman questions me as we get out of his car and start making our way into this adorable Japanese restaurant that just recently opened in a neighbouring town.

"Because Huxley choked on his words while asking Kennedy out, and ended up saying that we wanted to take her out for food to thank her for all the help."

"Wait." Roman halts and grabs my elbow, making me stop in my stride too. "Are you telling me the girl doesn't even know this is, what, a double date?"

"Not exactly. No."

"Oh, this is going to be fun." Roman declares as a wicked evil smirk comes out to play. "Ouch." He utters after I land a punch on his gut.

"Be nice, Roman. I really want these two to end up together. I have a feeling they are simply meant to be. And I mean, I am sure you wouldn't fancy Huxley's attention coming back to me, right?"

"What do you mean by that?"

"Oh, only that he has had the biggest crush on me since we were kids," my words get cut short as Roman throws me over his shoulder and begins walking back to the car.

"Right. We are out of here. And you are not allowed to see him ever again."

"Roman," I shout his name as I attempt to get out of his arms. "Put me down, you buffoon. Ouch. Did you just slap my ass Roman Waterhouse."

"No." He so did. Jerk. He eventually puts me back down, which happens to be right next to his car, after he swung the passenger side door wide open wide. "Get in." He commands.

I cross my arms under my boobs, lifting the girls up. "No.

Roman you are being silly. Don't you think if I wanted to jump on that massive stick I would've done so already."

"Excuse you, Sheila. I don't think I heard you right."

"What I meant is, I don't like Huxley like that, ok? Furthermore, since you came into my life no one else even holds a candle to you. Damn, they are not even in the same league as you, Roman. So, jealousy is not necessary, ok? But Huxley is my friend, can we please just go inside and support him."

Roman frowns, grunting, "Fine," and slamming the car door shut. "Let's go. But when we get home you are going to have to explain what you meant by massive stick." Oh, shit.

"Is he going to kiss her or what?" I shush him. "Did you just shush me, pretty she-devil?"

"Yes. I am trying to hear what he says to her."

Dinner was lovely, we talked, laughed; none spilled any drink over any one, surprisingly, even though Huxley ended up with a soy sauce stain on his light grey skinny chinos from a rogue onigiri that slipped through his chopsticks as he got distracted listening to one of Kennedy's many dig tales. For quite ungraceful people those two were great with chop-sticks. I gave it a try that lasted five seconds and rice winded up everywhere, so I stuck to traditional cutlery as did Roman. All in all it was a great night.

At the present time, Roman and I are sitting in front seats of his car staring at Huxley and Kennedy while they speak by her car. Our windows are open so we can listen to the whispers the cold British wind sends our way.

"You know we are always in need of a mortician or forensic guy down in London. You are probably one the best I have met in either field. I could put in a good word and maybe you could move there." Kennedy says to Huxley.

"I don't think a guy like me would do well alone in a big city environment. I was at Oxford for university, and that was scary enough. I like the smallness of my hometown, it's a," Huxley takes a breath and pushes his glasses up with his middle finger, "safe and sound little moth cocoon."

"Is this guy for real?" Roman comments.

"Oh, you wouldn't be alone. We would be together. I mean, I would be there for you, hold your hand through the daunting big city. I really want you to come."

"You do?" I swoon in the car when Kennedy nods eagerly at his question, with a sweet smile on her face.

"Just bloody kiss her, you idiot," Roman screams as he pokes his head out of the driver's side window.

"Roman," I call out his name forbiddingly.

"What? Just be glad I didn't shout something else. They need to get a room, baby. I mean, you can cut the sexual tension emanating from them with a knife." He's not wrong.

Huxley's and Kennedy's gazes lower to the ground when they realise they have an audience just prior to them looking at each other in the eyes. I hold on to Roman's upper arm with considerable strength, sinking my nails in his flesh. "Oh my God, Roman," I utter as Huxley's hand grabs Kennedy's throat to pull her closer to him and their lips meet. I yelp in excitement.

"About damn time," Roman announces.

"Don't ruin the moment, baby," I remark, circling my arm around his upper arm now, shifting on my seat so I am alongside Roman, and placing my head on his shoulder.

"You are way too engaged in this." He tells me, placing a kiss on my forehead.

Those two are really going at each other. It's unquestionably a feverish effing kiss. You can just about perceive their tongues going in one another's mouths as if they are seeking to devour the other person. Huxley's hand is still holding onto her throat, while her hands are on his waist, fisted in his white button-down, most definitely creasing the material. She's tall, but he still towers over her at 6' 4. I wouldn't be surprised if they end up in the same bed tonight. Good for them.

"Fuck, this is turning me on." Roman notes as he adjusts himself in his pants. "What do you say we go home, so I can make you swoon for a different reason, pretty she-devil?"

"Oh, Waterhouse," I moan that part, "you do know the way to my heart." I finish teasingly.

"Your heart? Nah, but I do know the way to your warm and wet core, baby."

TWENTY-NINE
ROMAN WATERHOUSE

I glared at the stubborn slab of concrete, my arms sore from swinging the sledgehammer like some crazed demolition man. Sweat dripped down my spine, but the bloody door wouldn't budge. I cursed under my breath, a string of profanities that would've made a sailor blush. After an hour of fruitless attempts at prying open the stubborn basement door, I flung the hammer aside with a loud clatter. "Bloody hell," I grumbled under my breath. "Let it stay shut for now." The mysterious contents behind that unyielding barrier gnawed at my curiosity like a relentless itch, leaving me determined to uncover its secrets.

"Throwing in the towel, Roman?" Ackles' voice echoed from the stairs, her lilt wrapping around the words like ivy.

"For now." My chest heaved as I caught my breath, eyeing the impenetrable barrier. "Bloody thing's more trouble than it's worth."

"Never took you for a quitter," she teased, descending into the basement, those forest green eyes sparkling with mischief. Her copper curls were a wild mane framing her face, and I couldn't help but admire the way she filled out her uniform, all lean muscle and perky round tits.

"Quitting's one thing. Wasting time's another." I wiped my brow with the back of my hand. "Builders and plumbers can finish up now, anyway. No more of the dead to worry about."

"Except for the mysteries we haven't dug up yet." She stepped closer, her gaze fixed on the sealed doorway. "Like this one."

"Let it go, Ackles. Not every secret needs airing out." I sighed, my frustration ebbing away in the face of her curiosity. "Some things are better left buried."

"Speaking of buried..." Her lips quirked up into a half-smile. "You remember that safe I told you about? My Papa's?"

"Yeah, the one you reckon has all the answers?" I crossed my arms, leaning against the cool wall.

"Right. Well, I've been meaning to get a locksmith, what with the bodies keeping me busy and all." She fiddled with the badge pinned to her shirt. "But maybe it's time to crack it open."

"Should've done it ages ago." I pushed off from the wall, feeling the pull of her enthusiasm. "You need a number, I can hook you up with a bloke who's good with locks, I used him for the cottage."

"Appreciate it, Roman." Ackles smiled, then glanced back at the door. "As for this little mystery, I'm not giving up that easily."

"Stubborn as a mule, you are." I chuckled despite myself. "Alright then, siren. Have at it. But when you find nothing but cobwebs and old wine bottles, don't say I didn't warn ya."

"Deal." She beamed, that flirty, tough-as-nails spark igniting something within me. "And when I find something incredible, you owe me a drink. Preferably a virgin mojito."

"Fine. But it's your round either way." I shook my head, amused by her relentless drive. As I watched her examine the door with a detective's keen eye, I knew there was no changing her mind.

Ackles Harris was a force of nature, and God help anyone – or anything – that stood in her way.

)O(

I WAS out on the verandah, scanning the grounds of the estate when I heard the gate creak open. The real estate mob had been a pain in my arse, traipsing through the cottage like they owned the joint. Not one had the guts to make an offer though. James Beaufort reckoned it was the mess; the endless digging and uprooting that spooked 'em. But once the land was sorted, he said they'd be queuing up to slap their money down. "Just beautify the beast," he'd said with a wink.

Ackles' car screeched into the front, as she slammed on the brakes with a skid that echoed through the empty air. She leapt out of the car, her fiery locks a wild tangle in the wind, and her forest green eyes gleaming with determination.

"Oi, what's got you grinning like a shot fox?" I called out, propping myself against the railing.

Ackles' green eyes sparkled with mischief as she closed the distance between us. "You won't bloody believe it. I've only gone and nabbed that locksmith. He's set to crack open Papa's safe come tomorrow."

She barrelled into me with such force I almost toppled over, her arms wrapping around my neck as if I were the mast in a storm. Blimey, this woman could knock the wind out of you with nothing but excitement.

"Easy there, tiger," I laughed, steadying us both. "You really reckon there's treasure hidden away in that thing?"

"Who knows?" she said, stepping back but holding onto my forearms. "I'm itching like mad to find out."

"Hope it's worth all the fuss." I ruffled her hair, which earned me a playful swat on the arm.

"Either way, it's a win," she said, the twinkle in her eye telling me she relished the mystery more than whatever might come of it. "And if it's full of old rubbish, we'll have a laugh, yeah?"

"Too right," I agreed, wondering if anything could ever really dampen her spirits. Ackles Harris was a firecracker—constantly alight with energy and curiosity. And I'd be lying if I said I wasn't keen to see what sparks would fly when that safe cracked open.

Her lips crashed against mine, fierce and demanding, a fiery urgency in every press that spoke of raw, untamed need. Ackles, she was something else when it came to the dance between the sheets. Never had I encountered a Sheila so bloody sure of what she wanted, her desire as blatant as a shark's bite.

"God, you're insatiable," I muttered against her mouth, a laugh bubbling up from my chest. She devoured that too, like everything I said or did was kindling for her fire.

"Can't help it, can I?" Her voice was a husky whisper, laced with that intoxicating British lilt that always sent shivers down my spine. "You're just too tempting, Waterhouse."

With a strength that belied her petite frame, she shoved me back into the house, closing the door with a kick of her foot, and pushed me back onto the couch. The cushions gave way beneath me, the springy resistance mirroring the tension winding tight in my guts. She peeled off her pants in a swift, fluid motion, revealing legs that were pale and freckled, but strong—cop's legs, made for chasing down trouble.

"Fuck, Ackles..." I groaned, my own hands betraying me as they scrambled to undo the button on my work trousers. My fingers were clumsy, all thumbs, but the sight of her standing there naked from the waist down, ready to take charge, spurred me on.

"Come here," I managed, finally freeing myself and feeling the air hit my skin. Coolness contrasted with the heat that was building between us, threatening to set the whole damn place ablaze.

She didn't need telling twice. With a predatory grace, she straddled my hips, her gaze locked onto mine as if we were the only two people left in the world. She lined herself up and in one fluid movement, she sank down onto me, enveloping me in warmth, in wetness, in the pure, unadulterated essence of her.

"Christ..." The word was a half-groan, half-prayer as I felt every inch of her surrounding me. She was all sensation and power, taking what she wanted, giving as good as she got. And bugger me if it wasn't the most intoxicating thing I'd ever experienced.

With Ackles astride me, my world narrowed to the heat of her body, the primal rhythm she commanded as she rode me. Bloody hell, this woman was a drug, something fierce and addictive that I couldn't get enough of. She was drenched, soaked through with desire, and I hadn't even laid a finger on her yet.

"Fuck, you're perfect," I grunted, as her warmth enveloped me, tight and slick. Her pussy swallowed me whole, so bloody eager, it was like coming home. I moaned deep in my throat as her lips flushed against mine, her juices cascading down, bathing my balls in her cream.

I could feel every bounce, every rise, and fall as she drove herself onto me, her police uniform still hugging her body. The sight of her, all authority and control, only fuelled my fire. I'd always had a thing for a lass in uniform, but Ackles... damn I can't even put it into words

My hands, rough from days of labour, skated up under her top, finding the softness of her skin. Her tits were round, warm, filling my palms as if they were made to be there. My fingers found her nipples, already hard and begging for attention. I pinched them, gentle at first, then harder as I sought to draw out every gasp, every shudder from her.

Each pinch was answered by her tightening around me,

her pussy clenching in sweet, rhythmic spasms that threatened to unravel me. Christ, she was squeezing me so damn hard, my dick felt like it might burst right there and then.

"Keep going, darlin'," I panted, lost in the sensation, the urgent need. "Don't stop..."

The pressure built, coiling tighter, ready to snap. And through it all, Ackles just kept moving, kept taking what she wanted, what we both needed. It was raw, it was fiery, and it was bloody brilliant.

Ackles' rhythm shifted, her hips grinding down in a slow, deliberate circle that drove me to the brink. "Fuck," I breathed against her lips, every nerve ending screaming as she worked herself on me, riding the edge of too much and not nearly enough.

"Keep that up, I'm gonna—"

"Good," she cut me off with a wicked glower, green eyes blazing like the torches in that bloody crypt we'd just cleared. "I want you to stuff my pussy full. And when it's full, I want more." Her voice was a silken promise, filthy and sweet. "I want it to run down my legs all day, so I can sit in a puddle of your cum knowing you stuffed me well."

Bloody hell, that talk of hers did me in every damn time. My hands shot to her hips, gripping hard enough to leave marks. I helped her and forced the grind faster, harder. "Fuck, Ackles, I can't hold on," I groaned, feeling like I was being milked by her insatiable heat.

"Good, because I'm cumming," she announced, her inner muscles clamping down on me like a vice. It was almost painful, this tightness, this stranglehold she had on my dick.

And then I exploded, giving her exactly what she

demanded—filling her, flooding her, marking her in the most primal way. My head fell back, and a guttural shout ripped from my throat as I lost myself in her, everything else fading away but the sensation of being utterly consumed by this fiery woman who commanded both my body and my heart.

The waves of her climax ebbed, and she nestled close, her breath hot against the stubble on my jaw. "Roman?" Her voice was a whisper lost in the storm we'd just weathered.

"Yeah?" I replied, pulse still racing, skin slick with the aftermath of our recklessness.

"I love you," she breathed out, the words hitting me like a freight train.

"Fuck, Ackles..." Emotion welled up, fierce and raw as a riptide. "You nicked my heart that first night at the local, didn't ya? Love you too, siren." It was a confession torn from the depths, a truth laid bare.

She stood then, and I felt a part of me slip away with her, slick and warm, leaving a trail down her thigh. Her fingers, deft and daring, scooped it up, pushing it back inside her with a wicked grin. "I want to see how much you can fit in me," she challenged, eyes alight with mischief.

Heart hammering, I grabbed her hand, soft in mine, and let her pull me up. We stumbled towards the stairs, all fumbling steps and ragged breaths, a pair of desperados chasing a high only the other could give. "Show me then, darlin'. Show me how much this Aussie can give ya."

Thirty

Ackles Harris

I love you. Those three fateful words that make you bleed for the soul. They rip your heart out of your chest to sunken it deep into the other person's as he does the same. I hold Roman heart now as he holds mine.

I have been in Chief's office for a good ten minutes, sitting on one of the chairs that face his desk, bereft of speech and movement, staring ahead but not really looking at anything. After he called me in for a chat, he cut straight to the chase and told me the one thing that I was worried about hearing, more so after last night with Roman. My transfer to Edinburgh police force had been approved.

"Harris, did you hear me? They want you." Oh, I heard you alright, Chief. I just feel like I can't breathe. "I mean they were reluctant at first, small town detective where nothing ever happens in a big city filled with corruption, perversion and turpitude. Dark tales drenched in blood and other bodily fluids. What might've sold it to them is the brilliant job you are doing with this whole Device case."

"How did they hear about that?" I ask as I look at Chief Bargrave.

"Well, I called Chief MacVicar personally and told him all about it, of course. Ackles, I did promise you I would do everything in my power to make this happen for you. This town has a way of sucking people in, capturing them, and never letting go. You deserve so much more than this folklore you are living inside of."

Maybe I like being part of this story. Yes, there was a time when I longed, desperately, to leave this small dot in the map of Britain, but that was when I didn't have anything gripping me here other than an obsession that was driving me crazy because I couldn't get through the monstrous blacken rusty iron gates. Now, not only do I have the key to said gate and the houses it disguises within, but to the heart of the person whose family blood pours through every cranny and nook of the place.

"How long do I have to make a decision?"

"Decision? Ackles, you requested this and it's been approved. You are set to start in three months." Fuck.

"Can we delay it? The Devil house has more to give, the story isn't complete yet, there are still a few pages missing. I can't just leave without knowing the ending."

"Ackles," Bargrave begins, sounding a bit unhappy with the things I am saying, but I interrupt him.

"There's a second basement inside the one we found. There's something else to unravel here. I can feel it. And whatever it is, beyond that trap door, it's bigger than what we discovered so far." The excitement in my voice as I utter this is evident.

"You can't rely on a feeling forever, Ackles." Chief leans his upper body forward, placing his elbows and forearms flat on the desk and clasping his hands. "What if there is nothing but cobwebs and old wine bottles down there. Are you prepared to lose a great opportunity like the one that is being handed to you for that?"

"You sound just like Roman, Chief." I state as I get up, and start pacing the room.

"Smart lad then, even he can see that not every room holds a body." I can tell he is getting exasperated with me. "Why don't you talk it out with him? You're together, right? I am sure, if he is serious about you, Ackles, he will follow you to the bowels of the earth itself."

Yeah, he would, and that's the problem. This would be another fucking reason added to the million he already has to get rid of the houses on the Device estate. I don't want him too. I've set my heart on us making it our home. Is it too disturbed of me to desire that, considering all the death that taints that place? We can make it beautiful though.

"Delay it." I tell Bargrave as I halt on my back and forth walk of his office, and stare straight at him.

A stern warning from Chief follows my words, "A hold back could cost you the position altogether. Harris, I strongly recommend you don't do that."

"Noted." I say as I start making my way to the door. Once I turn the knob and half open it, I peer at him and declare, "But I still need time Chief, so shall I inform Agnes Grey to write up an email to them saying I need to postpone the transfer, or would you prefer to make the phone call to your friend on the other side, and tell him yourself?"

"Sometimes I forget you're a Harris."

"I don't know how you can, Chief. We Harris' leave a more sizable stain in this town than the Devices." I chuckle at what just crossed my mind. It's like our two families were always meant to dance together to the sweet melody that the Devil plays.

I DON'T KNOW how long I have been down here; staring at the trap door that refuses to open no matter how many punishing sledgehammer hits Roman lands on it. Time seems to move differently here, almost as if it stands still awaiting something.

"What could you possibly be waiting for?" I ask the slab keeping the secrets inside hidden.

When I got to the Device estate Roman wasn't around, so I just let myself in. Instead of going for a piping hot shower to wash away the day, and then get changed into whatever I have in my drawer in the bedroom, my feet lead me straight here. Why? I don't know. I feel this pull, this pulsating energy echoing around me that gets stronger the closer I get to the basement, and once before the trap door, as I rest my hand on the cold slab, it's like there's a heart beating within.

"I know you are in there." I speak to whoever is inside. "You keep telling me to come for you, yet," I pause, turning the flat palm that was against the trap door into a fist and knocking three times on it, "I can't find you if you won't let me."

"Lilith." I hear a deep voice murmur from within.

At the same time someone else calls for me, "Ackles."

"Please, let me in." I whisper to the door.

"Ackles." Roman says again, as his front meets my back and one of his arms comes around my middle. "Baby?"

My body feels heavy, and every movement I seek to make it's a struggle. I turn my head slightly, tilting it back so I can look at the green pools of the gorgeous Aussie guy behind me when I ask, "Why won't you let me in?"

"What? Ackles what do you mean?" His words and pretty face are full of concern. With his free hand Roman holds my face, brushing his thumb over the skin just under my eye. "Baby, are you actually with me right now? Your eyes are dilated as fuck."

"You're the one that is not fully with me. Not until we discover the piece of you that is missing."

"Ok. You are scaring me. What are you talking about?"

"Lilith." There goes that gravelly voice again, which makes me giggle.

"You should stop calling me Lilith, I'm Ackles." I tell Roman.

"What? I haven't." Roman eyes dance between mine for a second, before they gaze, with unease, at the trap door.

"Don't be scared, baby. You like spooky stories, remember."

"Not when we are part of it." His eyes return to mine. "Pretty she-devil, I need you back with me, please." In one swift motion, Roman spins my body around and pins me to the slab, his lips connecting with mine without a wasted second. This kiss is a demand, he's asking me to come back to him. I didn't even know I was lost.

I moan, when his tongue starts darting in and out of my parted lips. That heaviness lifts off of me, and I throw my arms around his neck. "Roman?" I call his name when he breaks the kiss.

"Ackles?" Our eyes meet, and Roman expels this big puff of air. It's as if what he sees there makes him breathe easy.

"When did you get home?" I ask him.

"Where did you go?" He tosses a question my way without responding to mine.

"Hmmm work, like I do every morning during the week. I mean I know we said I love you and all that, and fucked like crazed bunnies all night, but this bad bitch still needs to get her ass to her job." I inform him with all of that Ackles Danneel Harris charm.

Roman closes his eyes and shakes his head. "Do you recall the conversation we just had, before I kissed you?"

I frown at his question, because I don't understand it. "Before? Roman, one moment I am standing here trying to figure out how to open this bloody trap door, the next I am pinned to it by your yummy bod, being kissed like you were seeking to bring me back to life or something."

"Or something." He repeats after me. "We should get out of here."

"Baby," my words die in my mouth, because the slab behind me shifts. Luckily Roman's arm was still around me and he kept me from falling into the void that just opened up at my rear.

The fucking trap door we have been trying to break through for days, just swung right open.

Thirty-One
Roman Waterhouse

A gaping maw of darkness yawned before us, the basement door hanging off its hinges like some crooked grin. My eyes raked over the abyss that beckoned, and I could feel it, that prickly sensation crawling up the back of my neck, a shiver that didn't quite sit right.

"Oi, Ackles," I murmured, my voice barely above a whisper in the still air. "Reckon we should nick off, round up a proper mob for this, yeah? Get our hands on a couple more flashlights or somethin'?"

But Ackles, with her fiery curls and that relentless curiosity sparkling in her forest greens, was already fishing out her flashlight, strapped to her belt like a knight's blade. "It's okay, I have one," she said, her voice cutting through the silence as if to challenge the shadows themselves.

I squinted sceptically into the void, every instinct screaming to take the piss and bolt, but there she stood, all five-foot-sod-all of her, poised to leap into the fray. The torch clicked on, a beam slicing through the pitch-black, and I knew right then, whether heaven or hell awaited us down those steps, I'd be bloody well following her lead.

Her boot was hovering over the threshold. Instinctively, my hand shot out, fingers clamping around her wrist, yanking her back against me. "Don't reckon that's smart," I grunted, peering over her shoulder into nothingness. "I've got a gnarly feeling about this."

She twisted, looking up at me, sun-kissed freckles danced across her nose, her curls a wild mane against the stark back-drop of the unknown. "Mysteries are only mysteries 'cause no one's sussed out the answers yet," she countered, bloody stubborn as ever.

"Right," I scoffed, heartbeat drumming in my ears. "And some answers are better left bloody buried." Her body was taut and ready to explore.

"I'm just not sure about this," I muttered, the words barely above a whisper.

"Roman, let's go and live our own scary story." Her voice was an electric charge, sparking the air between us as she stepped forward into the gaping maw of the basement door, tugging me along.

"Strewth," I grumbled, feet shuffling reluctantly over the threshold. This woman, this pint-sized spitfire with nerves of steel, could march me straight through the gates of hell and I'd probably thank her for the warm welcome. The torchlight bounced off concrete walls, casting eerie shadows that danced like Devil's waiting for a waltz partner.

"Oi, hold up," I said, planting my boots firmly. Ahead, the beam revealed stairs winding down into the abyss. "Might not be stable, love. Let's nick off back upstairs, grab some reinforcements, hey?"

Her laughter echoed, a sound that would've been music in any other place. "Come on, Roman. Where's your sense of adventure?" She flashed that grin, the one that always seemed to say she knew something I didn't.

"Right behind the sense that's screaming 'this is a bloody awful idea'," I shot back, but it was no use. The pull from her hand was insistent, and so was the pull in my chest—a mix of recklessness and desire that had me stumbling after her into the dark.

Ackles' chuckle ripples through the dank air, a teasing sound that pricks at my nerves. "I need to follow the voice..." Her words are half-whispered, like she's caught in some trance only she's privy to, and I feel her tug on my hand as she descends the staircase.

"Bugger me," I mutter under my breath, but there's no resisting. She's got this pull about her, this flame-haired siren calling me into the depths. Like a moth to a bloody inferno, I'm drawn in, feet clomping against stone steps that spiral down into who knows what hellish pit.

The light from her torch flickers ahead, casting an orange glow that licks the walls with each step we take. It's a dance of light and shadow, exposing alcoves where candles squat, untouched for God knows how long. Dust motes dance in the beam, swirling in a mad waltz around us.

"Christ alive," I swear quietly, my breath misting in the cool air. The stairs seem to go on forever, winding down into the bowels of the earth. Each echo of our footsteps bounces back, distorted, as if mocking our descent. Ackles doesn't falter though; she's relentless, an unstoppable force pulling me further into the abyss.

Suddenly, the bloody stairs give way to solid earth, and I'm spitting out dirt that's kicked up into a cloud around us. The torchlight catches on something massive—a gaping maw of a cave opening right under my ancestral manor. Who would've bloody thought?

"Look at this place," Ackles whispers, her forest eyes wide as saucers. She ain't scared though. She's buzzing with excitement, like a kid who's found a secret passage in a storybook.

"Would ya look at that..." My voice trails off as I take in the scale of the hidden lair. Ackles' flashlight dances across the floor, revealing more candles than a bleeding cathedral lining the way. She strides over to one, yanking a lighter from her utility belt with a flick of her wrist.

"Since when do coppers carry lighters?" I jibe, trying to knock some of the edge off my nerves.

She laughs—one of those musical sounds that shouldn't belong down here in the dark. "It's for Austen. Daft bugger loses hers every day. But it's come in handy, turns out."

I watch her move from one candle to the next, setting each one ablaze. The small flames cut through the darkness, throwing shadows against the walls. It's almost beautiful, in a creepy, 'bout-to-get-murdered-in-a-hidden-cave sort of way.

Candles flicker to life, one by bloody one, casting a soft, eerie glow that crept like tendrils through the cavernous space. I can barely hear my own heartbeat over the crackling wicks. The room's lit up now, but it ain't exactly comforting

—it's like we're on display for whatever spectres fancy watching.

"Christ," I mutter, taking a tentative step forward onto the packed earth. It's dry as a bone down here—no dampness, no mustiness. Just the faint smell of soil and... something else. Something ancient.

To the left, there's this stone altar, standing like a silent sentinel against the cave wall. It's an odd thing, out of place in its grandeur amidst the dirt and shadows. How the hell they managed to lug it down here is beyond me. Feels like the sort of thing you'd find in an old church, not buried under a manor house.

Ackles strides over to it without a moment's hesitation, her boots kicking up little clouds of dust. She's got this look about her, like she's just stumbled upon the bloody Crown Jewels instead of a creepy rock slab in a hidden cave.

"Reckon this could be a crypt?" she queries, running her fingers along the surface. Her touch seems to dance with the flickering candlelight.

"Looks more like a damned altar to me," I say, eyeing the thing with suspicion. Cults, sacrifices—it all feels too real now, too close to home.

"Maybe it's both?" Ackles shoots back at me, her tone light but her eyes dead serious. "Could be where the women offed their husbands?"

"Let's not give you any ideas, eh?" I say with a half-hearted chuckle. But deep down, the thought sends a shiver up my spine that's got nothing to do with the chill air.

I shuffle closer to Ackles, the altar's stone biting cold against my palm. But as I drag my fingers over the etchings, the bloody thing's warm. That's bonkers—it should be like a meat locker down here.

"Can you read runes?" I ask, not expecting much.

Ackles chuckles, all light and breezy, then squints at the scribbles I'm pointing to. "Read runes? Nah—wait..." Her brows knit together in concentration. "Actually, maybe yes... Dunno how, but that one there," she taps the stone, "says 'Here lies,' and this squiggle? Says 'Tibb.'" Her voice drops, like she's telling a secret.

"Like the Tibb?" I mutter, but my question dies on my lips. Ackles' eyes have gone glassy, like she's staring through the stone into another bleeding dimension.

"We need to let him out," she whispers, her pupils massive in the candlelight.

"Let who out?" I grip her shoulder, trying to yank her back to the here and now.

She shoves at the stone lid, huffing with effort, but it might as well be glued down. "We need to let him out," she repeats, more frantic this time.

"Oi, Ackles, snap out of it!" My voice is sharp, trying to cut through whatever's got a hold of her.

That's when I spot the shadow slinking behind her—a darker patch in the dark, moving wrong, like oil over water.

"Quick, Roman, he needs to be let out," she urges, pushing against the immovable stone, eyes wide and pleading.

"Strewth, this isn't good," I mutter, every muscle tensing. I'm ready to pull her away, shadows be damned. We're messing with stuff we've got no right to, and my gut's screaming to leg it before we find out why.

THIRTY-TWO
ACKLES HARRIS

"Strewth, this isn't good," I just about hear Roman say. These voices have been shouting in my ear, mellowing everything else, urging me to let him out.

"I am trying," I tell them, either out loud or in my head, I am not sure. The damn thing just won't budge, just like the slab up there, keeping him from me. "Roman, you gotta help me." The chilling gust of air at my back gets replaced by this warm body engulfing me. Strong arms go around my middle and pull me away from the crypt. "No. Out. We need to let him out."

"No, Harris, we need to get out of here. The shadows are alive in this hell pit. They're bloody moving." I felt a shred of unease creep up my spine as Roman muttered those words. Shadows? Are they the ones speaking to me?

He starts walking us back to the stairs that lead up to the main house, to the Devil house. His arms still hugged me with vigour, making it impossible to disentangle myself from his brutal clasp. Just before we reach the first stone step, I at least manage to turn around in his embrace to tell him, "But Tibb." Tibb's in there. In that tomb. The main character of this whole eerie narrative, he's been sleeping under the Devil house this whole time. How fitting, like a pharaoh resting in the bowels of a pyramid, a monument not only erected in its name but built to be a means to immortality and a portal to the afterlife.

We stop in our stride. "Screw Tibb. Baby, please, I beg of you. Let's go upstairs." His fear is palpable. "Something's got a hold of you, again." The way Roman's jade green eyes are looking at me, he might be spooked by the things that surround us, but he seems more afraid of what they are doing to me.

"Roman, the only thing that has a grip on me is you. And can't you hear them? They are so loud. The voices."

"Voices? Ackles, all that echoes over the dead silence is our heavy breathing, the sound of our fast beating hearts and the crunch of the dirt under our feet as we move around this God-long forsaken chamber." So Roman cannot hearken to the whispers of the darkness?

From the corner of my eye, I see a shadow move beyond Roman, by the altar. Looming over the crypt it's the goat man, crouched down, with his all masculine bare torso, cloven hooves feet, hairy legs, serpentine tail and curled goat horns in his head. "You came. Now free me, Lilith." The malformed blackened image that wanes with the passage of air, the one that haunts my awakened and asleep dreams, commands me.

I am shaking my head, either attempting to get rid of the apparition or intending to tell him no. I hunger to do what the voices are bidding me to do, but not if that goat man is what I unleash. I want Tibb, not that thing.

"What if they are one and the same?" I think to myself.

I don't believe it likes my response. All of a sudden the devilish creature shifts into nothing but a low-lying dark cloud, falling down from the top of the crypt to the ground. This nagging weird feeling begins settling itself within me. My Roman is in peril. "Hey Waterhouse, I think you are right. We should leave." I seek to keep my worry at bay so it doesn't slip out when I state that, as the black fog slowly slithers our way.

"About damn time. Come on then, pretty she-devil." Roman says, grasping one of my hands, which have been clenching to his sweater by his waist, moves past me and shepherds me up the stairs.

An evil crackle chimes behind me, followed by, "He can run, but he can't hide. I'll have him soon enough and we can be together once more, my pretty charmer."

I hesitate in my steps. "What?" I ask, peering back at the chamber, but the shadow forged out of the murk is gone. Or most likely it's lurking just out of sight. It wants Roman, in what way? So it can end up with me? I think whoever this ghost is, it's getting me confused with someone else. I ain't Lilith. And how dare it, call me that?

"Ackles, what is it?" Roman questions.

"Nothing." I turn tail to face Roman, and we resume our hasty climb.

Once at the threshold of mind-fabricated safety, the Aussie hunk lets go of my hand, spins around, and waits for me to be fully out of that hellhole and standing by him before he thrust out a hand for the trap door to close the chamber of dark secrets.

"Fuck." He utters in a hushed tone. "Please tell me you can see the disturbing contortionist shadows crawling up the steps too?"

The what? I don't have time to ask that or even have a proper look at whatever haunting echo he just saw, because the next chain of events happens so fast I can't even comprehend them. This shadow comes out from within the darkness and lunges at Roman, passing right through him.

"Roman," I call out, latching onto his arm with both of mine to keep him upright as I see him stumble from the invisible force that just knocked into him. "I got you, baby." I lift my eyes to his face, which is set in a scowl as he vacantly gazes ahead of him. Now that's a scary sight. "Hey Roman, are you ok?" I ask, concern dripping from every word that cuts and runs from my lips. I remove one of my arms from the grasp around his so I can brush my fingers through his cheek, seeking to give comfort.

"I don't know." He declares, massaging the exact spot the shadow just travelled through, with his free hand.

Fuck. I think this tomb is like a Dybbuk box, but what lays dormant inside is sadly not wine.

THIRTY-THREE
ROMAN WATERHOUSE

Bloody hell, it's been a bloody full two days since that flaming shadow slipped right through my chest. In the flicks, they reckon when a ghost does a walkthrough, you're meant to feel colder than a dead dingo's donger. That's a load of bull.

I was down in that dark basement with Ackles by my side when it hit. Not a damn thing like those flashy movies make out. It was a heat, akin to that first gulp of steaming brew on a bitter arvo, seeping deep within me, reaching every inch of my body. For an instant, I was electric—stunned like a shot fox, sensing a wholeness I never knew existed. It felt as though every fragment of me slotted into place perfectly.

But then, just as sudden, the warmth buggered off, skedaddled without so much as a by-your-leave. Left me feeling hollow, like someone had nicked a chunk of me inside. Couldn't make a head or tail of it. There I was, a grown bloke, feeling like a lost Joey missing his mum. And that ain't a feeling I take kindly to, not at all.

"Strewth," I muttered to myself, rubbing my chest where the shadow had passed. "What the bloody hell was that all about?"

"Pull yourself together, Roman," I grumbled under my breath. The sound reverberated through the grand manor, mixing with the clinks of tools and muffled voices of workers echoing in the background. England, a land of perpetual grey skies and relentless drizzle, had a knack for seeping into your very being, playing tricks on your mind. As I stood amidst the ongoing renovations, it felt like the veil between reality and something more sinister was thinning, revealing secrets long kept hidden within these ancient walls.

"Nothing but shadows and dust," I said, shaking off the unease. But even as the words left my mouth, I couldn't shake the feeling that something was missing—a part of me I didn't even know I had, now gone without a trace.

I walked out the manor's back door, heart hammering like a jackhammer on hot asphalt. The shadows were at it again, slinking around my feet, crawling up my legs like they had a mind of their own. "Bugger this," I muttered, feeling the prickle of sweat snake down my spine despite the chill in the air. England's gloomy skies offered no comfort, just a canvas for the bloody shadows to dance on.

"Roman, focus," I growled to myself, trying to shake the creeping dread. I had a job to wrap up, a cottage to flip, and a ticket home to the sunburnt country waiting for me. But the shadows weren't having it. They clung to me, whispering of unfinished business, of roots sinking deep into this cursed soil. The trees swayed, casting their long, gnarled fingers across the ground, and I swear they shifted shape right before my very eyes—morphing into something sinister, then back again.

"Christ," I exhaled sharply, shoving my hands into the pockets of my jacket. My mind raced with thoughts of Ackles, with her fiery hair and that stubborn glint in her forest-green eyes. She was tough-as-nails, that one, but sweet as a lamington when she let her guard down. And by crikey, she'd worked her way into my heart, sure as anything.

Would she come with me, though? Back to Oz, away from this land of cold mists and colder memories? I could hardly bear the thought of leaving her behind. "Ackles, love, you're the piece I didn't know I was missing," I whispered to the wind, hoping somehow it'd carry my words to her.

The idea of living without her twisted in my gut like a knife. She was perfect for me, in a way no Sheila ever had been. But would she see it that way? Would she be willing to leave all this behind—the cobbled streets, the history-soaked pubs, the life she knew?

"Damn it, Roman, get a grip," I chided myself, watching the shadows stretch out toward me like they recognised a kin. Was I one of them now? A creature of this place, bound to the whispers and the chill?

"Shut it," I snapped at the encroaching darkness, quickening my pace. "You're not getting the better of me." I needed to finish what I came here for, sell the damn house, and bugger off back to where the sun shone fiercely and the ocean roared loud enough to drown out these shadowy bastards.

Every day I wake up in this godforsaken house, it's like the walls are whispering my bloody name. I can't explain it, but fixing up the old wreck is making it feel more like home. And that's exactly why I've gotta leg it out of here. The longer I stay, the deeper the roots sink into me, and that's a game I'm not keen on playing.

Today, the tradies were here giving the far wall a facelift, all rocks and mortar. That's the final call for the outside—a full stop to the exterior muck-up. Inside, it's another story; there's still plenty to do before it can scrub up nice for show. Haven't found a mug to take off the cottage yet, though the agent reckons it's a dead cert once the whole property is all spick and span. But I don't reckon I'll hang around to see the SOLD sign hammered into the turf.

I watch them work, muscles bunching under sweat-stained shirts, and I can't help but think, maybe I should flog the lot as a package deal. Manor, cottage, the house I'm in. Could be less of a headache, and I've got enough of those without adding more to the pile.

"Oi, Roman, careful with that beam!" one of the lads yells, and I snap back to the now, nearly copping a wooden monster to the noggin. "Thanks, mate," I shout back, dodging the near miss. It's a bloody circus, this place, and I'm done being the ringleader.

The unease is creeping up again, like ants up a sticky bun, and it's telling me it's time to cut the cord. Australia's calling me home, and not even Ackles' fiery hair or cheeky grin can hold me in place, or I swear I'll snatch her and bring her back with me, no matter what it takes. Not when every shadow feels like it's trying to nick a piece of me for itself.

This isn't just a renovation; it's a bloody exorcism. And I'll be damned if I let this house—or whatever's lurking in its shadows—claim me as one of its own.

I hoof it back to my digs, leaving the manor's chaos behind like a bad dream you can't shake. The sun's taken a dive, and the shadows are having a bloody field day, stretching across the lawn like they've got minds of their own. My shadow's a bloke on a mission, long and twisted like he's desperate to leg it from this place too.

"Strewth," I mutter under my breath, eyeing the ground warily as that cold shiver from before bobs up again. It ain't right, the way these shadows dance about, reaching for me with fingers made of dusk. It's like they're whispering, "Join us, Roman. Be one of the crowd." But I'm not buying what they're selling, no way.

The air's thick with the scent of damp earth and something else—something off. Can almost taste the bloody rot on my tongue. It's the house, gotta be. It's been festering here, soaking into the soil, into the roots of those gnarly trees. The workers don't feel it; they just see stone and mortar. But me? I'm copping it full force.

"Bugger this," I say, quickening my pace. My boots thump against the path, heartbeat loud in my ears. Don't want to admit it, but there's a proper panic fluttering in my chest.

"Like calls to like," they reckon. Well, I ain't like them— not by a long shot. I came here to fix up a wreck, not join the local spook squad. Ackles better have her wits about her when she cracks open that safe. We need to sort our business and nick off back to the land down under. This English manor can find another mug to haunt.

As I skedaddle closer to my place, I can't help but glance over my shoulder. The shadows cling to my heels, hungry-like. They're playing a game, and I'm the bloody prize. Good job I'm not one to roll over easily. This Aussie doesn't scare simple, and it'll take more than a few dodgy shadows to make me stick around.

I revved up my old ute, the engine growling like a hungry beast, and tore down the road towards Ackles' place. She had called needing me to swing by to settle the payment since she wouldn't make it back from work in time. The dilapidated van of the locksmith was carelessly parked near the entrance, a clear sign that Ackles had enlisted his help to crack open the stubborn safe. Ever since she started avoiding the main house like it was plagued by ghosts following that unsettling shadow incident, I completely understood her reluctance. Each creak and groan of the accursed old estate sent shivers down my spine as I arrived outside Ackles' enigmatic residence.

I strolled into Ackles' father's office, the musty scent of old books and leather hitting me square in the face. There he was, the locksmith, hunched over the ancient safe like a vulture eyeing its prey. Shadows danced on the walls, making me itch with unease.

"Any luck yet?" I barked out, trying to mask my impatience beneath a layer of forced nonchalance. Each creak of the floorboards echoed like a drumbeat in the tense silence that enveloped us.

"Nearly there," he grunted, more focused on his tools than the fact that the very air in here tasted like dread.

"Righto," I muttered, pacing the hall like a caged dog. The

tick-tock of the grandfather clock was like a bloody metronome for my rising panic. I used to be all keen to see what secrets that safe held, but now? Now, the thought made my guts churn.

Ackles would rock up any minute, fresh from her shift, with that flirty quirk to her lips and her forest green eyes that seemed to see straight through to my soul. Or whatever was left of it after that shadow felt me up from the inside out.

I glanced out the window, watching the sun dip low, casting long fingers of darkness that crept closer to the house like they were alive and reaching for... What? Me? Ackles? The very warmth of our bodies?

"Strewth," I cursed under my breath. This bloody town and its ghost stories can get stuffed. The longer I stayed, the more they seemed less like tales for the kiddies and more like bloody gospel truth.

"Roman, we are in business!" The locksmith shouted, breaking through my brooding thoughts.

"About bloody time," I replied, though the relief I expected to feel was smothered by a thick layer of unease. What would Ackles find in that safe? More importantly, did I really want to know?

"Cheers, mate," I said, handing over a few notes.

The bloody locksmith, feeling as relieved as a kangaroo in a downpour, shoots me a nod before legging it like a dingo chasing prey. Not once does he look back, almost avoiding the safe's insides as if there were mysteries even he didn't want to confront.

About 20 minutes later, Ackles strolled in, clad in her police uniform, a vision of beauty that could stop traffic. Her forest green eyes sparkled with determination, and her long ginger curls framed her face like a fiery halo. As I gazed at her, a faint voice whispered in the depths of my mind, *"Lilith"*. Shaking off the eerie thought, I couldn't help but admire Ackles' presence, her aura exuding strength and confidence that was undeniably captivating.

"Ready to see what's inside?" she asked, that flirty, sweet lilt to her voice belying the steel underneath.

"Sure," I lied, because ready was the last thing I felt. I followed her into the room where the safe stood open like a dark maw, waiting to swallow us whole.

Thirty-Four

Ackles Harris

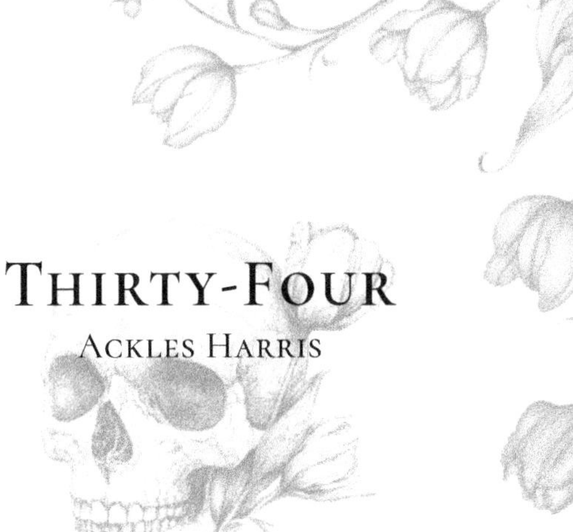

Roman has been acting weird since that bloody blackened smoke went through him. He's always looking around him, chasing shadows with his eyes that I can't perceive with my own. He seems worn out, like something is slowly chipping away at his soul. I keep telling myself it's from all the long hours and hard work he's been putting on the houses to get them done and dusted, but deep down I know that's a big fat lie.

I feel guilty. This is on me and my stubborn nosey ass. Going down into that chamber in the bowels of the Devil house was a mistake. I should've left it the hell alone. I should've not hearkened to the whispers from the darkness and instead listened when everyone told me that some stories are best left untold, some secrets are best left buried, and some demons are best left in the shadows they were bound to. I woke critters that ought to have stayed in the arms of Morpheus, and now they won't shut up. I am having a bit of an inner war, not really a body versus mind since my whole core vibrates in blind compliance and submission to the siren call from the Device ghosts, especially from him, Tibb, the goat man, and the Devil himself. I want to do what they ask, free him, with every fibre of my being, but I am scared for Roman. What will happen to him if I do? He's the long lost half of my soul, and now that I've found it, I can't sacrifice him, I can't lose him. I love him.

I haven't told him that I keep hearing them, the voices. He obviously can't, and I don't want him to think that I have gone completely mental. One thing is catching their haunting hushed words in the eerie confinements of the Device estate since that place is undoubtedly jam-packed with phantoms, thanks to the gruesome bloody imprint left on the dirt by, well, them when they were living. Another is them talking to me everywhere, all the time. But they are louder where the Devil sleeps, in Roman's family grounds, which is why I have been avoiding going there.

As I stand before Papa's stupid antique rusty cast iron floor safe that is finally wide open, I am having second thoughts. What if what's inside is somehow worse than bags of dried and shrivelled human fingers, a basement crammed with dirt and offered-up old bones, and a dark chamber of secrets that probably holds God's first fallen angel?

I am trying to act cool and collected, speaking with a flirty undertone and giving Roman the fearless and lion-hearted version of myself. "Ok. Let's dig into this bad boy then." I utter, kneeling before the safe and grabbing all its contents. My intention was to take the stuff to either Papa's desk or the kitchen table and look through them there, but Roman sat down cross-legged next to me. I guess we are going to do this on the cold hard floor of the office then. "Here goes nothing." I declare as I mirror Roman's sitting position.

Two folders, that's it. We go through the first. There isn't a lot in terms of papers, but what's written on them is plenty. From my birth certificate to Mama's, to every single one of my maternal foremothers, until we reach fucking Polly's.

"I don't get it." Roman states.

"Polly," I say, looking from the documents before us to Roman. He shakes his head, which tells me he doesn't know who I am talking about. "She is Lilith's twin sister." After those spoken words, his face snaps to mine.

"As in Lilith Device, Tibb's first wife?"

"The one and only. Now I get Papa's obsession with her, I am related to her. But why lock this away." I lift the folder that contains all these certificates from the floor, and as I do so, something falls from between the pages.

"What the hell?" Roman blurs out.

I drop the file and pick up the rip book page. The inscription at the bottom of the piece of paper claims they are Lilith and Polly Tulipa, while intricately drawn out above it, in black chalk, are two identical women, with long messy curly hair cascading down from their heads. Their faces... I am freaking out; I see those exact features look back at me every time I gaze in the mirror.

"Harris, they look just like you." He comments.

"So that's why you keep calling me Lilith." I quietly say to the voices in my head. I wonder if Roman looks like Tibb, wouldn't that be eldritch. "It seems we are more entwined than we thought, Waterhouse?" I remark to Roman, raising my forest green eyes to him.

"It certainly seems that way. Do you think we were always doomed to repeat history?" He asks, looking me in the eyes. "Fall for one another, like the ones before us did?"

"Those who forget their history are condemned to do so. I mean we keep saying we are bewitched, maybe there's something else at work here." Roman simply hums at my statement. "So what if we were guided to each other by supernatural forces," the reason for it, still unclear to us, "that doesn't lessen how I feel. They don't control my heart. I love you, Roman Waterhouse. Everything else is ancient dusty history."

Roman chuckles. "I love you too, Ackles Danneel Harris." He professes as he leans towards me, brushing his lips to mine softly, delicately, like easily broken butterfly wings. "Everything else be damned." He tells me once his mouth parts from our kiss. My tongue darts over my lips, licking the lingering taste of Roman from them, which makes him groan and avert his eyes.

"What skeletons do you think this folder holds?" He asks, gathering the other stack of papers that was in the safe alongside the one we just finished, and flips through them. He pauses on a page as he furrows his brows. "You know what,' he notes, closing the file, "I think we've had enough twisted revelations for one day. How about I draw you a nice hot bath, and while you relax I do dinner, then we can cuddle up on the couch and watch a movie, hmmm baby?"

"Wow, Roman that bad?" I ask him, playfully, but when he utters, "Baby," like he's grieving for me and I snap, "What the fuck does it say?" I don't even allow him time to reply. I grab the stuff from his hands and read it myself. I shouldn't have. I never learn. It's another thing I should've kept six feet under. Isn't it funny? I listen to the voices in my head, but what the people around me say, warn me about, I don't hear a thing at all. Amongst the pages is the truth about Mama. It's her medical records.

"Baby?" Roman's words sound muffled, like they are spoken underwater, or perhaps I am the one drowning. "Baby." He repeats again as I shoot up and run out the office, out of the house, and get into my truck. I know my gorgeous Aussie boyfriend was chasing after me, if the rapid stomping feet at my rear was something to go by, but he wasn't quick enough, by the time he got as far as my front door I was already speeding away.

How the fuck did I get here? How did I know how to get here? Time wasn't kind to this place. 'Tearsmith Mental Hospital' the protruding letters above the main entrance tells me. They give the illusion of crying, as if the stone they are made off is melting away. The vines that scale up the walls of the imposing red bricked building are all dried up and very much dead, withered as the fingers in Roman's walls. Most of the windows are broken, sharp tips poking out ready to stab you from all angles.

I am standing outside, by the steps that lead into the abandoned hospital, in the pouring rain, my uniform clinging to my body like a second skin. There are instances where the old structure morphs before my eyes, showing me the ill-omened beauty it used to be and the decaying ruin it is now. I am starting to question if I am there or here, in the past or the present. There seems to be a glitch in either my brain or the scenery around me, and I can't anchor myself to either.

Snippets from Mama's files keep flashing in my mind. Papa's letter requesting Mama be hospitalised here, the reason why she was put in this place noted down in his written words. Reports from the doctors from all the failed attempts to quiet the voices she claimed to hear. Like mother, like daughter. It looks like I took after my dear parents, in the main, all the good traits at least.

My footsteps echo in the silence of these empty halls. Wait. I halt in my stride. When did I get inside the building? It's as if I am sleepwalking, one moment completely unaware of the path I am taking, being shepherded by six sense alone, and the next, I am awake.

"Room 1408, sweetie." A nurse informs me from the nurses' desk. When my eyes meet hers, she gives me a kind-hearted smile.

I spin around, taking in my surroundings. What the fuck? What happened to all the cob webs, the layers upon layers of dust, the peeling plaster and all the broken dumped shit that was all over the hall? It all looks unstained by the passage of time.

"Today is actually a good day. Your mom has been in high spirits." The nurse speaks again. I should fall apart here, right? A full body apparition is bloody talking to me. But is she a ghost? She appears so fucking real. Maybe I am stuck in a dream. Maybe I am lost in a memory. "Ackles? Are you alright, sweetie?"

"Yeah, hmmm room 1408, was it?" I ask her.

The nurse nods, "Down the hall. Last one to your right." I thank her as I begin walking in the direction she told me to.

Once at the door to room 1408 I pause. Mama is on the other side. I was so young when she passed that she's but a murky figure in my mind. Or, after what happened at the morgue, I am starting to believe that maybe my brain has just been blocking out certain things to protect me. Well, it's time to wake up now.

The room inside is bland and dull. White walls bare of anything, to my right there's an antique Victorian mahogany wardrobe, at the fore of it, along the wall, a brass frame single bed size with a window just above the headboard that takes most of the wall in front of me, to my left a Gillows chamber writing table with a chair, and next to it a dark brown leather Victorian armchair rests, where my Mama is sitting looking out the window.

The pine wooden planks creek below my feet as I approach. "Mama?" I call out, but get no response. She seems lost in the downpour outside, the rain tapping mercifully against the window. Actually, she appears very much drugged-up. Is that what the nurse meant by a good day? How is this being in high spirits?

I kneel at her feet and look up at her. She looks like a haunt, dressed in a white sleeping gown, hollow-cheeked and ghostly pale complexion. Her ginger hair is in a relaxed fishtail braid, but its hue has lost all vibrancy.

"Oh, Mama, what have they done to you?"

"I was trying to save you, baby. I was trying to change the prophecy." Mama utters all of the sudden in a detached voice, but doesn't look at me.

"Prophecy, Mama?" I ask her.

"He always wanted to live forever, return from the cold embrace of death. So Lilith set out to obey her master and lover. She put a spell in place. One male son and a witch would do the trick." My mother gazes stone-heartedly at me then. "Polly didn't kill her sister and hexed the Device just so you could come along and wreak havoc on it all, Ackles."

"I'm sorry?" Why is Mama mad at me? I don't understand.

"She had to bloody leave, didn't she?" Who? "Once away from that hellhole the curse laid upon the Device family tree, it wouldn't work no longer, and he was born. The first male heir to the Device throne." Wait. Is Mama talking about Roman's grandmother? "And then you came along, my dear Ackles. And you had to look just like her, a mockery really. Why couldn't you just drown like a good girl?" I get up to my feet then.

"She can't hurt you no more." I hear Papa say in my mind.

"You tried to kill me." I state, tears streaming down my face.

"Oh no, baby. Save you. You should've heard the voices. They were so happy you two were brought forth into the world. Finally, he could return. The Device son and the Tulipa witch that loves him so. Your souls are doomed to forever belong to him." Mama's hand grips my wrist with an inhumane strength, digging her nails into my flesh. Wasn't she supposed to be dopey with drugs?

"Mama." I beg. "You're hurting me."

"Ackles." I hear Papa shout from the depths of the hospital, which makes me turn my attention to the ajar door of her room. "My pretty charmer, she can't hurt you no more." The hand on my wrist vanishes, like the veil of the past. Now I find myself in a decrepit and ramshackle room. I lift my wrist to my chest and massage it with my other hand. It throbs with pain, and as I peer down, I can see that it's bruised, a clear hand imprint marks my skin along with half-moon indentations that cry blood.

A breeze brushes wild ginger curls over my face. Moving the strands behind my ear, my eyes shift to the shattered window. Unlike the other ones, no fractured pieces of glass lay on the wooden floor of 'Tearsmith Mental Hospital', it's as if this one broke outwards. Mama's room is on the second floor of the hospital, so as I near the window sill I look below, and a wail flees my lips. My mom's dead body lies on the ground outside, glass scattered all around her, her white gown bloody, muddy and wet as the sky weeps down on her.

THIRTY-FIVE
ROMAN WATERHOUSE

I was always one step behind Ackles, tearing through the streets like a madman after the wild flicker of her tail-lights. The way her truck swerved and danced across lanes, you'd reckon she was three sheets to the wind.

"Strewth, girl, what's got into ya?" I muttered to myself, my grip white-knuckled on the steering wheel. Her ginger curls had been a fiery blur as she'd stormed out, all spitfire and brimstone, flinging herself into her truck without so much as a backwards glance. And me? Well, I was the mug hot on her heels, wasn't I?

There it was – in the distance – the red beacon of her brake lights pulsing an urgent SOS as she came to a screeching halt. The massive gate loomed ahead, wrought iron and as foreboding as a tombstone. She hopped out of the truck with this kind of desperate grace, a copper-haired banshee charging headfirst into the unknown.

"Fuck me dead," I breathed as she slipped through the gate like a shadow and bolted up the path. My heart hammered against my ribcage, each beat screaming for me to follow. That abandoned building stood there, silent and brooding, straight outta some horror story where no good ever comes to those who enter.

But this wasn't just any old tale of terror. This was Ackles, and if she was plunging headlong into the belly of the beast, then bloody hell, I was too. Whatever secrets were shacked up in that godforsaken place, they'd lured her in, and I'd be damned if I let her face them alone.

I skidded to a stop, gravel spitting out from under the tyres like it had a personal vendetta against the stillness of the night. The rear of Ackles' truck loomed in front of me, her tail lights blinking a fading warning. I bailed out of the ute before it even rocked to a complete standstill.

"Fuck's sake," I cursed under my breath as I sprinted towards the gate, my boots pounding the dirt track. But there it was—chained shut, thick links woven through the bars like steel snakes. My brain couldn't make sense of it. Ackles had just ghosted through here. How in the bloody hell?

Anger flared up inside me, hot and unyielding. I reared back and gave that damn gate what-for, rattling it like I could shout it open. But the iron didn't so much as groan. "Move, you bastard," I snarled, clenching my jaw tight enough to crack teeth.

My gaze shot upwards, and there, biting into the sky with rust-stained teeth, was the sign: Tearsmith Mental Hospital. Each word etched a deeper furrow in my brow. This was the hellhole those medical documents had spat out, the ones about Ackles' mother. It had to be.

"Right," I muttered, feeling the weight of history pressing

down on me. I grasped the cold metal, giving it one last futile shake. Nothing. A desperate glance leftward caught the crumbled edge of the stone fence line. Looked climbable—if you fancied a dance with tetanus.

"Here goes nothing," I grunted, surging toward the weakened masonry. Hands found jagged holds, feet scrabbling for purchase. I heaved myself up, cursing every god known to man as stones shifted treacherously beneath me. But I wasn't about to let some decrepit barrier keep me from Ackles. Not when she might need me.

"Better than any gym workout," I gasped as I reached the top, taking a moment to steady myself. Below lay shadows, stretched long and dark by the moon's unforgiving light—a path leading straight to the heart of a nightmare. And there was nothing for it but to jump right in.

The rocks crumbled under my boots as I hurled myself over the top, landing on the other side with a thud that jolted right up through my bones. What loomed before me was like something out of a bloody horror film—a great, hulking monstrosity of a building choked by dead vines that clung to the red brick like skeletal hands. Another sign hung there, paint peeling away to reveal those damned words again, "Tearsmith Mental Hospital." A shiver shot down my spine hard and fast, like a bolt from a crossbow.

"Strewth," I whispered under me breath, feeling the chill of this place seep into me marrow. It was like walking into the belly of some ancient beast, all teeth and darkness. But Ackles was in there somewhere, and I'd crawl through the pits of hell for that girl if I had to.

"Here we go then, ya old pile of bricks," I muttered, stealing myself for what lay ahead. The movies always have you yelling at the screen, "Don't go in there!" But when it's you it's a different story, ain't it? You can't just sit back and shove popcorn in your gob.

"Come on, Roman, find the girl," I coaxed myself, taking a step towards the entrance. The air was thick with the stink of decay and something else—something rank and metallic. Blood, maybe. Or fear. My heart hammered a wild rhythm against my ribs as I pushed forward, every sense on high alert.

"Fuck me sideways, this is nuts," I said to no one, my voice a low growl swallowed up by the vast emptiness of this cursed place. But there was no turning back now. Not with Ackles in the clutches of this godforsaken hospital. I was walking into the bowels of hell, alright. And I was gonna bring my maiden back out with me, or die trying.

The moment I crossed that threshold, the darkness clung to me like a second skin. The air was dank, heavy with the musk of rot and neglect. My boots crunched on debris, every step stirring up the ghosts of dust and decay. This place was a bloody mausoleum to madness, walls tattooed with graffiti like the scars of its past inmates.

"Didn't think you were a scaredy-cat, Roman," I scolded myself, my voice a low murmur lost amidst the whispers of the damned. Inside, I felt like a joey caught in the headlights —not quite sure if running or staying would save me.

The cobwebs were like curtains to the macabre, draping from every corner, dancing lightly as I brushed past. Leaves crunched beneath me, a reminder that nature was reclaiming this forsaken place. Rubbish—tin cans, broken bottles, syringes—a testament to the vices of those seeking refuge in the belly of this beast.

I could still taste the dust kicking up into the back of my throat, each breath a struggle as if the very air was trying to choke the courage from my lungs. Didn't fancy finding out what sort of blighters might call this hellhole home now. But it wasn't about me anymore, was it? It was about Ackles, that siren who'd somehow managed to shipwreck me in this ocean of fear.

Then it hit me, faint but clear—the sound of a voice drifting down from above. "Mama..." it called, soft and aching, pulling at something primal deep inside my guts. "Fuck me dead, that's her." Ackles' voice, no mistaking it, even if it did sound more like a frightened Sheila than the tenacious copper I knew her to be.

Adrenaline surged, kicking my arse into gear. I bounded up the stairs two at a time, the wood complaining under my weight like the groans of the long-gone loonies. Each step closer to that voice felt like a step further from reality, like I was diving headfirst into some twisted fairytale.

"Keep it together, mate," I muttered, heart racing like a greyhound on the track. "Almost there, Roman. Almost there."

The voice grew louder, more insistent. "Mama... Mama..." Bloody hell, the way she said it—it was nothing short of haunting. Like hearing your own eulogy whispered through the walls.

As I neared the top, that icy finger of dread traced my

spine again, making me shiver despite the sweat dripping down my brow. Ackles needed me, and I wasn't about to let her down—not now, not ever. If this hospital had taught us anything, it was that sometimes the real monsters are the memories we carry with us, weighing us down like chains.

"Comin', Ackles," I breathed, reaching the landing, ready for whatever fresh horror awaited me. "Hold on, love. I'm comin'."

I skidded to a halt in front of the door, heart hammering like a jackhammer. "1408" stared back at me, the numbers crooked and sneering, as if they bloody knew something I didn't. Pushing it open, the creak sounding like a death rattle, there she was. Ackles—my fierce little firecracker, looking like she'd seen a ghost.

"Oi, what are you doin'?" I barked, rushing towards her. The sight of that broken window, the sheer drop beyond—it was enough to turn my guts to ice. Wrapping my arms tight around her middle, I yanked her back, safe into me, away from the edge where sanity slips into nothing.

"Mama jumped," she whimpered, her voice trembling like leaves in a storm. "Mama jumped out the window..."

"Yeh, I know, love," I murmured, remembering the stark lines of black ink on those medical records. "It's the medical records from the safe."

She twisted in my grasp, her eyes—those deep forest greens—shining with unshed tears. "She tried to kill me," Ackles choked out, the words heavy as lead. "My Mama tried to kill me so I wouldn't meet you."

"Wha—?" My head spun, trying to wrap around her words, the implication sending a shiver through my core.

This place, these walls, they were poison. We needed to get the hell out.

"Come on, Ackles. We gotta bolt!" Urgency clawed at my throat, each word a command as much as a plea. Hoisting her up, I started dragging her back through the decay, stepping over scattered memories and the debris of broken minds.

"Leg it, darlin'," I urged, half-carrying her down the stairs. Every echo, every shadow felt like it was closing in, whispering secrets best left buried deep. But we weren't gonna be another pair of skeletons for this mausoleum.

"Almost there, Ackles. Just a bit further," I grunted, my muscles screaming in protest as we fled the clutching fingers of Tearsmith Mental Hospital. It was a race against ghosts, and by hell or high water, I was winning this one for her—for us.

Bolting out into the bitter night, the frigid air slapped against my face like a wake-up call. We were nearly there, the gate—our ticket out of this godforsaken place—was just ahead.

"Nearly free, Ackles," I panted, my lungs burning with each heaved breath.

Then we were there, at the damn gate that'd been chained up tighter than Fort Knox when I arrived. But now? The bloody thing swung open, as if it was waiting for us all along. What the fuck?

"Wasn't that—" My words got caught somewhere between confusion and disbelief. Ackles strolled through the gate as if it had always been wide open, her coppery curls catching the moonlight, casting an otherworldly glow around her. "Oi, you seein' this?" I gestured at the open gate, brows knotted in suspicion.

As she passed me, Ackles turned, her forest green eyes glistening with a dreamy quality. "I wanna go home," she whispered in a voice that seemed to float on the breeze, "I need to go home."

Thirty-Six
Ackles Harris

I wanna go home. I need to go home. As I get in my truck, I lead the way, with Roman's car right at my tailgate, his headlights casting an almost blinding glare weakening the darkness of the cabin of my car. But I don't go to my childhood home, no, I drive us straight to the Devil house. Home is where the heart is, right? At least according to Mister Elvis Presley.

Mama's words are still ringing in my ear. A Device son and a Tulipa witch, that's all it takes for Tibb to rise from the dead, to awaken from his eternal slumber. Am I the witch in this equation? How? I hold no magical properties, I think. And what does that entail, bringing him back? Are we talking some zombie shit, or does Tibb spirit need a body to host? She called it a prophecy, but who the hell is foretelling this? Who decided that me and him are meant to play this out like fools on a fable? What are we destined to bring forth, a bad ending to the Tulipa's story or a happy ever after conclusion to the Device's tale?

"She tried to usher me to fucking Davy Jones's locker," I speak to the nothingness that surrounds me, "to my watery grave, because of a haunting augury."

Makes sense now why Papa got so obsessed with that damn house. The ghostly whispers from within totally fractured what was possibly an already ill mind, eliciting Mama to almost end the life of her 4 year old little girl. According to Papa's letter to the mental hospital, he stated that Mama always had weird dreams about that place, but that the voices that spoke to her in her head, the sleepwalking where she would end up at the corroded black gates of the Device estate, these episodes only began after she became pregnant with me. Perhaps I broke her.

I think Roman Waterhouse was the piece that was missing from Papa's Devil house puzzle, without him, nothing marries. He's the skeleton key that opens all the doors to the hush-hush stories of the Device family. A tall tale about a devil boy, witches and their trials, luring shadows, and a murderous cult. A bloodline with a malediction that only got severed the moment his grandmother left the ratchet Devil house, granting a long-awaited Device son to be born.

I park my truck in front of the house in question, while Roman's car comes to a stop beside the driver side of mine. Once out, as I am shutting the door Roman comments, "I thought you said you wanted to go home." My eyes turn to the bewitching handsome man, watching him appear by the bonnet of his car.

"I am home." I state. "We are home."

"Ackles," whatever was about to follow my name being

uttered like he was about to shove a bitter pill down my throat, gets cut off by me stating that we should head in, get rid of the damp clothes that hug us so tight, take a hot shower and go to bed. It's been a long fucking day after all. "Fine, but we need to talk about stuff in the morning." He informs me.

"Fine." I tell him, heading to the building Roman has been staying in.

Sleep never comes. I am feeling like the every last drops of an ink pen leaving incomplete words on the pages of my narrative. I won't have that. We are getting to the epilogue sooner rather than never.

I am lying on my back, looking up at the painted white ceiling, with Roman's body against my side, his strong and shredded arm draped over my middle, one of his legs in between mine, his warm breath leaving sweet caresses on the skin of my neck.

The chamber we'd stumbled upon in the ancient manor next door is calling me back like a siren's song, the voices from within are relentless tonight, "It's time, witch," they say. "Let him out. Unbridle him from his tomb."

"I won't harm him, Lilith. I promise."

"You can start by calling me by my name, you idiot. It's Ackles." I mutter to the devilish deep voice that I know now belongs to Tibb. He actually laughs at my words. I shouldn't want to do it, but I am as much under a spell by him as I am by Roman. I guess, Mama was right for not having faith in me to not fall for the Devil's charms.

"Hey Waterhouse, we need to go back down there." I say with unyielding resolve. He grunts somewhat half asleep, as I detangle myself from the cocoon he had me in. "Baby, come on, get up." I order once my feet touch the bitterly cold floor. Even with chunky woollen hand knitted socks the chill creeps up my body. It doesn't help that I am only wearing one of Roman's tee to bed, but the guy is like a furnace under the sheets.

"Hmmm wait, what's happening?" Roman asks me, rubbing his eyes.

"We're returning to the chamber." I inform him, pulling the bed sheets away from him.

"Now? Ackles, can't this wait until dawn?" He observes at the same time as I begin my retreat from the bedroom. "Fuck. Harris, wait up then. Goddamnit, woman."

As we tread past the last step of the long stairway to hell, our bodies are slick with sweat from fear and anticipation. I go about lighting up the candles amongst the wall of the darkened jaws of this cave. The flames must've flickered out after we left, instead of consuming the whole candle to nothing but a small puddle of melted max gathered around its wick. Once the room is cast in a dim glow, my eyes zero in on the crypt straight away.

"Can't believe you dragged me down here again, Harris." He utters, his eyes bouncing around every inch of this eerie space.

"I did no such thing, Waterhouse." I remark. "You follow me like a good boy." That's when something embedded in the walls above the stone coffin catches my eyes. "Were those there before?" I ask, making my way to it so I can get a closer look.

"What?" Roman asks back.

I am greeted by a sight that freezes my blood. "Unholy fuck. Roman these are urns." This wall is littered with them, like forgotten toys sunken into the carved surface.

"I am sick and tired of finding bodies in this bloody place, Ackles. There better be preserved fruit in those things."

I chuckle at his words, reaching for one of the urns and opening it up. But what lies inside is far more horrifying than mere ashes. The object slips from my shaking hands, and when it hits the ground, shattering into a million pieces, a cloud of dirt lifts masking the secrets it held for a little while longer. The moment the dust settles you can perceive it, the minuscule skeletal remains of infants. A wave of revulsion sweeps over me, and I lift my forest green eyes, locking them with Roman's jade ones in scared terror.

"Fuck." Roman quietly murmurs. "Are those baby bones?"

"I don't see them being leprechaun ones." I say jokingly, seeking to perk up the fast dampen mood. I kneel in front of the mess I made and grab one of the tiny bones that snapped on impact, making one of the ends sharp as a knife.

I don't get it. Assuming every urn holds a dead infant, and that they are of Device blood, there's at least a good baker's dozen so the math doesn't add up, the Device body count exceeds the number we know about from papers we have. The only way this makes sense it's as if the first two Device daughters of every generation had children of their own too. But why keep that buried? Was this some gory attempt at breaking Polly's curse? A murderous bunch that's what these bitches, I mean witches, were.

"I am done, Harris." Roman declares all of the sudden, as

he begins taking steps back. "I'm done with this bloody estate and its houses, this bloody horror story that I don't see having a happy fucking ending. Ackles we should leave, run far away, and never come back."

"What?" I stand up straight, staring at Roman distancing himself from me.

"Come with me to Australia. Let's forget all about this soul eating hellhole."

I walk to the crypt, rooting myself right next to it, as I tell Roman, "No."

"No? Ackles," his words die in his lips as he gazes at me with panic written all over his face, "Baby, what are you doing?" My hand stings, why? As I peer down at it, I notice that I just slashed my palm with the knife-like bone. I drop the, now dripping red, part of a dead child, as Roman strides over to me. "Shit, how deep did you cut? There's so much blood."

The heavy feeling is back, gripping my whole body, the one that makes every movement on my part a grueling effort. My eyes land on the stone coffin, as Roman seeks to put pressure on my self-inflicted wound. "What are those on the lid?" I ask numbly.

Roman's jade colour eyes journey to me and then to the crypt. "The runes? You read them to me, remember? You told me they say 'Here lies Tibb'."

"Not those. The other ones. The incandescent ones." I free my gashed up hand from his clasp, bullying the blood that pours from the wound to flow to the tips of my fingers, and begin drawing up what I see.

Once I am done gracing Tibb's, supposed to be, perpetual bed with new writings, that's when all hell breaks loose.

THIRTY-SEVEN
ROMAN WATERHOUSE

I could feel the heat in the air, like the bushfire's breath on a scorching arvo. The blood runes sprawled across the ancient stone of Tibbs' crypt were alive—aglow with a sinister light that danced across the walls and bathed us in a red hue. Ackles, caught up in the madness swirling around us, stumbled back into me, her solid frame a sudden weight against my own.

"What?" She muttered, as the red glow lit up her pale skin.

"Steady on, love," I grunted, my arm instinctively curling around her middle, anchoring her to me. It was a protective move, but also one that kept me grounded as much as it did her. Her presence was reassuring amongst the chaos.

The runes—those bloody hellish things—flared with an intensity that had us both squinting. I threw a hand up, trying to shield our eyes from the blinding light, feeling like I was staring straight into the sun on a scorcher of a day back home.

"Christ, what is that?" Ackles gasped, her forest green eyes wide as saucers beneath the fringe of her ginger curls.

"I don't know," I replied through gritted teeth, the brightness intensifying until spots danced behind my eyelids.

We were caught in a stand-off with something far older and more powerful than either of us. Power oozed from the ancient stone, and I could almost hear it whispering secrets from long ago, promising power—threatening destruction.

"Roman, this isn't good," Ackles said, her voice barely above a whisper but clear over the hum of energy that filled the room.

"Understatement of the century," I shot back, my attempt at humour falling flat even to my own ears. This was no time for jokes. There was something here, something waking up, and it wasn't going to be friendly.

Bloody hell, the sound hit us like a freight train—a sharp, ear-splitting crack that echoed through the chamber. The lid of Tibbs' tomb, bloody heavy and solid it was, split right down the middle, and I swear the ground beneath our feet shuddered.

"Christ," I muttered, tensing as Ackles gripped my arm tighter. Dust, or what looked like it, billowed from the fissure, spreading like a thick fog across the floor. It wasn't just dust, though; it swirled with intent, with malice. You could almost taste the centuries of darkness in it.

"Roman, what the—" Ackles started, but her words were swallowed by the sudden chill that descended on us.

"What the fuck," I whispered, my voice hoarse. The dust

was alive, moving with purpose, coalescing into something that sent a shiver down my spine. A shape emerged from the cloud, growing, solidifying into a form that belonged in nightmares.

It was like staring into the abyss and finding the abyss staring back—a half-goat, half-man figure materialising in front of us. Thick, shadowy tendrils rippled outwards from its body, as if it wore darkness like a bloody cloak. Its eyes, though... they were the worst part, glowing with an unholy light that seemed to bore straight into my soul.

"Strewth," I breathed out, the Aussie in me retreating behind a wall of primal fear. This wasn't just any old spectre; it was ancient, a legend made flesh—or whatever twisted mockery of flesh it had conjured for itself.

"Is that—?" Ackles couldn't finish her sentence, her voice a mix of awe and terror.

"Bugger this," I muttered under my breath, every muscle in my body tensing as I started to edge backwards. Ackles was right there with me, her back glued to my chest, her breaths coming out in sharp bursts that told me she was just as rattled.

"Move, love," I urged, trying to keep the panic out of my voice as I tightened my grip around her and shuffled us both away from the chilling spectacle.

The shadowy figure swelled before us, its form becoming clearer, more defined, as if it drew strength from our fear. It was like watching the Devil himself stepping out of a bloody painting, only this was no artwork—it was our reality, stark and terrifying.

"Roman..." it boomed, the sound echoing off the stone

walls. Its finger—long, gnarled, and freakishly human-like—pointed right at me. "I've been waiting for you. Welcome home."

"Home? You're off your rocker," I shot back, my voice a mix of disbelief and raw anger. Every instinct screamed to leg it, to get as far away from this nightmare as possible. But there it was, that bastard of a demon, calling this cursed place 'home' and acting like we were long-lost mates.

I could feel the power emanating from the figure, a dark pull that tugged at something deep inside me. But I wasn't about to roll over and show my belly. Not now, not ever. Ackles and I—we were getting out of this madhouse, even if it meant taking on the Devil himself.

The bloody thing lunged, a swirl of dust and shadows that took form as it moved—a twisted sight, half goat, half bloke. Bloody hell, this was it. Heart thundering a mad drum solo in my chest, I spun round, shoving Ackles hard towards the stairs. "Move!" The word ripped from my throat, all guttural and desperate.

But she didn't budge, her feet like they were sodding cemented to the dirt floor. Panic clawed up my spine as I stumbled, nearly toppling over myself, scrambling to follow her, but Ackles...she was stuck fast, rooted to the spot as though some unseen force had claimed her.

"Run, damn you," I hissed, terror gnawing at my insides. But it was like she couldn't hear me, or worse, couldn't move even if she wanted to.

And then she crumpled. Not like someone falling, but sinking—slow and graceless to her knees, as if every bit of fight had been sapped from her. There she was, my fiery-haired Ackles, looking small and defeated on the cold ground.

The goat-man-thing—it stopped, just a hair's breadth away from her, its grotesque form towering over Ackles like some kind of sick guardian from the depths of a nightmare. Its hand emerged from the shadowy mass, long fingers ending in points that could slice through flesh like butter. But it didn't harm her. Instead, it brushed against her cheekbone ever so gently, an obscene tenderness that made my skin crawl.

"Welcome home, Lilith." The words slithered out, oily and dark, sending shivers down my spine. It was talking to Ackles, but those bloody eyes—beady and black—stayed locked onto mine, drilling into me with a malice that spoke of things no bloke should know.

"Get your filthy mitts off her," I spat, voice barely above a whisper, but it might as well have been a shout. It echoed in the thickening tension between us, a challenge laid bare. There was power there, under the surface, a battle of wills that had nothing to do with physical strength.

Ackles, still kneeling, looked lost—her forest green eyes wide, her usually vibrant curls dulled in the crimson glow. She was silent, but her gaze cut through the chaos, meeting mine with an intensity that screamed louder than any cry for help.

I stood frozen, every instinct screaming to snatch her away from that creature, to protect her from whatever sick game this bastard was playing. But I was rooted just as firmly as she was, caught in a standoff that chilled me to the bone.

"Stay the fuck away from me, Tibb," I growled, my voice rough like gravel as the red glow from the runes cast eerie shadows across the chamber. "I'm not a part of this sick game you're playing."

Tibb's laugh was like thunder, cracking through the tense air, reverberating off ancient stone walls. "Yes, you are, Roman. You're me. My blood runs in your veins. We're cut from the same cloth. Don't you feel it? This place," he gestured around with a sweeping, dramatic flair, "is your home. It's where you were always meant to be. Polly might've cursed us, but your nan, she did me proud—she ran when I told her to, broke the curse so I could walk among you all again."

I blinked hard against the blinding light, every word from Tibb hitting me like a punch to the gut. "What?" The single word escaped me, half disbelief, half dread curdling in my stomach.

"That's right. This whole thing—it was planned. Down to the last detail. Down to you standing here, right now, where you belong." Tibb's eyes gleamed with something wild, untamed. "You and me—and this beautiful witch here —" His gaze slid to Ackles, still on her knees, her breath coming out in short bursts. "She carries the same blood as Lilith. She was always meant to be yours, her soul belongs to me, as it does to you."

My heart hammered against my ribs, a caged thing desperate to escape. I felt the pull, the undeniable connection that tethered me to this accursed place, to Ackles, to the very blood that coursed through my veins. But hell would freeze over before I let this demonic bastard claim what was mine.

The bastard lunged, and in that heartbeat, I knew what it was to be hunted. Tibb's form, no longer solid but a twisting wisp of shadow, surged towards me with the ferocity of a storm. It slammed into my chest, seeping into my flesh like smoke drawn by a flue.

"Fuck," I grunted, the sensation akin to a hit of something too strong, too warm. It was like stumbling into a heated room after being drenched by a merciless downpour, or sinking your teeth into a hearty meal when hunger had clawed at your insides for far too long. A twisted sense of belonging wrapped around my heart, squeezing until I could hardly breathe from the pressure of it all.

My gaze snapped to Ackles, her fiery curls cascading around her as if they were flames licking the ground. Her forest green eyes pierced through the darkness, locking onto mine with an intensity that scorched my soul. Her lips parted, and even though the chaos deafened us, I read the silent confession on her trembling mouth: "I love you."

"Ackles..." The words died in my throat. Every fibre of my being strained against the pull of Tibb's essence, but it was like wrestling a bloody riptide. Powerless, I watched Ackles crumple before me, her body kissing the dirt floor as if in surrender.

"Ackles," I rasped, the plea lodged between desperation and command. But even as I reached out, trying to bridge the gap between us, darkness crept into the edges of my vision, spreading like ink in water.

"Roman..." The sound of her voice was faint, a ghostly whisper carried away by the shadows that now claimed me.

"Fuck this," I spat, the fight still raging within me despite the encroaching void. I wouldn't let this end here. Not like this.

But it was too late. My world went black, and I fell into an abyss where only Tibb's laughter echoed, a sinister reminder that some curses were bound by blood, and some fates were sealed with a kiss from hell itself.

THIRTY-EIGHT
ACKLES HARRIS

What a bizarre nightmare. Roman and I were down in the dark chamber of secrets again, and I wrote some shit in my own blood on the lid of Tibb's crypt and it broke, and the spirit of half-goat half-man of my dreams came out.

Someone brushes some of my strands away from my face, dragging them behind my ear. "You were such a good girl, Lilith." This gravelly voice tells me. Weird, it kind of sounds like Roman, yet the Australian twang is all gone, replaced by a posh old English elocution.

I groan, my body twitching and my hands curling in the hmmm dirt? Wait. That was a dream, right? Then why does it feel like I am lying on my belly on a gunky hard floor, instead of being in bed tangled up in the sheets with Roman. My eyes flutter open, and thanks to the faint soft glow of lit candles I can just about perceive Roman crouching down beside me. Shit, we are indeed in the hollow grotto beneath the Devil house.

I slowly get up, my whole body aching, as Roman does the same. Oh my God, it's as if I just been hit by a fucking truck or something. "What happened?" I ask, my voice coming out throaty, like I just swallowed a bunch of the dirt and dust I was resting upon.

"You did what you were supposed to, my little pet." Roman says to me.

"Did you just call me pet?" I ask him a bit dazed by his choice of endearment. When my eyes journey up the full one foot height of difference between us, the air in my lungs gets knocked out of me. His eyes have lost their alluring jade green hue, now a jet-black shade, dark as the moonless and starless night sky, paints his iris. It's like I am staring into a deep as fuck abyss. "Roman?" I question with a shaky voice.

"Try again, love." He comments, an unholy evil smirk popping up in his face.

My heart is racing as the next gasping words flee my lips, "Tibb?"

"In the flesh. Or in your boy's flesh to be precise. How do you like our spooky story now, pet?" Rather than answer my possessed companions' question I bolt from the chamber in sheer panic, taking two steps at a time. "Aww you still remember how to please me, baby. I love the chase. Run my delicious prey, I will catch you, always and forever."

Once upstairs I seek some sort of sanctuary within the house's winding corridors, my heart hammering against my chest in terror. What have I done? Shit, is Roman gone? It was my Aussie hunk's body moving, it was his lips parting and speaking, but the person doing so it's not him it's Tibb, he's pulling the invisible strings that control my Roman.

"Can I tell you a story, pet?" Fuck, Tibb sounds close, hot on my heels, yet as I draw to a sudden halt and spin around, almost tripping over my own feet and falling on my ass, he's nowhere to be seen. I barge into the first room I come across and hide at the core of an old oak wardrobe. The perks of being a tiny skinny bitch is that you fit in pretty much any poky hole.

"Once upon a time," he begins narrating his story, "there was a poor sickly boy, ill-fated to waste away to nothing by a dark ghastly corner of the horrible world he was born upon. Abandoned by the only family he had left, his grandmother." His spectral whispers send icy tendrils down my spine. "He prayed, while lying down on a pissed filled ditch, dying, not to end up like his Mama and Papa. They died of the terrible plague, you see. The same putrid disease adorning his sun-kissed skin black." The floorboards creak as someone enters the bedroom I found refuge in. "He would give anything, he said." A looming present takes fore just on the other side of the wardrobe doors, I can perceive this arresting shadow through the crack where the hinges are. Roman, or Tibb to be exact, came straight here, to me, like he knew where I was the whole time. "I suppose something answered, out of pity or perhaps it saw something brewing within him, apart from the rot. I did become this after all, a demon made in the dark prince's image. And the rest," he utters, hurling the doors wide open, grabbing me by the throat and pulling me out of my hiding spot, "you, my cute sitting duck, know all about it." He ends just as he pins me to the wall right next to the wardrobe.

I whimper. His body is crushing mine, whilst his hand is

verging on strangling me. I grab his wrist with both of my hands, trying to pry him away from my throat. I can't breathe, so I dig my nails in and scratch like a madwoman. To no avail though, blackened dots are starting to float around in my vision, soon I will lose consciousness. He's choking me to death, then why the fuck am I wet between my legs? Why do I tremble, not in fear, but in need?

"I am home sweetheart, and so are you." He informs me as his face lowers, his lips hovering just above mine. "Together we can conquer it all. Just submit, Ackles, and I will give everything your heart desires."

I look up into his black eyes and in its cavernous depths reflected back at me, like a beautiful motion picture, it's our whole future. I don't know if he's the one who's conjuring it up or I am, in my state of delirium, but it doesn't matter, I cave nonetheless, "Ok."

"Ok, what, pet?"

He eases off the pressure on my throat, so I can properly answer him, "I submit, master."

"Good girl. Shall we seal it with a kiss." I nod at his words and his lips waste no time crashing into mine. It's a violent and possessive kiss, no easing into anything, he bites my lower lip straight off the bat which makes me part them and grant his tongue entrance into my mouth. I can taste a sweet metallic tang as he swirls his tongue with mine.

I moan just as he groans, shoving his tongue so deep down my throat I almost gag. "Hmmm, love that sound, how about you get down on your knees and kiss something else, pet? Gag on that instead." Tibb doesn't wait for a reply, with the hold he has on my throat he forces me down. That hand then moves to the top of my head, his fingers punitively tangling themselves on my ginger curls. He releases his cock from the confinements of his grey joggers, dangling the already fully hard dick in front of my face. "Open wide."

I do as I am told, and just like the kiss he doesn't procrastinate, or even gradually creep in, no, he thrusts himself all the way in my mouth in one go. "Look how well you take me, baby." Only when I start to choke does Tibb pull out. Once I get some needed air, he begins thrusting in and out, fucking my mouth mercilessly.

I am drooling like a bloodhound, as I let the Devil get his way with me. "That's it, pet, get me all wet and ready to sink myself in your lower lips." That statement makes me moan, which in turn sends sweet vibrations to the dick in my mouth. "Fuck. Trying to make spill my seed down your throat won't save you from the punishing drilling that is coming your pussy's way, witch." Tibb announces, tugging on my hair, pulling me off his dick and into my feet.

In a split second he spins me around so my front is to the wall now, rips my panties, but doesn't bother to remove the tee I borrowed to sleep in and didn't get changed out off when we went down to the chamber. "Hands on the wall, pet." He orders, jerking my ass back whilst pushing down on my spine, bullying me to arch my back. His cock moves up and down my wet folds, before penetrating my core, stuffing me to the limit.

"Shit." I scream.

"Actually, now I'm home." Tibb tells me as he aggressively kicks off driving in and out of my pussy. He is ramming into me with such vehemence that I have to push back on my hands against the wall, so I don't bash my head to it. While one of his palms stays on my spine, keeping me in this position, the other has buried its nails on the flesh of my hip.

Before you can say knife, I am losing it, the ember in the pit of my belly metamorphoses to a flame and then to a darn inferno that puts the bible one to shame is that blistering hot. My legs buckle as I orgasm, but Tibb doesn't give me the time to succumb to my trembling legs and collapse. He withdraws, leaving my pussy empty and grasping for it to return. He spins me, lifting a single one of my legs first by placing one of his arms in the shallow depression on the back of my knee, and penetrates my dripping pussy. Once he bottoms out, Tibb waits for me to get my arms around his neck before picking up the other leg. My bent legs rest on the crook of his elbows, as my back is flushed against the wall.

Instead of boring into my core in a harsh and rough manner, like he has been doing since this whole fuck fest began, Tibb sways his hips in a slow and intoxicating way. I don't know what's worse this or the unforgiving way he was fucking me. They both drive me wild.

"Master" I purr out, tucking my face in his chest. That's when he starts swinging my pelvis in his direction, making me slam down on his cock over and over again. "Yes." I shout.

"I am going to cram so much cum inside you, pet, there's no way I won't impregnate you." His words trigger me to rupture once more, but on this occasion I bring Tibb along with me. "Fuck, witch." He breathlessly utters, as he settles himself far in my pussy. "You are milking me so damn hard." His dick swells ahead of twitching and erupting, his hot seed gushing out of me by virtue of the sheer amount he's pumping within my core. "Do you like the idea of us begetting our own little spawn?" I nod, because the ability to speak has long been lost amongst all the shagging. "Good. We waited long enough for this story to conclude, why wait to bring another pretty charmer into the chaos we are going to fabricate."

Thirty-Nine

Huxley Davis

Beep beep. The insistent horn of a cab punctured the quiet of my Newchurch town centre apartment—a stark reminder that I was about to embark on an unsettling adventure, one that beckoned from the cobblestone streets of London. This humble abode, with its mismatched furniture and towering stacks of forensic journals, was my sanctuary ever since university spat me out with a degree in hand.

With a final glance at the cramped space that bore witness to countless nights hunched over case files, I seized my battered suitcase and a carry bag stuffed with essentials: notepads, a collection of true crime books queued up for the journey, and, of course, my most lurid tie featuring a tableau of famous murder weapons. It was a conversation starter—or stopper, depending on the company.

"Okay, Hux, time to put those mortician muscles to use," I muttered, hoisting the luggage like a body on the slab. A nervous chuckle escaped me as I double-checked the pockets of my slacks for my phone and wallet. Check and check.

I yanked the door shut behind me, the familiar click of the lock a small comfort. My descent down the steps was less graceful gallop, more controlled tumble, each thud of my worn shoes echoing in the stairwell. By the time I burst through the entrance of the building, the cool morning air slapped some sense into me, and I paused to adjust my slipping glasses.

"Doctor Davis! Time's ticking!" the cab driver called out, an edge of playful impatience in his voice.

"Right you are," I replied, sprinting the last few metres and nearly tripping over a crack in the pavement. Safety hazards—my old nemesis.

The cab was a musty black in the pale dawn light, a chariot ready to whisk me away from the sleepy town of under five hundred souls. With a practised heave, I lobbed my baggage onto the backseat and then clambered in after it, the scent of leather and pine air freshener invading my senses.

"London, eh?" the cabbie said with a knowing grin, his eyes meeting mine in the rearview mirror. "Big city's got nothing on Newchurch's charm, but I reckon it's got its fair share of secrets."

"Secrets, and so much more," I agreed, the corners of my mouth twitching upwards.

"Good luck, Doctor," the driver said, his tone earnest now. "Find those answers you're looking for."

"Answers, closure, and maybe just a dash of horror," I murmured, half to him, half to myself.

The highway stretched out before us, a grey ribbon tying me to the heart of an enigma. My leg bounced with anticipation; I was eager, like a kid on his way to a candy store, only my sweets were shrouded in morbidity and wrapped in crime scene tape.

"Kennedy's going to flip when she sees me," I chuckled to myself, picturing her bright hair, that distinct orange-teal ombre nearly as vivid as her personality. Six months had crawled by since she'd last graced Newchurch with her mismatched socks and fascinating diatribes about decomposition rates.

We'd kept the lines burning, phone calls filled with her rapid-fire updates on London's latest horror show—a killer mirroring Jack the Ripper's ghastly waltz. Kennedy's voice would crackle through the line, animated and breathless with details I probably shouldn't have known without a badge.

"Did you know he left the same kind of...," she'd start, and I'd hang onto every word, piecing together the gruesome puzzle from across the miles. Emails too, always signed off with 'Wish you were here!' Like I needed more temptation.

"Obsessed" doesn't quite cover it. Like a moth to a flame, I was drawn to the grotesque ballet of Jack the Ripper's copycat killer, each snippet Kennedy sent feeding the fire. She had this way of dropping tantalising clues in my inbox, breadcrumbs leading me through a forest thick with intrigue and horror.

"Come on, Hux," she'd urge over the phone, her voice a siren call laced with the thrill of the chase. "You've got that criminology degree gathering dust. Put it to use."

And so, I did what any self-respecting enthusiast of the macabre would do—I rallied someone to man my post at the mortuary, packed my bags, and didn't look back. The old university course on criminology might have been for fun back then, but Jack? He was personal. A dark fascination turned academic pursuit turned... well, here I am, barreling towards London with the zeal of a kid at Christmas.

"Kennedy," I whispered to myself, thumbing the edges of my carry bag where I'd stuffed the latest case notes. "We're going to crack this one wide open."

I could almost hear her laughter, picture the gleam in her green eyes as we would dive into the abyss together. The Ripper had nothing on us—Brennan and Davis, an unstoppable duo in the making.

The cab's engine hummed like a purring cat, eager to set off. I leaned back against the worn leather seat, the familiar scent of lemon wipes and city life filling my nostrils. London beckoned with its labyrinth of mysteries, and I was more than ready to lose myself in its embrace.

"Mind if I roll this down?" I asked the cabbie, gesturing toward the window.

"Your ride, mate," he grunted, eyes fixed on the road ahead.

Cool air rushed in as I cranked the window down, chasing away the last cobwebs of hesitation from my mind. There's something about the onset of an adventure that makes you feel alive—like every pore of your skin is buzzing with anticipation. And the fact that it involved murder most foul? Icing on the cake.

As we zipped past quaint storefronts and sleepy cafes, Newchurch's small-town charm flickered by like a slideshow.

The familiarity was comforting but constricting, like a well-loved sweater that shrunk just a touch too much.

"Almost out of the sticks now," I muttered to myself, catching sight of the Device Estate walls through the left window.

It was impossible not to look. The place was a landmark —an enigma shrouded in whispers and ivy. Three buildings, each more impressive than the last, stood proudly behind that imposing stone wall, their windows glinting in the sun like eyes keeping secrets.

"Done quite a number on the old joint," I remarked, more to the wind than to my driver.

"Yep," he replied, nonchalant. "Place was falling apart at the seams before."

I chuckled at his understatement. 'Falling apart' was kind to what that estate had been—a Gothic relic filled to the brink with bones and ghost stories. Now, it was all polished stone and manicured lawns, a phoenix risen from historical ashes.

"Can't even see the bloody house anymore," I added, craning my neck for a better view as we passed the grand iron gate. It stood sentinel, as if guarding the world within from prying eyes like mine.

"Privacy is a luxury these days, isn't it?" The cabbie's words hung in the air, and I found myself nodding in agreement.

Luxury indeed. But then again, so was freedom—the freedom to chase down demons of the past and present, to unravel the threads of a killer's mind.

I pressed my nose to the cab window, the cool glass a

welcome reprieve from the jitters that danced in my belly. That place was now Ackles' sanctuary, her private nook in this quaint little town. Since shacking up with Roman, she'd become something of an enigma, tucked away behind those towering stone walls.

"Roman's done quite the number on the old joint, hasn't he?" I muttered to myself, recalling the whispers that trickled through Newchurch like a chilling breeze. The Australian bloke who blustered into our lives with a toolbox and a dream had certainly stirred the pot. He dredged up tales of Tibb, the son of Lucifer himself, as easily as one might recount family folklore over a Sunday roast.

"Supposed to flip it for a profit, wasn't he?" I continued the one-sided conversation, unable to shake the image of Roman, sleeves rolled up, pride glinting in his eye as he spoke of renovations and real estate ventures. But the siren call of England, with its fog-wrapped mornings and history-soaked streets, had snared him good and proper. Now here he was, rooted to the spot, with Ackles by his side.

"Probably thought it'd be a quick buck," I chuckled, shaking my head. Who would've guessed that a man with an accent thick enough to spread on toast would trade sunburnt plains for a life within these ancient, whispering walls?

"Trading kangaroos for ghosts," I said under my breath, the cab's engine humming a steady tune as we left the estate —and its spectral occupants—behind us. "Not your everyday fixer-upper story."

A flicker of something passed through me then—curiosity, perhaps, or the remnants of a half-forgotten fear. Whatever it was, it danced away just as quickly, lost to the road and the thrill of the hunt that awaited me in London. With Kennedy's voice ringing in my ears, promising mystery and mayhem, I couldn't help but grin.

I let out a sigh as the cab wove its way through the winding roads leading away from Newchurch. The rearview mirror flashed with the last glimpses of town, drawing my thoughts back to Ackles. Funny how absence digs a deeper hole than we care to admit. It had been a good five months since I last saw her, striding into the police station with a steely resolve that belied the tremble in her voice. Resignation letter held like a white flag, she surrendered to a different life.

I remembered the last time I saw her, walking the grounds of the Device estate, hand resting on the gentle swell of her belly, carrying Roman's child. The estate stood imposing and secretive, like an ancient beast keeping watch over its new wards. Rumours swirled among the locals, speaking of the transformation that seemed to have bewitched the couple—a particularly juicy one suggested that Roman's Aussie twang had all but vanished, replaced by an old English accent that didn't just hint at antiquity; it fairly screamed of another century.

"House claimed them again, they say," I mumbled to myself, recalling the hushed gossip exchanged over pints and pool at the local pub.

"Sorry, what was that?" the cabbie inquired, glancing back at me.

"Nothing," I waved him off, "Just town talk about the Device place. They reckon it's got its hooks in 'em."

"Ah, sounds like a proper mystery novel, that does," he said with a grin.

"Or a cult classic," I added, thinking of Tibb, the son of Lucifer himself, supposedly tied to the estate's dark history. "Guess every town needs its legends, especially ones as small as ours."

The cab driver hummed in agreement, leaving me to my thoughts as we merged onto the road leading to London.

"London awaits, Dr. Huxley," I whispered to myself. "And so does the next chapter of this bizarre tale."

To Be Continued...

About Cassandra Doon

Cassandra Doon hails from New South Wales, Australia, where she was nurtured between the bustling streets of Sydney and the serene snowy mountains of Tumut. Today, she finds inspiration in the breathtaking Scenic Rim of Queensland's Gold Coast. A versatile author with a lifelong passion for storytelling, Cassandra has penned over 16 novels and 5 children's books, exploring a variety of genres. Known for her daydreaming and a head often lost in the clouds, she admits to being more at home in her fictional worlds than on social media. Outside of her literary pursuits, Cassandra is a devoted mother to two boys, dedicating her days to their endless energy as both a soccer mom and Pokémon master.

Standalone:

The Boys Of Hastings House

The Kings of Willows Peak

Damaged Goods

Tuesday May

The Devils Cut

The Detectives Mate

Bittersweet Snapdragon

Phantom Navis

Obsessed Shadows

Aces (Coming Soon)

The Dead Zone (Coming Soon)

Second Chances at The Riverbend Café (Coming Soon)

Still Waters (Coming Soon)

Lavender (Coming Soon)

Dark Dahlia Rite (Coming Soon)

Shadow Prince (Coming Soon)

Ravenwood Manor (Coming Soon)

Summer (Coming Soon)

Oakland Harbour Series:

Missing

Found

Home

Second Chances Series:

The Waterfall

Wicked Bonds (Coming Soon)

The Restaurant (Coming Soon)

The Queens of Ombres Series:

Follow Poppy

Protect Poppy (Coming Soon)

Crown Poppy (Coming Soon)

About Mimi Baptist

I am half Portuguese half French girlie, with maybe somewhere else sprinkled in there, but I wouldn't know, living in the UK.

Indie author and a bibliophile. All around bookish to the bone.

If you don't find me snuggle up in a couch reading a book, then I am in front of my laptop writing whatever crazy land of make believe my wild imagination has come up with.

I swam in the deepest waters of 'Fall Apart' for a good year until I decided to put pen to paper, and after that words just poured out.

My second book 'Just Always Be Waiting for Me' a reverse harem retelling of Peter Pan's, is the first retake on a Disney story, I intend on taking on others. But Peter Pan was my first love, may as well start there. All to say, I am a Disney fanatic, don't judge me to hard for it.

Please join me in this insane ride.

ALSO BY MIMI BAPTIST

Awfully Big Adventure Series:

Just Always Be Waiting For Me

Standalone:

A Field of Tulips and Bones

Bittersweet Snapdragon

Dark Dahlia Rite (Coming Soon)

Follow Poppy

Somethings Got To Give:

Fall Apart

Fall Together

www.ingramcontent.com/pod-product-compliance
Lightning Source LLC
Chambersburg PA
CBHW072042190726
48294CB00005B/1364